Up The Wrong Tree

Brandy Ayers

Contents

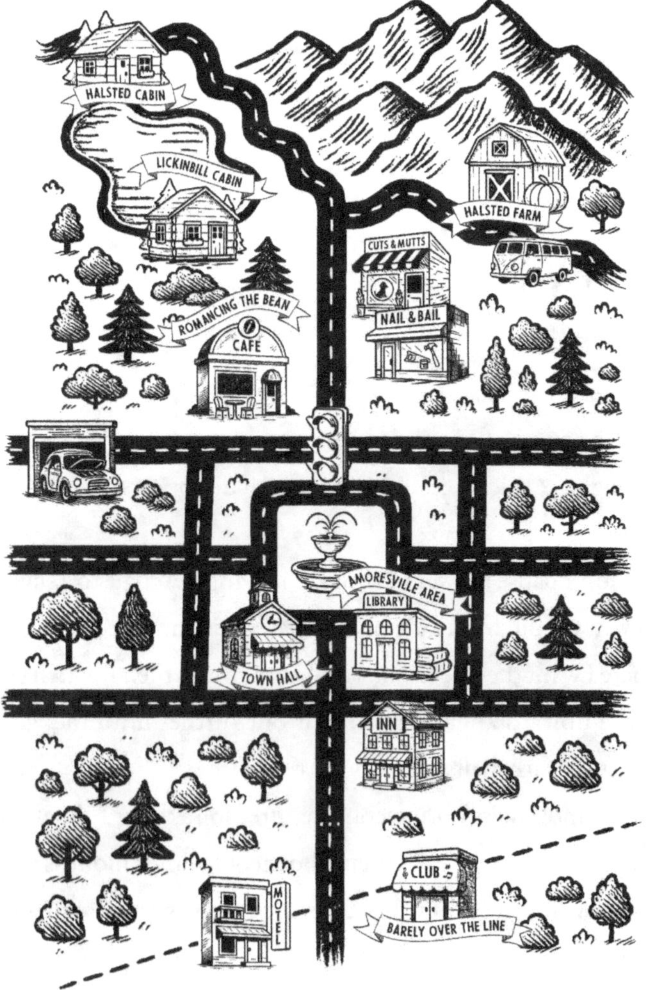

WELCOME TO
Amoresville
HALSTED CABIN
LICKINBILL CABIN
HALSTED FARM
CUTS & MUTTS
NAIL & BAIL
ROMANCING THE BEAN
CAFE
AMORESVILLE AREA
LIBRARY
TOWN HALL
INN
MOTEL
CLUB
BARELY OVER THE LINE

Chapter 1

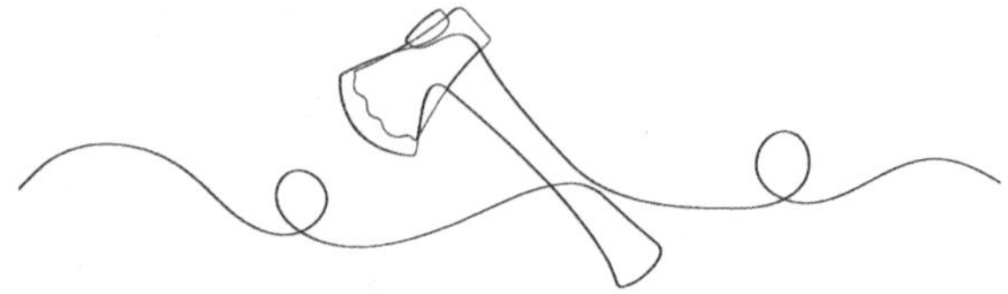

Orion

Thwack!

The sound of metal ax hitting stubborn wood reverberates through the thick trees, echoing until it disappears deep into the forest.

I don't pause between swings, changing my angle to a slightly downward pitch, cutting out the wedge on the side of the trunk where I want the tree to fall. Five more swings then I switch back to the upward angle, notching it out further until the wedge makes it nearly halfway through the trunk.

The movements are second nature, something I do at least once a week every week except those cold winter months when the snow on the ground prevents me from wandering too far from my cabin.

Those are the months I question my life choices. As they creep closer and closer with every degree the temperature falls this time of year, I begin to wonder if it isn't time for me to move down from this mountain, at least for the months when the snow and ice cut me off from civilization.

Not that Amoresville is very civilized.

Another swing of the ax and I push the thoughts away, concentrating only on the task at hand.

With each chop I get closer to the spot I've mentally picked where I will switch to the back of the tree.

On another back swing, I realize I've pushed my hair behind my ear, exposing my face to the camera. I pull the swing short before making contact with the mighty oak tree that looms above me, already half dead from disease.

Covering the hiccup in my movements, I reach up stretching over my head, making a point to flex all those muscles the strangers on the internet love to compliment me on. It was weird at first having anonymous women and men comment so blatantly about my body, but I've become almost numb to it at this point.

I let the long curtain of red hair that hasn't gotten more than a trim since I was discharged from the Marines five years ago drape across my face before angling my head slightly to the camera set up to my side.

I never show my full face on camera. I've found hilarious ways to keep my identity hidden. My hair is the most obvious one. Hats, branches, an ax, even my own arm, have all helped served as a wall between myself and my followers. Not because there is anything wrong with the way I look, but because I am holding on to the delusion that if I don't show my face, I'm not actually an internet celebrity.

Five million people across various social media channels say different.

It also helps to camouflage the infamous Halsted Blush. Even out here in the middle of nowhere with no one around, filming my videos never fails to make me feel like an idiot. As the younger kids on the apps would say, it is totally cringe.

The rest of the job goes by fairly quickly. This tree doesn't give me much resistance, and before long I hear the telltale creaking sounds that precede it falling to the floor of the forest. I stand back, letting gravity do the rest of the work for me as the trunk arches down to the ground exactly where I wanted it to land away from the healthier growth around it.

With it finally down, it's time to do my trademark closing. Ambling over to the far side of the trunk, I bury my axe into the thick bark and call my best friend and co-star, Spruce Campbell, to my side with a whistle. The three-legged pitty mix comes trotting over from where he had been faithfully waiting on the passenger seat of my truck.

Before he makes it to me, I pull my soaked shirt up to wipe away the sweat pouring down my face, making sure to keep my face angled to the forest floor so it is mostly concealed from the viewers, not that they will be looking anywhere north of my abs. I earned those puppies in the Marines and have maintained them mostly thanks to boredom.

Spruce takes his place of honor, hopping onto the tree trunk and sitting on it so he is perfectly framed by the camera. I swear, it's like he knows his angles better than any model. The few people that don't watch my videos for my body are watching for my dog. He appears in almost every video at some point, but the ones where I'm bringing down a tree he stays at a safe distance until the sign-off. We take our places, with him blocking half my face while my arm draped across the handle of my ax blocks the other half.

One intrepid follower took screenshots from various videos and photoshopped them together in quite possibly the creepiest headshot known to man. My anonymity is one of the things that has helped garner a following; everyone is waiting for the day that I give in and show my full face. Hell, I've shown nearly every other part of me, even damn near my whole ass once. But never my whole face at once.

"I can't wait to get this beast into my shop and make something beautiful out of it. It never ceases to amaze me that something that has been wasting away here alone in the woods can be turned into something beautiful again, with nothing but my hands and a few tools. "

I bite my lip and pat the tree trunk, then turn to Spruce, letting my long hair shield the camera view of my profile, and give him a vigorous pet as he gazes up at me with so much love it kills me. "What do you say, buddy, ready to go home?" At his favorite word, he jumps up, placing his paws on my shoulders and leaping up until I catch him in both arms. He licks my face like crazy and I laugh even though we've done this same routine countless times.

I can already feel the comments being typed out on dozens of keyboards. *I'd like to lick him too. Lucky dog.*

"See you next time, everyone."

After getting out of the service I had no intention of becoming a content creator, but the world works in mysterious ways. Not all of that was total bullshit. I do find it amazing that the diseased, dead trees I harvest from the deep woods of northern Pennsylvania can be turned into beautiful, ornate pieces of furniture.

Not sure I need to say that to the whole of the internet with my abs showing, though.

With my shoot done, I get down to the part of the job that isn't nearly as glamorous. Getting this huge fucking tree back to my cabin three miles away through the woods.

"Spruce, place." At the command, my dog hops down from my arms and runs back to the truck, curling up on the seat. But his eyes never leave me as I work. As used to my work as he is, Spruce remains vigilant when I'm dealing with my tools. I swear, he's like a mother hen trying to make sure his chick doesn't accidentally off itself. If he could sit on me to keep me still, I'm sure he would.

Dog safely in his spot, I gather my hair back into a messy bun and put my shirt back on, because lets me real, it is safer that way. Ax in hand, the first order of business is getting the tree stripped. Would a chainsaw make this job a lot faster and easier?

Yeah, probably.

But even if my viewers didn't hate the things, I don't like them either. There is something much more satisfying about using the strength of my own muscles and the leverage created by the perfect wedge of an ax head that makes me feel better about bringing down a part of the forest. Someday, sooner than I want it to, my body is going to fail me and I won't be able to do this anymore. So I'll cherish the burn of my muscles while I can.

Plus, Spruce hates the noise.

This is the part of my day I treasure. Most people talk about the outdoors with a reverence for the silence. I don't see it that way. All around is noise. The chirps, squawks, and screeches of various birds. The hum of bugs. Wind through trees. It's a cacophony of chaotic noise. I love every single bit of it.

It takes a good hour to cut off all the branches from the trunk. I bundle some of them up to use for smaller projects and leave the rest on the forest floor to become part of the earth once again.

Another thirty minutes and I have the trunk secured to the tow hitch of my truck. I'm lucky because this tree is close to a long-forgotten access road that I easily maneuvered my truck down. I try not to go this far from the cabin when I'm harvesting a tree, but I came across this one on one of my many off trail runs and knew it needed to come down. I only take a specimen that is already diseased or dead and this one had obviously been struck by lightning at some point, most likely killing it instantly. If I had let it stand, it would have been a danger to the surrounding trees or any people that might wander out this way.

Everything secure at last, I climb into the driver seat, giving Spruce a pat as he sits up next to me and I attach his harness to the seatbelt for the trip back.

It might feel like I am completely secluded out here, but the truth is these mountains aren't nearly as untouched as they look. The town I grew up in, Amoresville, is only fifteen miles to the south. The state park with its crowded campsites and cabins for rent butts right up against the border of my land, ten miles to the west. Other small towns dot the area as well, but by most people's standards, I truly live in the middle of nowhere.

My father's family has owned this land for generations, along with the farm my brother inherited when Pop passed away five years ago. I never felt like I earned this land as much as my brother did the farm. Knox was out in the fields every day from the time we were kids, helping with all the chores that go into maintaining a working farm. I ran around causing trouble with my friends.

The first time I ever stepped foot on this land was the day we laid Dad to rest. I've been doing my best to bring it back to life ever since.

My closest neighbor is an empty cabin on the other side of the pond from mine. The place sits on the edge of one acre of land right smack in the middle of the over two hundred acres that belong to me. For generations it's been owned by our family nemesis and long line of town mayors, the Lickinbills.

My great-great-uncle lost the single acre and cabin to Chester Lickinbill during a poker game nearly a hundred years ago. To this day, Uncle Buck's name is forbidden in my family.

The difference between the two sides of the pond is like night and day. For a while the Lickinbills kept up their side; a few generations back the family wasn't totally full of assholes. But once it was passed down to our current mayor, Burt Lickinbill, that all stopped. I don't think I've ever seen the man step foot on the property since the deed was signed over after his father passed.

The weeds grow unchecked around the small cabin. Fences of former gardens lay broken and scattered around the small clearing. I refuse to mow the grass that grows wild out of principle. Burt or his nephew Wesley can get their asses up here and mow it themselves. The cabin itself is well built, which is probably the only reason all four walls and the roof are still standing. But the shutters are barely hanging on, and I'm fairly certain a family of squirrels have taken residence over the chimney.

The shake of my head is a reflex at this point as I make my way through the last of the trees and the Lickinbill cabin comes into view. Burt's offered to sell the cabin and single acre of land back to me more times than I can count. If the amount he was asking for wasn't ten times its worth, I might have considered it. But he doesn't really want to sell it to me. Being able to hold the decades-old embarrassment over my family's head is just about as much of a family tradition to him as being mayor of Amoresville.

As I draw closer, my foot slides over to the brake to slow down the truck, because for the first time in the five years I've lived here something is different about the Lickinbill cabin.

Parked directly next to the south wall is a Honda Civic that looks like it's seen more action than I did while enlisted. Attached to it is a small U-Haul trailer, and I'm frankly shocked that combo made it up the rough mountain road to our clearing.

Next to me, Spruce stirs a little, giving a little yip. He probably notices my trepidation.

The front door to the cabin is open, which might be the first time I've seen signs of life in the place since I got back from my time in the Marines. A moment after that realization, a high-pitched scream cuts through the peaceful clearing, echoing out across the mountains.

My truck jerks to a stop when I slam full force on the brakes, sending dirt and rocks spraying out behind me. I leap from the cab of the truck and sprint toward the cabin, sure in my gut that that was the unmistakable sound of a female in distress.

Behind me Spruce barks like crazy, probably straining at his harness holding him back while I charge forward.

As I draw even with the bottom of the stairs leading to the wrap-around porch, a blur of black and pink comes stumbling from the open door. A woman flies down the steps, her feet getting tangled together so she crashes down on top of me and we both go tumbling to the weed covered walkway. The breath is knocked from my lungs as the whole of her crashes onto me and I simultaneously realize she is wearing nothing but a bra and panties.

Her wild, panicked eyes swing up to my face. Pure unadulterated fear fills the beautiful, brown eyes looking down at me. She draws in a breath, and I expect her to let loose another scream. But instead, she mouths silently, "Help me!"

Chapter 2

Brigid

I will admit, more than once I have fantasized about having a hot, plaid-covered lumberjack pinned beneath me. But not in a single one of those fantasies was the reason said man was underneath me because I literally fell on top of him after running out of what was supposed to be an adorable cottage in the forest but is instead one step above a condemned shack.

I am no stranger to a good DIY project. I love taking the abandoned and neglected things of this world and turning them into something beautiful again. Whether it is furniture, jewelry, thrifted clothes, hell, even a few people that I took under my wing. But this cabin is not a DIY project. It's a knock it down and light a match project. The pictures on Facebook were obviously a few years old. Or digitally enhanced.

When I arrived at the cabin a few hours before my current predicament, I still had a sense of optimism about this whole thing. True, at first I thought the much larger and much more well-maintained cabin across the pond was where we would be staying. But the smaller cabin came into view and I knew the truth. The pond is gorgeous, the surrounding woods pristine. So what if the cabin needed some cleaning, paint, and maybe an entirely new roof? I can do hard things.

But the optimistic me of just a few short hours ago is now long gone, replaced by a pissed off woman who has been lied to by one too many men. That woman had yet to discover that the electricity and water weren't turned on. She hadn't discovered the dead rabbit petrified in the oven. Not to mention the second bedroom has a giant hole in the floor that goes straight through to the ground beneath. But worst of all was the nest of mice living in the couch. A couch which I dragged out onto the porch, then down into the yard, by myself.

That woman had yet to have the world's biggest spider drop from the ceiling onto her arm. Yeah, I watched frozen in horror as the ginormous, hairy arachnid scurried up under the sleeve of my t-shirt. Which is when I let out the blood curdling scream that undoubtedly attracted the man lying among the weeds beneath me.

It was also when I started pulling off my shirt, then pants, to try and find the eight-legged creature and banish it from this realm. But I can't find the damn thing. I can feel it crawling all over my skin though. It might have multiplied and now it and its ten thousand babies are covering my skin while I stare at the man below me, silently begging him to help me.

Mr. Mountain Man sits up with me still in his lap, a move that has me momentarily distracted from the venomous killer probably sinking his teeth into my flesh at this very moment. Because now I am straddling this stranger while in nothing but panties and a bra and he holds me tightly against his chest and glares into the open door of the cabin.

"Is someone in there hurting you?" Every muscle in his body is rigid beneath me. Well, almost every muscle. His voice is a low dangerous rumble that I can only compare to the growl of a bear. "Did someone bring you here against your will?"

I'm struck dumb when the guy climbs to his feet, my legs still wrapped around him like a damn kola bear clinging to a tree trunk. For a moment, I struggle to remember why I was running from the cabin in the first place. Maybe it was just so I could run into this big, burly, sexy man who looks like he would be willing to murder whatever villainous man is inside the cabin.

Something skitters across my shoulder and all the terror from ten seconds ago comes rushing back. "Get it off, get it off," I whisper while also slapping at my neck and shoulders to try and kill the damn thing.

Lumberjack man puts me down, finally, and peers at me from what feels like five feet above. "Get what off you?"

"The spider," I hiss at him, turning in a circle to try and see my own back. "The world's biggest spider, with huge pointy fangs." I hold two fingers up in front of my mouth, hooked to mimic said fangs. "It's probably poisonous. I could be dying as we speak."

Two large hands reach out and grip my shoulders, holding me still so that my back faces him. "Don't move," he whispers against my ear.

My heart pounds so hard I'm sure it must be sending shock waves through the mountains. There is probably a landslide happening somewhere on the other side of the range because my heart is trying to burst out of my chest in an attempt to escape the spider too.

Eyes squeezed tight, I do as the stranger asks and stand as still as possible. He pushes my hair up to expose my nape. Involuntarily a shudder ripples through my body and goosebumps appear along my arms. Because of the fear and the terror. Not because that move was really sexy.

"Got it." The man walks around me so I can see the sizable spider wriggling on his cupped palm. "I'll admit, she's big, but I don't think this little lady will be breaking any records. She looks scary, but orb weavers are harmless. Locals call this a pumpkin orb weaver." The stranger's mouth quirks up into a little grin, and he huffs out a breath that is half laugh.

"So, not poisonous or venomous?"

His eyes shift to my face. "You aren't dying as we speak, promise."

Now that I know I'm not in any danger, I take a closer look at the little creature that caused so much panic. In my book, the thing is huge, the bulbous orange and yellow body alone is about the size of a dime, and with the legs it stretches to the size of a quarter. But it doesn't try to hurt or bite the man holding it.

"They rarely bite, and when they do it's no worse than a bee sting." He walks over to a clump of branches and weeds that might have at one point been a flower garden and gently turns the spider out of his hand and onto a branch. "Great for keeping pests under control though. You probably have her to thank for keeping bugs in the cabin under control."

Spider safely stowed away, the man turns back to me, and I don't miss the way his eyes track up and down my body. Which reminds me, I'm practically naked after ripping my clothes off trying to find the spider. Too late, I cross my arms over my chest and try to kind of hunch over to block his view of my nether region in my black boy shorts.

"Here." He unbuttons his plaid shirt, revealing a white tank top clinging to the many muscles along his stomach.

The stranger is unfairly gorgeous. Tall, and not just compared to me, but actually tall. Like over six feet. He has beautiful hazel eyes and I wonder if they change with his surroundings.

A dog that I hadn't noticed in the commotion lets out a long, mournful whine from behind the stranger. He turns in that direction, giving the dog a single command that appears to reassure the creature enough that he quiets.

I should stop staring. The man rescued me from a completely harmless spider and is now literally giving me the shirt off his back, so I shouldn't be ogling him. Not to mention my track record with men is truly heinous. Which is why I have sworn them off for good.

He steps forward and drapes the flannel shirt around my shoulders, holding out the sides so I can slip my arms through the sleeves, then tucks it around me like a wrap. The thing is comically long on my five-foot three frame but barely covers my chest and belly thanks to my generous curves.

"I'm Orion, by the way." He holds out his hand for me to shake. "That's my cabin just on the other side of the pond." He nods in the direction, even though my sad excuse for a cabin blocks the view. I had noticed his place when we first got here. It's about twice the size as the cabin I'm renting, and significantly better cared for. His side of the pond also has several other buildings, not to mention some rather large machinery.

As our palms slide together in greeting, another round of goosebumps spreads up my arms and down my legs. Thankfully, he can't see now that I'm covered in his shirt. His shirt that smells like leaves and grass and vanilla.

"Brigid, I'm renting this... well, this pile of sticks, for the next month." Neither of us has broken the contact yet. Our hands still pressed together, slowly moving up and down in a sad imitation of a handshake. A heat is building between us, palpable and heady. I know I'm not every man's cup of tea, but there is no mistaking this man, Orion, would drink me down given the chance. I have to admit, the attention is kind of nice after nearly two years of self-enforced celibacy.

So of course, right at that moment, the mewling cry of my nine-month-old baby echoes out from where I left him napping in his car seat in the cleanest part of the cabin I could find. Surprisingly, the bathtub.

As if in slow motion, I watch in fascination as Orion's interest in me turns to confusion as his gaze darts toward the sounds of my son waking up. It's like a car crash happening right before my eyes that I can't look away from. The confusion turns to realization; he drops my hand as if he's been scalded and takes a step back.

Ah yes, the instant boner killer that is the knowledge that a woman is also a mother.

Chapter 3

Orion

"And that is the reason I was trying not to scream. Or at least tried not to scream after that first one." Brigid turns toward the door, my flannel more or less covering the delectable view from behind I had been enjoying while I took the spider from her shoulder.

In retrospect, it might have been a dick move to check out her ass while the woman was in distress. I can't help it though; Brigid is unlike anyone else in Amoresville. Her pale skin is covered in a patchwork of colorful tattoos along both arms and down her back. Smooth, black hair is cut in a blunt line just below her chin with bangs above her eyebrows. A silver ring pierced through one nostril, and at least a couple others on each ear. I could look at her all day and find endless interest in her features and adornments.

"Thanks for the help." With a backward wave over her shoulder, the beauty disappears into the cabin, not even giving a backward look at me, the man who saved her life. Or at least saved her from a harmless spider bite, thanks to her flailing.

Why does her departure and lack of a goodbye rankle so much? I'm used to being a bit of an afterthought. Living up on the mountain, far away from town and my family, results in a bit of an out of sight, out of mind situation. So it shouldn't hurt that a stranger could turn and leave me behind without a thought.

I should probably check around the cabin to see if there are any more predators. It's the neighborly thing to do, after all. It has nothing to do with the memory of her body in the skimpy bra and panty set. Or hoping that I'll get another glimpse of her.

Carefully, I climb the rotting wooden steps and onto the porch. The beams are so old and soft I'm a little worried one of my gigantic feet is going to punch right through the floorboards. Brigid left the front door open, but it's wrong to walk in without saying anything. Especially when she's dealing with a crying baby. And yet, leaving feels just as wrong.

Instead of waltzing right into her living space, or going home, I stand awkwardly on the porch inspecting the door frame. The door itself is in solid shape, though it sags slightly on the hinges. The frame is a different story. There is some obvious rot toward the floor, and the threshold has water damage as well. Fall is just ramping up, and the temperatures are still pretty warm during the day, but at night it gets downright cold up here in the mountains. If the wind picks up, this doorway is going to be more of a wind tunnel than a barrier to the elements.

Crouching down, I take a closer look at the rotting parts. The slightest touch of my finger to the wood causes chunks to flake off. Thankfully, no sign of termites though. It should be a fairly easy fix. The items I'll need are probably already in my workshop.

"Listen, this place is falling down well enough on its own, I don't think it needs your help." Now that she isn't quaking in fear or whispering to prevent her baby from waking up, Brigid's voice is like honey dripping from the hive, sweet and thick. But with an undeniable edge that makes clear I'm not especially welcome. Apparently, my good deed is already forgotten.

"I was just taking a look at the place." I glance up to find my new neighbor standing a few feet away, the baby who had been crying a minute ago now propped on her hip flashing a gummy smile.

My knowledge of babies is confined to the few times I've been around by best friend Sam and his wife Paula's kids. This one is especially adorable with its blonde hair and chubby cheeks. Like it belongs on the label of baby food. He wears a pair of footy pajamas in a bright yellow and green print, contrasting severely to his mom's new outfit, a pair of ripped black jeans and a black t-shirt that says *Witch Way to the Coffee?* in big white cursive letters.

"Trust me, it looks better the further away you are." Brigid holds out the flannel shirt I had lent her, and for some reason knowing the first thing she did after going in was to take it off rankles. "I could have just dropped this off later, you didn't need to stick around for your shirt."

Slowly, I rise to my full height and cross into the cabin to retrieve the piece of clothing from her. Reluctantly. I want it back on her skin with nothing beneath. "Wasn't waiting for the shirt, I wanted to make sure you were okay."

Goddamn, am I so hard up that I can't stop obsessing over the first non-local woman I see even if that woman is holding a baby? For all I know she could be married. I'm fairly certain that kid didn't blink into existence without the help of another person.

A glance at her hand confirms she isn't married. Or at least she doesn't wear a wedding ring.

"This place isn't fit for habitation. I didn't realize Burt had been trying to rent it out." I wander further inside the musty, dark space, testing a couple of the light switches and confirming my suspicion. The electricity isn't even working.

"Yeah, I found the place on Facebook Marketplace, but let's just say the photos might have been a little out of date." Brigid wanders over to the kitchen to rummage through a massive duffel bag with an astonishing number of pockets that sits on the dusty island. "Or possibly enhanced with AI."

"Trust me, Burt does not have the technical know-how to use AI. The only intelligence around here that is artificial would be his. He probably used photos from before he inherited the place."

I watch in fascination as Brigid pulls out various mysterious baby paraphernalia and somehow mixes up a bottle with only one hand while she does that elephant sway thing. I always see the moms in town do that sway with their kids. Is that shit instinctual? Does it download into a parent's brain when the kid pops out?

"I already left a message for the owner to try and get someone up here to turn on the power and water. After that it will just be a matter of some cleaning, and the place won't be half bad." She sounds like she's trying to convince herself as much as me. She glances up from her work and scans the small cabin. "I do wish I hadn't sold all my furniture though. This place was supposed to be fully furnished."

I follow her gaze's path. The main living area is open concept, like mine, but about half the size. A stone fireplace along one wall, a couple chairs and a table that look like they might collapse if someone even thought about sitting on them. A few end tables here and there, but no couch. There are three doors off the living area. I know from blueprints I've found of both cabins that two of the doors are to small bedrooms and one is to a bathroom.

Once the bottle is deposited in the little guy's month, Brigid glances around the space as if she can see something no one else can. "Considering the price on this place is about a quarter what I was paying in monthly rent in Pittsburgh, I can deal with its shortcomings."

"Is that where you are visiting from?"

"Not visiting, Mica and I plan on making Amoresville our home." She tickles under the baby's chin, and he giggles around the bottle nipple. "Aren't we, dude? No more city life for us, isn't that right?"

Why does that tidbit of information make my heart pick up speed and my brain go fuzzy?

"That explains the selling the furniture comment."

She raises one eyebrow and shoots me a *no shit dumbass* look.

Transplants to Amoresville aren't very common. Occasionally someone marries into the small-time life, like my soon-to-be-sister-in-law, June. She had just been passing through and quite literally crashed into my brother's life, then never left. It only took a year for Knox to put a ring on her finger.

But June is definitely an anomaly. There aren't a ton of people clamoring to live in a town where the nearest Target is almost an hour away. The opposite, actually. Townies have been fleeing from Amoresville more and more each year. Though, I have to admit, tourism has picked up thanks both to June acting as the town's one-woman tourism board and the book she released a few months ago about the history of small towns in Pennsylvania.

"You look kind of familiar. Is it possible we've met before?" She gives me an all too familiar look. The one that strangers get when they look at me a little too long. She has undoubtedly seen some of my videos. That's not my ego talking, it's a fact. If she's even semi-present on social media, then one of my videos would have made it across her feed at some point.

I fight the blush that I can feel creeping up my face, but know it is a losing battle so instead turn to inspect one of the windows along the front of the house.

"I guess I have one of those faces. I'm pretty sure I'd remember running into you before. How on Earth did you decide to move to Amoresville?" I can deflect like a freaking ninja. Someone mentions anything even remotely related to my online persona and I am instantly doing flips to move the conversation on. "Most people don't even know this place exists." I hope she takes the subject change and moves on. I've yet to recognized as the stranger online who chops wood, but a part of me knows it is inevitable.

Brigid chuckles a little as she shifts Mica to her other hip. "Actually, the first time I ever heard of the town was when I moved to Pittsburgh five years ago. I used to live in Arizona and the weather changes on the East Coast fascinated me, so I tended to keep the news on in the background while I cleaned. During the weather segment on the news one Valentine's Day a few years ago—" She doesn't so much as give me a look as she tells the story, focusing instead on the baby in her arms as he drinks his bottle. The monotone tenor of her voice makes it more than clear she's being polite by continuing to chat with me, but would rather I leave. "—the weatherman had put all the weird Pennsylvania town names that had even a little bit to do with love on the map. You know, Pillow, Intercourse, Lover, Climax."

Yeah, I perk up a little at that last one, I'm completely embarrassed to admit. "And Amoresville?"

"That's right. The whole thing was kind of funny, and it stuck in my mind. I would run across the town name every now and again after that, and it always seemed to stick out to me. It became almost like a game, where will that town name pop up next? Then last year, I was on bedrest and was endlessly scrolling social media. I saw a post about a cute little farm in the town named after love that grows giant pumpkins and was hosting a fall festival." Brigid reaches back into the magic bag and pulls out a granola bar, ripping it open with her teeth between sentences. "I recognized the town name immediately and went down a rabbit hole looking at different posts from this travel influencer that moved here."

I don't mention that the farm belongs to my brother and his fiancée. Or that his fiancée is that former travel influencer turned author and travel marketing guru. "So you moved here because of a weather map and a couple social media posts?"

Brigid rolls her eyes and takes a bite of her snack, shaking her head as she does. "Course not, that would be insane." She swallows her bite and I'm paying way too close attention to how sexy the sight of her eating is. "But the town name just kept popping up. A vendor I use was going to have a booth set up at the fall festival. A couple weeks later a group I belonged to announced they were going to do a retreat and stay at the B&B in town. I couldn't go because I was due the same week they were going. Then Mica here came along right on Valentine's

Day. It was like the universe was insisting I look at the town named after love."

I'm trying not to make snap judgments about this girl who apparently believes in signs from the universe. Try and fail.

"The last straw was a tarot reading a friend of mine did a month ago. The Six of Swords landed right on top of The Lovers." She looks at me as if that sentence should mean anything to me. Which it doesn't.

But all at once a bunch of puzzle pieces fall into place. The t-shirt. The look. The signs from the universe. The group of women that descended on the town last summer and turned out to be a bunch of new-age hippies who got caught dancing naked in the woods around a fire.

My new neighbor is also a witch. Can't say I've met too many of those before.

"The Six of Swords can indicate a move of some sort, usually away from a negative energy, which certainly hit home. The Lovers typically means a choice needs to be made in a relationship. But I took it a little more literally. The town named after lovers."

Silence descends on the cabin as I take in the complete insanity of what this woman has said. She moved four hours across the state, with a baby, because of some coincidences and a couple of cards in a deck.

Completely undisturbed by the awkward silence, Brigid simply stands there making faces at her baby as he finishes his bottle, and she munches on her granola bar.

"What does Mica's dad think about you picking up and moving across the state because of a deck of cards?" As soon as the words pop out of my mouth, I wish I could grab them and shove them down my throat. It's like they spewed out of my mouth before I could even think about them. Something that is not like me at all.

You learn in the military to think before you speak. The wrong answer to a commanding officer's question and you'll find yourself doing unending pushups in the mud, or worse, the sand in a hot desert.

The slow slide of Brigid's smile from her face as she turns toward me tells me what I already knew, I absolutely said the wrong thing. Her borderline tolerance of my presence of just a few seconds ago has evaporated. Now she regards me as if I am lower than the spider she had been freaking out about earlier.

I don't believe in magic or witchcraft, or much of anything that I can't see and touch myself. But if I did, I would be absolutely terrified right now, because there is no doubt that Brigid is currently silently cursing my existence.

Chapter 4

Brigid

"Excuse me?"

The fuck did he ask me? Listen, I am used to the weird looks and eye rolls most people give me about my beliefs. Even in a fairly progressive city like Pittsburgh, Paganism isn't widely accepted. But most people have the decency to keep their thoughts inside their heads.

Not Orion apparently.

"Shit, fuck. Sorry, that came out wrong."

"Oh, there was a right way to insinuate I took my son away from his father against his will on a whim?"

To his credit, Orion does truly look embarrassed for his question. His face has lost a lot of its color and he has shoved his hands deep into his pockets, hunching his shoulders in on himself.

"That is *not* what I meant at all. I didn't mean anything. I was just curious about where the dad is." Orion shakes his head. "Not that that is any of my business. I can't ignore the fact that you two appear to be alone out here in the middle of nowhere. That isn't exactly safe."

I can feel my left eyebrow creeping higher onto my forehead in what my sister affectionately calls my "*Going to Explode*" expression. As in each tick of my eyebrow gets my target closer to a BOOM. The anger now wafting off me in waves is not lost on Orion, apparently.

"Not that I think a woman needs a man to be safe. Or at all. I'm a feminist," he ends weakly.

Why is it shitty men always like to think of themselves as feminists? As if that will save them? My ex loved to spout on and on about the need to uplift women artists in the industry, while also stepping on every woman in his way to being a celebrated artist. Including me. "Yeah, I can tell."

"Seriously, my mom and sister would kill me if they had heard that whole, well, disaster." Orion removes one hand from his pocket and pulls the tie from his hair. His hair flows down over his shoulders, the dark auburn strands falling in front of his face before he gathers it back into his fist and redoes the man-bun. "What I should be saying is, this place is a dump. Please let me help get it at least semi-livable before night falls so I won't be up all night wondering if the woman and her baby next door are being eaten by a bear."

"No thanks, we'll be fine," I return in a flat monotone. He's obviously exaggerating. A bear wouldn't be able to come in here. Right?

Orion drops his gaze to the floor, his hands going back to his pockets. "At least let me get the water going. And I can take a look at the electrical box, too. I guarantee Burt isn't getting anyone out here tonight, if at all. Both because he's an asshole but also because nothing happens that fast out here."

"Do you even know what you're doing?" Sure, he obviously has some well-crafted muscles and a face made for the cover of *Lumberjack Monthly* or something, but that doesn't mean he knows anything about home repair.

He nods his head and glances up at me from beneath his eyelashes. God damn, he truly is beautiful. There is no other word for it.

Shame he's an asshole.

"My family built both cabins and maintained them until my great-great-uncle lost this place in a poker bet." He inspects my new home, cringing at what it has become. "I know Burt hasn't replaced anything, so it should be all the same equipment I had at my place when I moved in. I did all the work modernizing my cabin. I don't doubt I can at least get you electricity and drinkable water."

Mica pulls my attention back to him by letting out a great big burp and then giggling. If we don't have power or water, we can't stay here. If I turn down this stranger's help then I would truly be as bad a mother as he thinks I am.

He fidgets under my scrutiny, shifting from one foot to the other. Strangely, there are no alarm bells ringing in my head or in my stomach. I ignored my intuition for years and it landed me in a horrible relationship that I am finally putting behind me. That is not a mistake I'll make again, so I take the time to tap into what my body is telling me, even if it does make Orion uncomfortable. Much to my surprise, everything inside me feels at ease around this man.

"Fine."

Orion has the good sense to keep his mouth shut and head to the door with nothing but a nod.

"His dad wanted nothing to do with him." The words come out even though I try to hold them back. I don't owe this man an explanation, but I also don't like anyone thinking I could do something as evil as take a child from a loving parent.

Gently, I press Mica's head to my shoulder so his ear is pressed against me on one side and my hand muffles the sound on the other. I know he's too young to understand any of this, but the idea that he might internalize any of this bullshit at such a young age still bothers me.

"I won't go into the details, but let me reassure you, my ex doesn't care to know where we are, and he made that more than clear when he gave up all parental rights before Mica was even born. I got the best thing that man ever had to offer the universe, and it is all right here in my arms." I let go of Mica's ears and give him a quick kiss on the top of his head, which my little sweetheart returns with a smacking wet kiss on my cheek.

I have made damn sure my son only knows love and that he will never feel the absence of his paternal side of the family.

Turning, I leave Orion staring after us and head into the larger of the two bedrooms, the one without a hole in the floor, to get things organized. Or just to do something with my hands before the burning sensation creeping up behind my eyes turns into tears. I refuse to cry in front of a stupid-hot stranger that happens to think I am crazy and is maybe the second biggest asshole I've ever met. An asshole, but not dangerous. I trust that instinct.

Thankfully, the bedroom isn't that bad compared to the rest of the place. A little dusty, light on furniture, but no noticeable wildlife or holes in the floors, walls, or windows. And at this point, a win is a win, so I'll mark this off in the win column.

The first thing I did upon our arrival was drag in the unbelievable amount of crap it takes to both care for and entertain a child. Mica falling asleep in his car seat ten minutes before we got to the cabin was a stroke of good luck. The kid has blessed me by being the absolute best sleeper and stayed fast asleep through me taking the car seat out, carrying him in, and placing the whole seat safely in the confines of the tub where he napped for nearly an hour. I know, I know, letting babies sleep in a car seat isn't the best. But given the alternatives all needed to be bleached, I figured one time wouldn't hurt too much. His impromptu nap gave me enough time for me to unload the car, but my goal of getting everything put away was interrupted by spider-gate.

Time to get back to it now.

It only takes a minute for me to get the Pack 'n Play set up in the corner with the least cobwebs and then Mica settled with his favorite toys. Which he promptly ignores in favor of performing his newest trick—pulling himself up to stand at the side of the playpen while babbling "Mamamamamama" over and over again. I was so excited the first day he said those two syllables. Now I would give anything not to hear my name on repeat every hour of the day.

But he's happy, so put another mark in the win column.

Pulling the musty old sheets and blanket that look like they haven't been changed in years off the full-sized bed, I'm pleasantly surprised to find a mattress that has zero springs sticking out or holes in the fabric. With my face as close as I'm willing to get it to the bed, I see no signs of mice or bed bugs. The wins just keep rolling in!

From a large black garbage bag, I pull out the four sets of sheets and two quilts I brought with us. Their clean scent wafts through the musty air as I snap them out and begin making the bed. Another garbage bag holds our pillows and some of Mica's stuffies. What can I say, I didn't see the point in going and buying moving boxes when I already had trash bags. It only takes a few minutes, and the bedroom is already looking more welcoming.

The whole time I work, I concentrate as hard as I can on ignoring the mutterings of Orion outside the cabin. There is a small utility room, more like a closet, toward the back of the cabin, just outside the bedroom window, which holds the mysterious utilities. I'd peeked in the tiny room when we got here to see if I could figure things out, but electrical boxes and water tanks are a little outside my wheelhouse. Plus, there were more spiderwebs than I was willing to contend with at the time.

An involuntary shiver runs up my spine at the thought of the spider crawling on me again. The irony of a witch and self-proclaimed lover of all things dark and macabre being afraid of a spider is not lost on me.

From the utility room, a not insignificant amount of swearing and banging around is happening. I hear at least three instances of *"Fucking Burt,"* a couple *"Goddamn Lickinbill,"* and at least one loud and distinctive *"As bad a landlord as he is a fucking mayor."* Between the cursing and complaining, Orion talks to his dog as if they are both working on getting the power working. *"Alright, boy, I think we just need to clean this off a bit."*

After all that swearing, a subtle hum precedes every single light in the cabin turning on all at once and Orion declaring, *"I still got it."*

In the next moment, the pipes running along the walls groan to life and a slight rush means he got the water going too. This place is so old it looks like it was built before indoor plumbing, and the pipes were an afterthought many generations later run on the outside of the walls. Not exactly my aesthetic, but I can make it work until we find someplace more permanent in town. I had originally planned on staying in this cabin for a month, enjoying the mountain air, then moving into the little town when my store was ready to open. But given the state of the cabin and the newly discovered obnoxious neighbor, I might need to move that timetable up.

Orion appears at the front door a few minutes later, knocking on the frame where I left it open to air the place out. The dog sits obediently by his side, but his nose strains into the cabin, sniffing the air. "Do you mind if I check some of the pipes in here? If the water's been off as long as I think it has, it's possible some of them have eroded or have leaks."

I stay where I am in the bedroom but have a clear line of sight to where he stands, the sun beginning to set behind him giving a halo effect around his tall, lean frame. I have a feeling he would stand there not stepping a toe into the cabin if I said he couldn't come in.

"Have at it," I respond coldly, waving him in.

As he enters, I notice he needs to duck down slightly so he doesn't hit his head on the top of the door frame. "Stay, Spruce."

Curiosity gets the better of me, and I make my way out into the living area to watch him work. The kitchen faucet sputters violently the moment he turns it on, but eventually settles into a steady stream of water. Orion stoops down to open the cabinet doors below the sink and nods in apparent approval.

Next, he heads to the bathroom, and with a glance back at Mica, who is now occupied with a crinkly baby book, I follow in silence.

I'm amazed to find his dog is sitting exactly where Orion left him. "The dog can come in. He can't make the place any dirtier than it already is. I feel bad he's just sitting there staring in at us."

"You sure?"

I nod, but realize he can't see me from the bathroom. "I'm sure."

"Spruce, relax." The dog immediately stands and does a combination trot/hop into the main living area. Which is when I realize he's missing one of his rear legs.

The dog's nose goes to the floor and he makes his way around the walls, smelling every inch of the house. I let him do his thing and follow Orion.

The bathroom is one of the better parts of the cabin, and was obviously added onto the side of the structure mere decades ago. It's very retro in a sixties kind of way with black and white tiles, a white pedestal sink, a toilet, and a tub that is only slightly chipped at the rim.

Orion is frozen beside the tub, staring at the car seat where my son had been napping earlier.

"Oh, sorry, I left that in here after Mica's nap." I squeeze past him, bending to lift it from the deep tub. "Seemed like the safest, and neatest, place for him to be when we first got here."

There I go again, over explaining things that are frankly none of his business. I used to pride myself on not giving two shits about what people thought about me. I was a goth witch in sunny Arizona through my teens, that makes a person grow a thick skin. But through the years, one shitty man wore down that armor until I almost couldn't recognize who I was. I even left my family and moved across the country for that shithead.

Mica's dad, William Walters. Never Will or Bill or Liam. William.

From the moment we met, I was mesmerized by him. So enamored with the brooding artist that I ignored the intuition that seemed to constantly be on edge around him. I thought I was simply intimidated by his brilliance, and the ten years he had on me. So, when he was offered a full-time professor position at the Art Institute of Pennsylvania, I followed. Left in the middle of my freshman year at the art school where we met when I had him for Figure Drawing 101. I had only known him six months.

He swore up and down he'd find a way to get me enrolled at the highly prestigious school, and until then I could get our new place set up. Yeah, it was one of many lies he told me along the way.

As I turn to get out of Orion's way, I catch him staring directly where my ass would have been while I was bent over. It takes him a second, but eventually his head snaps up and he stares at the wall just above my head, his cheeks and the tips of his ears slowly turning bright red.

He really does look familiar. I swear I've seen him someplace before, but can't quite imagine the place or circumstances we would have ever met before.

Chapter 5

Orion

Caught.

God damn it, there is no way this woman didn't catch me staring at her ass. Her round, luscious, heart-shaped ass.

The heat spreading up my neck to my face and ears signals the goddamn blush I have been cursed with my whole life is also probably not helping my case. I got so much shit in the Marines for my red hair and tendency to blush anytime I saw a woman that piqued my interest. The nicknames were lame and never ending. Carrot Top, Little Orphan Annie, Ariel, Gingy, the list goes on. Marines are not known for their creativity.

I keep my eyes glued to the space above Brigid's head, completely avoiding any eye contact. "I'll just test things in here and then get out of your hair."

"Sure." Yeah, she caught me. The cold demeanor that has been directed my way since letting those idiotic words leave my mouth chills further.

As she slips past me, I try my best to hold my breath. To not lean in and take a deep whiff of the spicy-citrus scent I noticed earlier.

Finally, alone in the small bathroom that is almost identical to what my own looked like when I moved in, I busy my hands with turning on and off the facets and the feed hose to the toilet. Everything fills exactly as I would expect with no obvious leaks or drips, which is honestly pretty astonishing considering I have no clue when fucking Burt decided to shut off the power and water where it comes into the house. He had already owned the place for a few years when I moved in. Even the hot water is in working order.

My checks take a matter of seconds, but the idea of walking back out there and facing this woman who I have not only insulted but now horn dogged over her like a teenager is almost too much to stand. I'm not usually prone to fits of embarrassment. Growing up in the most infamous family in a small town, you get real used to being okay with who you are real fast. It's that or try and bend to the will of everyone around you, and that just isn't how our mother raised us.

"You about done?"

God damn, this woman has no business talking in such a fucking sexy voice every damn second. It might be laced with barely contained contempt for me, but apparently that does something for my libido.

"Not too bad considering your landlord is an idiot." I turn all the faucets off again and reluctantly exit the bathroom to face my new neighbor. "The electrical panel was a challenge, lots of erosion and the contacts were fused together, so I had to work 'em loose again. I wouldn't plan on running several electronics at once if you don't want it to trip every five seconds. The water came back on with no problem, there might be a small leak in the water tank, but it won't affect anything in here."

I also already have plans to patch it once I get the things I need from the Nail and Bail tomorrow. I'm not quite sure how this woman will react to me doing work around the house, so I don't plan on bringing it up unless I have to.

"Thankfully, the two houses share a well and I make sure to maintain things on my end, so no problem there. Propane tank appears to be in good shape too and is about half-full. That will get you through a couple months of cold weather before you need a refill, but I have the truck coming up next week to top me off before the winter, so I'll make sure they do yours too."

"No need, we won't be here that long." Her words are flat, and leave me more than a little disappointed that she'll be gone before long.

"Well, just in case it takes you longer to find a place than you expect, I'll still have them fill it up. They don't like coming up here more than they have to."

"Fine, tell them to leave the bill if I'm not here and I'll pay it online."

The fuck she will. I am not letting this lady pay that bill after putting my foot in my mouth and considering Burt is probably charging her way too much for this shit hole

"Speaking of which, do you know where the Wi-Fi router is in here?" Brigid is in the kitchen, wiping everything in sight down with a bleach wipe. There is a little mound of them sitting on the corner of the island, all a nauseating shade of brown from how much dust and dirt there is coating every surface. "I tried looking for it on my phone, but the only network I found I assume is yours."

The blush had just gone away from my cheeks, and now I can feel it creeping back, only this time not because I've been caught ogling. No, this one is because my Wi-Fi network name is *Morning Wood.*

"Yup, that would be mine. I'll give you the password. I think there might have been a landline in here at some point, and I am willing to bet my life savings that Burt never upgraded when he inherited the place."

"Are you sure it will reach this far? I mean, you are all the way across the pond."

"Yeah, when I inherited my cabin, I had a buddy set me up with a pretty sophisticated mesh system. He specialized in comms in the Marines, so he knows his shit. It covers the whole clearing." I will not mention I had to make sure the signal was strong all the way to the tree line so I could reliably do lives once a week on TikTok. "If you want to hand me your phone, I can get you all signed in."

"Can you write it down? I'll need to sign in on my computer too once I manage to unpack and set up some semblance of an office."

If I could stop inadvertently embarrassing the shit out of myself with this woman, that would be awesome. "Fuck, okay, so you probably won't need me to write it down to remember it. In my defense, Tommy might be a communications genius, but he's also a complete asshole and has the sense of humor of a thirteen-year-old boy. He refuses to tell me how I change the network name or the password."

"Is it really worse than *Morning Wood*?" She gives me a disbelieving stare, one eyebrow hitched slightly higher than the other.

"Absolutely. It's *PolishMyKnob*. All one word. With an exclamation mark at the end."

Brigid tries her best to hold in her laughter, but as her face turns redder, and her cheeks puff out from the effort, she finally gives in with a loud cackle. "That's amazing. Yeah, definitely won't forget that."

"Well, glad I could help. I'll go jump in the pond now, and hopefully drown." Listen, if my own embarrassment means I've managed to crack her cold exterior for even a minute, yeah, that is worth it any day.

From the other room a constant babbling of *Mama-mama* gets increasingly louder. Brigid's smile widens a little as she glances back at her son.

"I need to finish getting things around here in order before that one—" she tilts her head in his direction —"starts demanding dinner."

"Right, sorry." Slowly, I inch back toward the door, for some reason reluctant to leave the cabin I've never once stepped foot in before today. "Listen, you need anything, I'm just across the pond. Obviously. And actually, here." I pull my wallet from my back pocket and fish out one of the business cards I make a habit of carrying with me but almost never hand out. "My cell number is on here, so if you notice a leak or smell anything off, seriously, call me and I'll come check it out."

Reluctantly, Brigid steps forward to take the card from my outstretched hand. The smile that had dominated her face slips back into that passive, blank expression I desperately want to banish permanently. Her thumb brushes slightly against mine, and I swear I feel that minuscule contact all over my body. Not even a half an hour ago this girl was lying on top of me in nothing but her underwear, asking for my help. I wish I had been aware enough to enjoy it while it lasted. Before I opened my big mouth and directly inserted my boot.

She pulls back the small rectangle of paper and looks down, one eyebrow arched in curiosity, or annoyance, I can't quite tell. "*Constellation Furniture*... You make furniture?"

I nod, shoving my hands as far down in my pockets as they'll go in an attempt to bury the desire to reach out and touch the woman before me again, in a more meaningful way than accidental brushes and fearful tackles. I want to touch her with purpose. A very certain purpose. I don't know why my reaction to this woman is so strong. I've been around beautiful women before, lots of times, but the way my entire body lights up with her proximity has me totally baffled.

"Huh." She shoves the card into her back pocket and shoots me a tight smile. One of those smiles that you know is an attempt at politeness when a person wants nothing more than for you to leave.

I take the hint.

Chapter 6

Brigid

Three hours later, and the cabin is finally in a state where I won't feel bad having Mica crawl on the floor. It took an absolute crap ton of scrubbing, dusting, and even a little hammering for some of the loose floorboards. There was nothing to be done about the hole in the second bedroom though, so I just locked the room up and Mica and I will have to bunk together.

The living room is pretty sparse thanks to the mouse condo, a.k.a. the couch, being hauled out onto the lawn. A rocking chair to the side of the fireplace, a small round table with two mismatched cafe chairs under the front window, and a side table that had been next to the couch. All that open space made for the perfect place to set up Mica's play area.

I can't help but chuckle as I look around at the myriad of toys strewn about the circular baby jail where Mica and I are playing together. The colorful gates connected into a sizable octagon are something I never thought I would have as a mom.

When I first found out I was pregnant, and decided I would keep it despite every one of my friends insisting I was crazy to do this alone, I had all these romantic ideas of only getting him wooden toys, nothing that required batteries. Nothing plastic. Nothing artificial. I was going to breast feed exclusively and puree my own baby foods.

But then my milk supply never came in, or at least not enough to sustain my quickly growing baby. The day the pediatrician told me I had to start supplementing formula because Mica wasn't thriving, I thought I had failed as a mother. I cried harder in that doctor's office than on the day I excitedly presented Mica's father with a gift bag containing a onesie and the positive pregnancy test. I had been so sure he would be thrilled with the news. But he dropped the test, disgusted that I would give him something I peed on, and told me to take care of the problem. He wasn't going to let a screaming baby stymie his career or his lifestyle.

That afternoon, I gave Mica his first bottle of formula and sobbed, apologizing to him over and over again for failing. He slept for more than a few minutes at a time because his belly was finally full. I slept too. After our nap I realized this mom thing was going to be hard. If making some compromises along the way made things a little easier, I wasn't going to beat myself up about it.

So, when the baby jail showed up at my local thrift shop right as Mica started crawling, and getting into absolutely everything if I turned my back for a second, I grabbed it and never looked back. With one of the many quilts my mom has sent across the country for her first grandson and some yoga mats underneath, it is actually pretty cozy.

There are some wooden toys, some plastic, and yeah, even a couple that require batteries. But my little guy is happy, fed, and thriving.

Mica rubs one of his little fists into his eye, a dead giveaway that he is getting tired. The cabin has grown gradually darker as the evening marched on past dinner. I ignore the begrudging gratitude toward my neighbor for getting the electricity going. It would have been pitch black in here without it. There are a few lamps scattered around, but only two have working light-bulbs, and an antler chandelier that only has one bulb missing, all of which give the place a soft, cozy glow. I wish I had been brave enough to attempt a fire in the fireplace, but Goddess only knows what state that is in. Plus, I've never started a fire in my life.

Or not an intentional one.

Maybe I could ask the judgmental lumberjack to check the chimney for me. Or teach me how to make a fire that would be safe.

I'm a feminist.

Just the memory of his feeble attempt at walking back his hurtful words gives me secondhand embarrassment. The look on his face when I caught him staring at my ass causes an entirely different feeling. One that starts low in my belly and radiates out to the rest of my body like wax dripping from a candle.

I shove the feeling away.

Was Orion attractive? Obviously. Did he also have all the hallmarks of a judgmental ass? Yup.

The only man I plan on having in my life from here on out is the one I gave birth to.

Mica, my work, and myself. That's all I need.

And I will keep repeating that to myself repeatedly until I believe it.

. . .

"Mamamama." Anytime Mica wants to learn a new word would be great. I squeeze my eyes closed, reluctant to see what time my little live-in alarm clock decided to wake me up this morning. Wrapped up in another of my mother's quilts, I'm so warm and cozy, I wish I had caved and let Mica sleep in the bed with me instead of in his Pack 'n Play. If I had, I wouldn't need to get out of bed to get him. There are many things I love about being a mother. The inability to sleep in is not one of them.

"Mamamamama." The telltale squeaks of Mica bouncing in his Pack 'n Play tell me he is not going back to sleep any time soon.

"I'm coming, my little jumping bean." With great effort, I manage to open my eyes and am greeted with warm sunlight streaming in through the windows. The disgusting curtains that had been barely hanging on were thrown out, so there is nothing preventing the early morning light from filling the room.

Blackout curtains need to go on the list for our excursion today.

I roll over to find my baby gumming the side rail of his playpen, the corners of his mouth tipped up in a goofy half-hidden smile. "Did you let Mama sleep until the sun was up?"

"Mamamama," he responds, which I interpret as *I sure did, aren't I the greatest kid on the face of the planet?*

"Let's see what time it is." I dig around in the blankets for my phone that I more than likely dropped while reading myself to sleep last night. Once I locate it, I pull it out of the folds of my sheet, and it lights up with the time.

"Holy shit, eight-thirty?! Is it my birthday or something, I got to sleep for eight hours straight?"

"Mamamama."

"You are right, you deserve an extra special breakfast for letting Mommy sleep in."

The very second my feet touch the wooden floors, Mica is reaching up with both hands, babbling non-stop as if telling me every single dream he had in the night. His little one-sided nonsense conversation continues as I pull him into my arms and give him a soft kiss against his blonde hair, all the way to the kitchen and through me strapping him into his highchair.

"Jeez kid, take a breath." From the fridge, I grab the container of strawberries I had diced before leaving our apartment in Pittsburgh, a cup of yogurt, and some pre-made banana pancakes. For two days before the big move, I did nothing but pack and cook easy meals to throw in a cooler since I knew it might be a day until I could find the closest grocery store.

As dismayed as I had been to see the state of the cabin when we got here, I actually love the kitchen. It's full of vintage appliances that miraculously still work. The fridge took some work to clean the mildew out, and I bleached the hell out of the oven after finding the mummified dead bunny, but otherwise everything is working great.

And all the appliances are avocado green!

Forget stainless steel, give me the tacky colored appliances and tiles of my grandparents' generation.

As I whip together Mica's breakfast, I start a mental list of things we need to grab in town today. More cleaning supplies are at the top of the list since I had completely depleted the supply I brought with us. Pantry staples like spices, oils, and canned stuff that would last a while.

Thanks to living on the thrifty side, my security deposit being returned, and money from some things I sold before leaving, I have a pretty decent nest egg to get us going here. If I planned right, I won't need to dip into my savings, my personal checking account, or business accounts at all. This little escape from the city is entirely funded from my fun account.

Mica makes quick, but messy, work of his breakfast, so I clean him and myself up, and we start in on our inaugural trip to downtown Amoresville.

Driving down the mountain to the valley where the town lays is an adventure in my crappy old Honda. The driveway and single lane road put the Pittsburgh potholes to shame.

Which is saying something.

After dropping off the rented U-Haul trailer at the local garage, we explore the town a bit. I manage to find a thrift store attached to the town's only church. That turns up some half-decent gauzy curtains, some area rugs, and a few other small items to make the place a little more homey. No couch, though, not that I have a way to haul a couch up the mountain now that the trailer is returned.

After popping in and out of some stores that are cute but don't have anything I need, Mica is starting to get grouchy and I know my time is limited before he gets hit with a nap attack. We need to grab groceries and head back up the mountain pronto.

A quick Google search shows the only grocery store in a thirty-mile radius is a little shop about a mile away from the town square. Not wanting to walk that whole way, we hop back in the car and drive the short distance.

Dolly's Market is a cute little box of a building. It boasts tons of beige siding, a red tin roof, and a porch-like area that houses hanging baskets of flowers, buckets of mums, and stacks of pumpkins along with other outdoor decorations for the fall.

Looking up at the sign, I have to tilt my head to make sure I'm seeing it right. Dolly's Pantry is spelled out in blocked letters which are surrounded by drawings of various fruits, veggies, eggs, and milk. Cute and normal, until you notice the eggs nestled up against a cucumber that looks vaguely phallic. Not to mention the cross section of a cantaloupe that looks awfully yonic. The peach isn't totally innocent either.

That had to be an accident, right?

Maybe I'm reading too much into it considering I haven't seen any action since Mica's conception.

With a shake of my head to clean the weirdly sexual images, I climb out of the car and pull the baby carrier from the trunk. When I first bought the thing it took hours for me to figure out how the complicated network of straps and buckles worked to secure my baby. I practiced with a stuffed bear a dozen times before I attempted putting my precious boy into the carrier. Even then I knelt in the center of the bed and hovered over a pile of pillows to make sure he would have some place safe to land if I messed up.

Now I'm practically an expert at strapping my wiggly baby to my chest.

Once I've got him all set, I grab my reusable grocery bags and head into Dolly's, side-eyeing the sign as I go.

The place is so cute I want to grab everything I see.

The floors are worn hardwood, with displays of fresh produce as soon as you walk in the door. Each display has the name of a farm, which I assume to be their local suppliers. Items that wouldn't be in season locally, like strawberries and more exotic fruits, have labels that tell you where they were grown. I grab bananas, a variety of berries, apples, a grin on my face the whole time. The prices here are so cheap compared to the city. Plus, to get anything that looked nearly this good you had to go to the fancy grocery stores that jacked up their prices for the bougie crowds.

A display across the aisle catches my attention. It's an adorable fall themed arrangement of mini-pumpkins, gourds, and garlands of leaves. The small chalkboard to one side is decorated with drawings of more fall items and a familiar name. *Happy Accidents Farm.* The farm I follow on Instagram that was at least part of my motivation to move. Unable to resist, I grab a few of the gourds to decorate the cabin and as a little reminder of why we are here, how I learned about the town.

As I wander into the rest of the store, I realize how small it actually is. Half the market was taken up by the extensive produce section, the other half holds meat and bakery counters against the far wall, half a dozen aisles with your basic grocery needs, and a small pharmacy window manned by a man that has to be going on seventy.

You could fit five Dolly's Pantries in the smallest Pittsburgh grocery store. But everything I need is easily located, and everyone we pass smiles and mentions how sweet Mica looks with his sleeping face pressed against my chest. Because, of course, he fell asleep before I could get us back to the cabin.

"Hi there, and what is your name? I don't believe I've seen you around before." The cashier, a woman a couple inches taller than me, with deep brown skin and warm green eyes, offers up a friendly smile as she starts picking up each item and tapping the prices into the register with her extra-long acrylic nails. No scanning or self-check outs here. They appear to do everything manually.

"I'm Brigid and this is Mica." I tilt my body so she can see Mica's face and she makes the appropriate cooing sounds in response. "We just moved here."

"Oh, how nice. We love newcomers. Helps break up the monotony of all us old folks." Honestly, she could be anywhere from twenty-five to forty-five. She has a youthful appearance thanks to her smooth skin and bright eyes, but the strands of gray glittering from her braids hint at a few more years. "I'm Dolly, it's so nice to meet you."

"Wait, Dolly as in Dolly's Market?"

Dolly smiles wide, showing off a bright white smile and delicate blush. "Well sort of, the original Dolly was my mother who opened the store. I'm Dolly Junior, and then there is my daughter Dolly the First."

Not every day you meet a lineage of women that do the whole junior, first, etc.

"Please tell me you have a granddaughter named Dolly the Second."

Dolly chuckles and pauses her work. "Not yet, my daughter is only sixteen, but who knows, maybe someday."

I chuckle along with her, loving the warmth the woman radiates from every nearly invisible pore. "Well, I love your store. I had to stop myself from grabbing everything I saw."

She waves a hand at me as if to dismiss the compliment. "My mama did all the hard work getting it up and running. Can you believe this all used to be a roadside stand? We only built the larger market about a decade ago when the chain grocery store closed up shop."

"Really? That is incredible." The conversation is cut short by Mica stirring against me, scrunching up his face and letting out a pathetic little whine.

"Oh, well, look who is finally showing off his baby blues." Dolly leans down to wave her fingers at Mica, who rewards her with a sleepy little smile.

"You let me know what brand of diapers and baby food he likes best and I'll make sure we stock it."

"No, really?"

Dolly pulls a pad of paper and a pen from beneath the counter and passes them over to me. "We don't have many young families around here, got to make sure you and yours want to stick around."

"Well, we've only been here a day, but I already love everything I've seen. The only thing that could make it better is someplace to get a good cup of coffee. My coffee maker broke during the move."

"Oh, darling, we have you covered. You'll want to stop at Romancing the Bean next. Best coffee in town." She rips off the paper where I wrote down the brand of diapers I prefer and tapes it next to the register. "I'll even throw your groceries in our walk-in so nothing spoils while you sit and drink a cup."

Is this how all small towns are? A glow builds in my chest, something like the love I feel for Mica, but smaller and not nearly as intense. I think I might be falling in love with Amoresville.

Chapter 7

Orion

My random sojourns into town never fail to be the highlight of my week. As a teen, I had itched to get out of this small town and what I thought were its equally small people.

After my dreams of playing football at college came crashing down, I thought the military was the only way out. That it would help me see the world, and it did, but what it revealed was that the people in Amoresville were just about the best around.

As usual, my quick trip to The Nail and Bail has morphed into a great conversation with Sam, my best friend from high school. He's the biggest fucking gossip, thanks in part to his wife, Paula, being the only hairstylist in town. She gets the dirt from whoever is in the chair that day, and immediately runs over to tell her hubby, who then tells anyone that comes into the hardware store.

I swear the only time those two aren't stirring up trouble in town is when they are working on making yet another baby.

What he doesn't learn from Paula is gleaned from the town council meetings he faithfully attends each month, town charter and a copy of Robert's Rules of Order in hand.

"Hey, have you heard anything about a newcomer to town?" Sam continues writing out each of the items in my order on his notepad. The man refuses to upgrade to a digital system and still insists on doing everything the same way his father had before him. Being old school appears to be something everyone in town takes very seriously. I can count the number of businesses that use digital inventory systems on one hand. As much as I appreciate his, and the town's, dedication to carrying on our charming small-town way of life, it also means that checkout takes three times as long since he has to pause writing each time he talks. The man is incapable of talking and working at the same time. "Rose was in to get her bi-monthly trim, and she told Paula she saw an unfamiliar car pulling through town yesterday afternoon with a U-Haul trailer attached to the back."

Knowing Sam as well as I do, I know better than to tell him anything about my new neighbor. The minute he gets the slightest bit of information it will be all over town. It was Sam that started the infamous rumor that my brother had picked up a hitchhiker on the side of the road and brought her to the farm to be his mail order bride. Don't ask me how she could be both a hitchhiker and a mail order bride. Gossip doesn't need to make sense, it just needs to be juicy.

"Nope. Haven't heard anything about that." Technically the truth. I hadn't heard anything about a newcomer to town. The mountain isn't technically part of the town proper.

Sam nods and puts his pen back to the ledger, writing out the description of the linseed oil I use to seal some of my pieces. Two words and he perks back up with yet another piece of information gleaned from his wife.

But my mind can't focus on whatever tall tale he's weaving now. The only thing occupying any space in my head this morning is why Brigid's car hadn't been parked by the cabin this morning. The first thing I'd done when I rolled out of bed was peer through my window in hopes of catching sight of my new neighbor. But the lights were out, and her car gone. Had one night in the forests of Tioga County proven too much for the city girl?

I didn't think so.

I took it upon myself to patch up the hole in her water heater, as well as change out some of the fuses in the electrical box since I had spares in my workshop. I also grabbed the items I needed from the workshop and replaced the front door threshold. Which is also when I noticed the front door lock doesn't work. Hence the lock on the top of my pile of purchases.

A vibrating in my pocket breaks my swirling thoughts. Pulling my phone out, my sister's name flashes across the screen. "Hold on, Sam. Delia's calling."

I answer the call. "Good morning, Brat."

"Good morning to you too, Dipshit." The trademark whistle of the steaming wand at our mother's cafe rings through the phone, which is odd considering Delia almost never crosses foot into the town limits before noon. "What are you doing today, Loser?"

"Now is that any way to talk to your beloved brother that you are obviously going to ask a favor of?"

"How on earth do you know that?"

"Because you never ask what I'm up to." It's true, Delia constantly has at least three or four irons in the fire and doesn't have time for small talk. I'm usually her first call when she needs help with anything from fixing something at her apartment to needing a fill-in bouncer at the club.

"Ugh, okay, you're right." The whistling stops and Delia goes quiet for a second. "Mom twisted her ankle this morning during Harley's pole working class. I think I should take her out to the urgent care in Wellsboro to make sure it isn't fractured."

I did not need the image of my fifty-eight-year-old mother pole dancing in my head. It is bad enough knowing my sister owns the only strip club in the entire county. Don't get me wrong, I'm proud of her for being a successful businesswoman and paving her own path in life. But Knox and I like to live in a state of denial about what it is she does for a living. Even when I work the door at the club, I like to pretend it belongs to her best friend and partner in crime, sometimes literally, Harley.

"Shit, is she okay?"

"Yeah, she's basically fine, resisting going to get it x-rayed, but her ankle is blowing up, so I think we should."

"Okay, you want me to pick her up and take her?"

"No, I'd rather go. I feel bad it happened when she was at the club." Delia is a caretaker through and through. She was the one to take care of Mom while Dad was battling brain cancer. They were always close, but after what they went through while Dad was sick, their bond is incredible. I'd be lying if I said I wasn't a little jealous of how close they are. "But could you come man the cafe? The girl she hired to cover in the mornings had to go to school and I can't get a hold of Knox or June." Our brother and his fiancé are probably off boinking in a field somewhere, another hot topic on the Amoresville gossip line.

"Yeah, no problem. I'll be there in a minute." I hang up the phone and turn back to Sam, whose pen hovers over the paper while he does a piss poor job of trying to look like he wasn't listening to my conversation. Without a doubt every detail will be making its way down Main Street before I walk in the door of The Bean. "Sorry, man, I gotta get down to the cafe. Could you finish writing this up and charge my usual card? If you bring it down to the Bean later, I'll even throw in a free coffee."

"That's a deal, man, as long as it is a preview of next month's special. Paula will be so jealous I get Roxy's new flavor before her." He ducks his head down, continuing to write out each item, and mumbles, "I fucking love a good latte."

. . .

Five minutes later I pull into the tiny parking lot at the back of the cafe. My mother prides herself on pushing the lines in our small town. Case in point, the sign she and Delia designed for her cafe, Romancing the Bean. The house that serves as the town cafe has been in her family basically since the beginning of time. Over the years the house has been home to the only doctor's office in town, a dress shop, a bakery, and my mother's favorite, a whore house. Each generation in my mother's family has put its own stamp on the large house. When the place changed hands to my mom, she opened the cafe.

Mom loved our dad like crazy, but farming wasn't something she had a passion for. Caffeine and books? That she could dedicate her life to.

Once us kids were old enough to help out on the farm, and not burn the house down without parental supervision, she opened The Bean.

Mom wanted the cafe to be an homage to the second love of her life: romance novels. So, Romancing the Bean was born.

We all pitched in painting and restoring the place. I was thirteen and learned how to strip and refinish the floors and built the bookcases with Sam and his sad. It was my first foray into my future career, woodworking. Our dad and Knox installed all the appliances. Delia painted, decorated, and helped Mom with her recipes. Various town members pitched in, too. The cafe didn't feel like it was just Mom's, it was a little piece of all of us. A little piece of the town itself.

When Delia was in high school, she got into graphic design for some reason and took it upon herself to update Mom's branding. The result was a hilariously suggestive logo featuring a book lying open and a coffee bean resting between the pages. At first glance it isn't offensive, but once you look at it closely, it very much resembles a clit nestled between a woman's labia. Mom loved it immediately and had the biggest fucking sign with the image front-and-center mounted to the roof.

Our stick-in-the-mud mayor fucking hates it but also can't prove it violates his insane decency laws. So The Bean and its slightly sexually suggestive sign have stood.

Silently, I pull open the back door, checking for my sister or Mom in the kitchen. With no sign of them, I creep out, spotting Delia with her back to me through the small window in the door separating the prep area from the coffee bar.

Behind the counter, Delia finishes up making Mrs. Winchester's usual order: The Slow Burn Latte. A hot honey and cinnamon latte with oat milk. Just like usual, Mrs. Winchester will take her mug to the side room where the books are held and sip it for a few hours while reading the filthiest erotica in Mom's collection. Then she'll hustle out of the cafe with her face beet red and run to the church down the street to confess her sins.

With a swift push of the door, I clomp up behind my sister and shout, "Hey sis, how's it going?" right in her ear. She jumps about a mile high and nearly tips over the freshly made latte on the counter.

"Jesus fucking Christ, act your age occasionally, Orrie." My sister punches my arm with a decent jab and flings my apron at me.

Mrs. Winchester narrows her eyes and shakes her head at our antics, clutching her drink to her chest as she wanders off to claim her spot in the Den of Sin.

We've all been trained to work in the cafe so Mom can have a day off. She also hires a teen or two from the high school, but if one of them can't work, and Mom needs help, Delia and I are her unpaid help. Hell, Delia practically ran this place for the three years Mom was caring for Dad. Knox gets an out because he runs the family farm. I don't mind, though. It's a great way to give back to the family I owe so much to. I might not have been here during the hardest years of our lives, but I'm here now and I will never stop working to make up for my absence.

"Everything is fine here. I got some fresh pots brewing for the self-serve carafes, but the syrups are going to need to be refilled before the rush, can you handle that?" she says as she begins wiping down the counter.

"No problem. Where's Mom? I want to check on her before you two head out."

My sister chuckles a little and shakes her head. "Back by the books. She found a new stray to take under her wing."

The first floor of the cafe is split into four sections. The two front rooms used to be the dining and sitting room back when the place had been a residence. Now they each house five cafe tables for patrons to sit along with the counter and prep station

in one corner. A door behind the work area leads to the kitchen.
It isn't huge, but big enough to prepare the homemade syrups
Mom is famous for and an area to make sandwiches and salads.

Behind the two front rooms is a huge set of French doors that
lead to the house's den, which we affectionately call the Den of
Sin. Bookshelves line the whole room all the way to the beams
in the fifteen-foot ceilings, complete with a ladder to reach the
higher selves. The place is positively overflowing with books
both old and new. Every single one a romance of some sort, or at
least has romantic elements. Supposedly the books are for sale,
but more often than not Ma simply lends the books out to her
customers.

On the back wall is a grand fireplace that we light on colder
days during the winter. Two lush club chairs sit on either side of
the mantel with a velvet loveseat facing the fire, creating a nice
little conversation area. Three other small tables are scattered
throughout the space as well.

To my surprise, Mom sits at one of the tables holding a very
familiar baby and making funny faces at him as he giggles. Behind them, almost at the top of the ladder, is another familiar
sight. A very shapely ass in tight black jeans, one that I had been
appreciating the day before.

Brigid leans over, holding onto the ladder with one hand as
she reaches for a book. "Is this it, Roxy? *Stolen* by Jaimie Hart?"

Almost in slow motion I watch as Brigid climbs back down
the ladder. She's only three rungs up, but misplaces her foot and
starts to wobble.

On instinct, I rush across the room, just in time for Brigid to totally lose her balance and fall backward from the ladder. I do my best to catch her, but in the end, we wind up both sprawled on the floor, my body cushioning her impact.

"I'm so sorry." My new neighbor sits up quickly between my legs and twists around to look over her shoulder, shock transforming her face as she takes me in.

"Seriously, you can just say hi next time. No need to leap at me every time we meet."

Brigid rolls her eyes and clambers to her feet. "How do you keep managing to be literally underfoot?"

I shrug in response. "Part of my charm." Something catches my attention from the corner of my eye. The book Brigid had been retrieving when she fell. The cover features a guy with a six-pack taking off his shirt. I hold the offending item up with the photo facing her. "At least this time you managed to keep your shirt on."

Brigid glares at me and for some reason the annoyed expression makes my smile grow even wider. She's like a grumpy little storm cloud, but for some reason she's lighting up my whole world like a ray of sunshine.

"I take it you know my new friend, son?" Mom's comment breaks our staring contest.

"Yup. Your new friend is my new neighbor."

My mom's smile beams, mischief glinting in her eyes. I've seen that look before and it ended with my brother on one knee proposing to the last woman who blew into town unexpectedly.

Chapter 8

Brigid

I might be rethinking this whole small-town thing. Especially if it means I literally can't escape my annoying, and annoyingly hot, neighbor.

Mica and I moved here because I wanted him to be closer to nature. *I* wanted to be closer to nature. The trees overhead and grass underfoot calms my soul. Pittsburgh was a great city to live in, and despite only moving there because of the shithead, I'll always love the city. But even when we first got there, I knew I wouldn't be staying forever. The traffic, the rush of everyday life, it wasn't ever what I wanted. Wasn't how I was raised.

But at least in the city the odds I would run into someone I knew without it being a planned thing were minuscule at best.

Now, not only have I run into Orion far from the mountain we both live on, but it also turns out he is the son of literally the nicest, coolest woman I have ever met.

"No offense, Roxy, but how is this oaf your son?"

The cafe owner bursts out laughing while Orion scoffs. "Well, the oaf part he gets from his father. The red hair was all me though."

Now that I am looking, I can see the resemblance. Roxy's hair is nearly white, with just the slightest hint of strawberry blonde. But her eyes are the same soothing moss green as Orion's. There is also a subtle mischief that seems to linger in their irises, as they could be hatching some plan for trouble at any moment.

"I am not an oaf!" Orion climbs to his feet, brushing his hands down his jeans, which calls my attention to his thick thighs straining against the denim. "I am not stupid, uncultured, or clumsy. In fact, you are the clumsy one here." He boops me on the nose and I swipe away his hand with a scowl on my face.

"Well, I didn't mean oaf like that."

"You mean like the actual definition?" His words are softened by a small smile on his face as he tilts his head slightly to the side.

"No, I meant like big. And..." My mouth opens and closes as I search for another word other than big. Suddenly I feel like the oaf in this whole situation. "Ugly! And who actually knows the literal definition for oaf off the top of their head?"

"Listen, I might be a lot of things, but I think we both know ugly isn't one of them." He leans in ever so slightly, and the same scent of wood and leather that I noticed yesterday wafts around me. "Big, however, that I will admit to."

"Son, please remember there are young ears in the room." I almost forgot Roxy is still holding my son. Okay, I forgot Roxy was here too. The physical reaction my body has to Orion's presence truly pisses me off.

"Sorry, Ma." Orion holds the book out toward me, and I take it, pressing the cover against my chest as if hiding it might make him forget that his mother was indeed recommending smut to his neighbor. "That's a good one. My favorite is the third in the series though."

"You read romances?" I shoot him a raised eyebrow, doubting this big mountain man could possibly be into Romance. He looks more like a Thriller guy. Or hunting and fishing magazines.

"When I was deployed Ma sent care packages full of them. We would pass them around the unit until the pages were practically falling out. Or sticking together." He nods toward my chest, or the book I'm trying to suffocate there. "That particular author got me through quite a few lonely nights."

An image of a younger, buzz-cut, fatigues-clad Orion lounging in bed with a romance in one hand and himself in the other barrels its way into my mind's eye before I can stop it.

"Too much information." The need to get away from Orion is equally as intense as the desire shooting through my body like lightning striking the ground. As smoothly as I possibly can, I step around Orion and reach out to relieve Roxy of Mica. With a slight pout she hands him over.

"Don't tell me you're taking this sweet baby away already." She plays peek-a-boo with my giggling son from her seat, and a fierce longing for my own mother on the other side of the country adds to my already distressed state of being. I make a mental note to call her as soon as I get back to the cabin. We have a standing call on Sundays, but always end up chatting mid-week at some point too. "We barely got to start chatting when my oaf of a son interrupted us."

Orion rolls his eyes and comes over to kneel next to his mom's chair, picking up her leg to inspect an alarmingly swollen, black and blue ankle. "Ma, no time for chatting. If you and Delia are going to make it out to the urgent care in enough time to get back here before she has to open the club you got to get on the road."

"Urgent care? What happened?" When I got here twenty minutes ago, Roxy had already been seated in the book section of the cafe with a cup of tea and a novel open in front of her. Almost immediately she started chatting with me about Mica, books, and her shop. But never did she mention needing medical attention.

"Oh, it's nothing." Roxy pushes her son's hand away and he shakes his head but relents. "I was practicing my inside leg hang at pole dancing class this morning but landed awkwardly."

"Ma, that looks like more than an awkward landing. I wouldn't be surprised if you have a fracture, you need to get it x-rayed." Orion stands to his full height, both hands planted on his hips as he glares affectionately at his mother. "No more pole dancing, floor work only."

Now Roxy rolls her eyes at her son, and this has officially clocked in as the weirdest conversation I've ever heard between a parent and their child.

"Nonsense, I am in the best shape of my life thanks to Harley and her classes."

"I'm sorry, but I'm still hung up on the fact that this quaint little town has a pole dancing class let alone a whole slate of what sounds like stripping classes."

"Exotic dancing, my dear," Roxy says with a gentle reproach in her voice. "It is a wonderful workout and a beautiful art form. The classes are held at my daughter's club just outside town."

"Club?"

The woman's smile widens and she beams with pride. "Club Barely Over the Line. It's a strip club just on the other side of the town line. Delia opened it about five years ago and it is a wild success. People come from all over the state to see it."

I'm not a prude, there are plenty of clubs and adult stores in Pittsburgh. Hell, I even heard there's a popular swingers club in the city. But I'd never in a million years imagine a small town in the middle of the mountains in northern Pennsylvania would have the demand to support something in the adult industry.

"You should come to a class sometime!" Roxy perks up even more. "You'd bring down the median age of students by at least a decade."

Orion coughs into his fist, obviously trying to cover up a laugh. "Mom, you can't just invite strangers to hang out at a strip club. It's a little weird."

Roxy scoffs and shakily stands from her seat. Now that she is standing, I see her genetics must have played into the height of her son as well. "Oh nonsense. I just recommended a book to the woman with a full-blown orgy scene. We're practically best friends." She takes one limping step closer to me. "Which reminds me, do you need a toy to go along with that book? I've got some great, quiet vibrators, so no risking waking the little one." She winks at me over Mica's head.

Jaw meet floor.

"Jesus Christ, Ma." Orion's face quickly turns bright red and he hooks one hand around the back of his neck, staring up at the ceiling in disbelief.

"Hey, mothers have needs too, son." Roxy hobbles toward the front of the cafe, calling over her shoulder. "Let me go check what I have in stock. Technically I can't sell them because of the stupid decency ordinances in this town, but if a Womanizer just happened to fall into your bag and a twenty just happened to make its way into the tip jar, we could call it even."

This lady can't be real. I love her.

"Actually, Roxy, I am all covered on that front, I promise." I avoid Orion's gaze despite its tractor beam-like intensity on my face. "I actually need to go down to City Hall and find out about getting a business license before they close."

Before Roxy could get out the protest obviously forming behind her lips, the girl I had bought a latte from just twenty minutes ago struts into the room with more sass than a Thursday afternoon really calls for. "Okay, Mom, you ready to head out? Orrie, everything is restocked and ready for you."

"Oh, perfect timing. Delia, this is Orrie's new neighbor and my new friend, Brigid and her adorable son Mica. Brigid, this is my daughter, Delia."

I don't know what I pictured when Roxy said her daughter was the owner of the local strip club, but it certainly wasn't the tall, curvy, strawberry blonde girl standing in front of me. When I'd seen her behind the counter earlier I assumed she was a high school student, not the fully adult owner of a strip club.

"Nice to meet you, Brigid. Welcome to the madness that is Amoresville." She reaches out her hand and I shift Mica over to one hip so I could extend my own for a firm handshake. "Wait, how can you be Orrie's neighbor?"

"She's staying in Burt's cabin," he says with unveiled hostility, but I don't think the anger is directed at me.

"That thing is still standing?" Delia lets out a shrill whistle.

"Barely." The word erupts from his mouth more growl than syllables.

"Good luck to you there, girl." Delia shifts her attention to Roxy, who is contemplating my existence rather intensely.

"Did you say you need to apply for a business license? What kind of business are you opening?"

Now it's my turn to smile with pride. "It's a crystal and metaphysical shop. I'm mostly online, but I've always wanted to open a brick-and-mortar store as well. I have a little money stashed away to finally make that happen."

Roxy's open, joyous face shutters slightly as she looks from me to her children, who also have strange expressions. "Have you looked into the requirements for opening a shop in Amoresville yet?"

"Only what I could find online, which wasn't much. Your town's website could use an upgrade. But it seemed like there are tons of open storefronts in the square, so didn't think it would be too hard." The air in the room turns suddenly tense; my intuition prickles with awareness as the mood turns. "Why? Is getting a business license hard around here?"

All three Halsteds look at me with something bordering on pity. Despite Mica being perfectly happy in my arms, I start bouncing and swaying with him to give my body even a small way to release some of the energy building up.

"I'm not going to lie, our mayor has made getting a business license a true pain in the ass." Roxy's hands ball into fists by her sides as she talks about the man. "I swear, the county, the state, and the federal government combined don't require as much paperwork as the town of Amoresville does to open a business."

"But there are lots of stores in town. I've been making a mental list of ones I wanted to visit as we explored today. And there really are *so* many empty storefronts. I would think the mayor would be eager to have one of them filled."

Delia nods sadly, her red lips tilting down at the corners. "Most of the businesses are family-owned shops that go back to before Burt took office. Or they are owned by one of his cronies who suck up to him, then turn around and complain behind his back."

"Shit."

"Yeah, I wanted to open a showroom for my furniture last year and I swear he took the paperwork and fed it right into the shredder." Orion's hands are buried so deep in his pockets I'm a little afraid they are going to rip the seams. "Granted, our families have been enemies for generations, but he could have at least pretended."

"And that is why all those free spaces will continue to sit empty and people will continue to leave town and start over somewhere new with more opportunity." Delia's whole body seems to be coiling into a big ball of rage, her face turning redder by the second. "The whole Lickinbill lineage is bullshit."

Roxy rubs her daughter's back in a reassuring manner. "There have been a few good eggs here and there. Burt's sister was wonderful, and thankfully her son seems to have leaned more in her direction than Burt's. With his and June's help, they've actually pared down the business application by a good twenty pages."

Twenty Pages!

Delia scoffs again and rolls her eyes, mumbling something under her breath that I can't quite make out.

"He had an uncle that I remember wasn't horrible either," Roxy carries on, ignoring her daughter's little rant. "But unfortunately, they are few and far between. And the good ones tend to flee from the Lickinbill legacy of running this town."

"So, I shouldn't even try?" I don't bother masking the despair in my voice. True, my store and livelihood will be fine without an actual physical shop. But I'm not ready to let go of the vision that's been growing in my mind as Mica grew in my belly.

Visions of a close-knit community, a little store where I could sell my products along with those of my vendors. Mica playing in the back room, doing homework as he got older, helping me in the shop once he hit high school. Each image seems to go translucent in my mind, like ghosts fading away.

"You should absolutely try." Roxy takes three limping steps to stand directly in front of me, both of her hands planted on my shoulders, Mica trapped between our maternal bodies. "You go down to City Hall, get the paperwork, and we'll help you wade through it all. I might even know someone that would be willing to help our cause."

"Maybe don't mention that you're opening a witchcraft store though. Don't think Burt would like that," Orion pipes up from behind his mother.

"Oh, so the two of you do have some things in common then." I shoot daggers at my neighbor, suddenly a little fed up with men who think their opinions are worthy of being spoken simply because of the appendage dangling between their legs.

"Seriously, son, what have you said to this poor girl?"

Chapter 9

Orion

"Here you go, Will. Tell Cynthia I said hi." I hand over the high school principal's usual order, a Dirty Hor (a horchata with a shot of espresso added) for himself and the Insta Love (an iced coffee with two shots of espresso) for his wife, who also happens to be the elementary school's principal.

Ten years ago, I was dodging detentions and egging both their cars. Now I'm working on a cradle for their first grandchild. Funny how life works.

The cafe has been quiet for most of the afternoon, just the normal trickle of locals popping in for a tasty treat and a spot of gossip. I was all too happy to oblige on both accounts. It took nearly an hour and assurances from both me and Brigid that I was being nice to my new neighbor before Ma finally agreed to go get her ankle x-rayed. Thankfully Delia texted a few minutes ago with the news that it is only a bad sprain, and Mom would be in a walking boot for three weeks to let it heal. Better than broken and a cast or surgery, so I'll take it. Knowing the matriarch of our family, it is going to be hell trying to get her to actually use the thing. But I have an idea to help with that.

With the cafe once again empty, the old antsy feeling of my youth creeps up my limbs, making it necessary to move. All the tables are clean, but I still drift between them with a rag, wiping away invisible crumbs.

Boredom has always been a problem for me. Without a project to occupy my mind I somehow always end up in trouble. As a kid if I didn't have something to do with my hands or my head then I was climbing shit, taking shit apart, or starting shit with my siblings.

Lady Luck had been on my side at birth though and saw fit to put me in a family with the absolute best parents who knew how to handle my ways. They put my energy to good use on the farm, found ways to help me keep my brain engaged at school, and dealt with the fallout when all our strategies and routines failed and I inevitably got in trouble. Not all kids were as lucky as the Halsted kids, and we all damn well know it.

I repaid them by hightailing it out of town the first chance I had.

A pang of sadness echoes in my chest, like a rock dropping in a cavern, the sound faint but repeating. That's what missing Dad feels like these days. No longer a large gaping wound, but a subtle, omnipresent ache that sneaks up in a flash to take my breath away when I least expect it. The guilt of not being able to be here for most of his illness never goes away. Turns out a brain tumor in your dad's head isn't a good enough reason for emergency leave from the military.

Before I can spiral down that rabbit hole, my eye wanders over to the spot next to the cash register where Mom keeps all her little notes on recipes, people that come into the shop, and random books she might want to stock. Sitting among all the Post-it notes is a business card for a business called *Tiger's Eye Herb and Gem Shoppe*. Picking it up, I turn it over to see my neighbor's name. Brigid Wolke. Before I can think better of it I'm scanning the little QR code in the corner and pulling up the website on my phone.

The design on the site is so Brigid I can't help but smile a little. The whole page is on a black background with the text in a smoky white. An aesthetically laid altar with dried herbs, little bottles of liquid, and an open book fill the top of the page. There are menu sections for books, tarot decks, crystals, herbs, spell kits, and tarot services. I click around the site, fascinated by this little peek into my new neighbor's world.

Just as I'm diving into the *About* section, the bell above the door rings, signaling a new customer.

"I cannot believe this town."

A familiar voice cuts through the silent cafe, causing me to close my phone and slam it down on the counter screen down as if I was looking at porn and not an e-commerce site.

"Would you look at this?"

Brigid drops a stack of papers at least an inch thick on the table in front of me.

"All this to get on the *list* for *consideration* for a business license." She slumps against the counter, Mica cradled against her chest in the fabric wrap I'm a little perplexed by.

How does that thing hold a baby so securely? Does she need help getting it on? Were instructions included with the baby at birth or was the knowledge downloaded into all mothers' brains? The kid obviously likes it; his little cheek is pressed against his mother's chest as he dozes snuggled up to Brigid. Lucky kid.

"Hey." Brigid snaps in front of my face. "Are you listening to my mental breakdown or just staring at my baby like you can see through him to my tits?"

"What is that thing called?"

Brigid tilts her head and gives me a look that very obviously translates to *what the hell are you talking about?* "A baby," she says slowly.

"Thanks for clearing that up. No, the fabric thing that you carry him in. How the hell does that thing work? It looks complicated, but it's like a giant scarf or something, right?"

"Seriously, you want to know about my baby wrap when my whole business plan is going up in flames?"

Baby wrap, well that solves that.

"Sorry, I've got a weird brain." I twist the dish towel in my hands. "Yeah, Lickinbill doesn't joke around about his forms."

"The guy didn't even have the nerve to meet with me. I had to talk through his receptionist." Brigid trudges away from the counter and plops down into the closest chair, propping her elbow on the table. "She kept going back to his office to relay messages then came back with his replies. Said he was dealing with important town business."

"He was probably counting the change from the fountain. I think they shut it down for the season last week and he insists on counting it by hand before taking it to the machine at the bank. Likes to make sure the bank isn't ripping off the town."

"Seriously? This town is so weird."

"Don't judge us all by the worst of us."

"Hey, you guys elected him."

"I mean, to be fair, he runs unopposed every election. So have most of his predecessors. Almost every mayor in our town's history has been a Lickinbill, with one or two exceptions." There was a write-in campaign once for the ornery goose that lives on my brother's farm to be mayor, but no one could spell his name the same way, so he ended up losing anyway. I don't tell Brigid that. She already thinks we're a town of backward hicks without that particular tidbit.

"Well, at least I know what I'll be doing for the next few days. Filling out forms in triplicate." She thumbs through the stack of papers, fanning them in rapid succession, looking less like her fierce storm cloud self and more like a sad, wispy cirrus cloud.

It's times like this I wish I knew the right things to say to people. Comforting wasn't big in the Marines, and I somehow missed the gene that both my parents had for talking through emotions.

"I could help."

Brigid glares up at me with obvious disbelief.

"I mean, true my own business license got turned down, but I think that has more to do with my last name than the way I filled out the forms."

Before the words are totally out of my mouth Brigid is already shaking her head. "I want to do it myself. If I let you help me and I get turned down I will always wonder if I should have just done it all myself."

The sinking sand pit of disappointment in my chest at her rejection of my help takes me by surprise. Around here neighbors ask for and give help easily; I'm not sure I've ever had someone refuse an offer of help. Other than my brother, but he's a grumpy asshole. Fuck do I hate being helpless. It makes my skin itch like ants are scurrying under the surface trying to get out.

"Well, maybe I could play with the kid? Watch him while you work? Take him for a walk around the pond. Although I have no clue how to use that contraption you use, so I hope you have a stroller."

Brigid straightens up in her chair, her spine snapping into a straight line that kinda makes me want to look around for a commanding officer that must have walked in the room.

"Have I somehow given you the impression in the last twenty-four hours that I'm not capable of both being a single mom and running a business?" Despite the obvious anger in her voice, a sliver of hurt shines through in her eyes.

"Fuck, no. Crap." How do I keep managing to step in it with this lady? "The only one here incapable is me. I am totally incapable of keeping my foot from inserting itself directly into my mouth when it comes to you, apparently."

Looking down to my hands I notice the dish towel I've been fidgeting with is now twisted so tight it has coiled around itself into a sizeable knot. I let go with one hand, shaking it out while avoiding Brigid's glare.

"It is more than obvious that you're some sort of hybrid bad ass and super mom. But I'm right across the pond and I work for myself, so I don't have regular work hours and I have time, and I've hung out with my buddy's kids when he and his wife need dates and stuff, so if you want a babysitter so you can do work or nap or whatever you would want to do with a few free hours I can absolutely help out." The words all spew out in a jumble, so I'm not sure she caught everything I threw at her.

My heart hammers inside my chest in the silence following my word vomit. But it eases just enough at Brigid's deep sigh to allow me to slide my glance up to see her face full of regret.

"Sorry, I'm still all wound up from my visit to the mayor's office." Our conversation has roused Mica, and he rubs his face against his mom's chest, squirming in the wrap. Brigid's hand goes to his back, and she rubs it in big circles in a way that has him soothed within seconds. "Honestly, though, I'm used to working with him around, so I should be good."

I nod, a little afraid to say anything that could come out in the wrong way.

"I should head back to the cabin and get started on this. Plus, Dolly's Market is still holding my groceries from this morning." She picks up the stack of forms and climbs to her feet. "I guess I'll see you around."

"Sounds good. Tell Dolly I said hi."

The small smile she shoots my way doesn't reach her tired eyes, but it makes me want to do something. That something could be anything from hugging her to finding a way to fix everything wrong in her world.

But since she has made it obvious she wants nothing from me, I just let her walk out the door, like an idiot.

Chapter 10

Brigid

Back at the cabin, I spend the rest of the afternoon doing yet more cleaning and decorating. Mica is stowed safely in his little play area, smashing two blocks together and laughing like the sound is the most hilarious thing ever.

On the island, the stack of forms seems to grow as they sit there. I know that isn't possible. Paper and ink can't procreate. But they loom in the space, using up all the oxygen in my brain.

Do I need the store to make a living? No. My online business is booming.

Five years ago, when I followed William to Pittsburgh I had to find a job, because as it turned out, setting up house for my former professor also meant paying half the rent and utilities. I lucked out and got hired at an oddities store down the street from our townhouse. I loved working there and meeting all the people that came in looking for the dark and spooky things we sold. The owner let me start stocking some items that were more on the metaphysical side of things.

But the shop was small, and I wanted to expand. So, within a year I built a website and started buying ethically sourced gems, minerals, and herbs. I had a consignment arrangement with smaller artists who designed one of a kind tarot decks and books by independent authors.

Within two years, I had expanded the website so much William began to complain it was taking over our townhouse and my life. By that, he meant I could no longer fawn after him like the legend he believed himself to be. I ended up contracting with a third-party warehouse to handle all my inventory and shipping. Much to William's annoyance, it was the best thing I could have done. Having the constant shipping of orders off my plate meant I could develop new products of my own to sell. Last year I became the number one ranking metaphysical store online. I'm never going to get rich off my shop, but I make enough to keep Mica and I comfortable, and that is all I want.

That and a physical store where I can host classes, give readings, be part of a community. I've thought about it for years. Got close to opening a store in Pittsburgh, but every spot I looked at didn't feel quite right. Something in my gut was telling me that it wasn't the time. It wasn't the right place.

That same something is practically screaming that I'm close. That my dream will be a reality soon if I just stay the course. That this *is* the right place.

But those forms. The damn mayor. I could hear him behind his office door telling his secretary that he wasn't going to come talk to a newcomer in town about a business license. *Not letting someone breezing through town take a spot one of our neighbors might want.*

If he had actually shown his face, I could have explained that I planned on becoming one of those cherished neighbors.

An insistent energy pulses through the air, pressing on my back. The damn forms. Stomping over to the small table by the window from where I've been folding laundry on the kitchen island, I scoop up the forms and shove them in one of the plastic totes I've unpacked. They thunk down into the bottom. *Click*, the lid snaps on tightly to the handles. With a huff of frustration, I pick the whole thing up and stomp out to the porch, practically throwing the plastic box into the corner of the rickety porch.

If I could throw them into the pond I would.

Now that they are contained, the pressure on my back, shoulders, and chest lightens slightly.

Hands on hips, I survey the sparkling water reflecting the tips of trees and the pinks, oranges, and yellows of the setting sun. It's not a large pond, probably about the size of a football field. From my vantage point on the porch, half the pond along with the dock on *his* half of the pond are hidden, along with the smaller dock behind my cabin.

I've tried my best not to glance over to his side of the pond too much. Aggravating is the nicest possible word I can think of for my neighbor. Aggravating and incredibly beautiful.

And apparently incapable of not meddling in my business.

After trying to convince me to let him, a complete stranger, watch my son, I came back to the cabin to find a brand-new threshold on the doorway to the cabin. I have a feeling if I looked around, I would find more things he's tinkered with.

I hate the implication that I need this man's help to survive. After William unceremoniously kicked my pregnant ass out of the townhouse I had decorated, cleaned, and ran like a well-oiled machine for five years, everyone I knew made it clear they thought I was incapable of taking care of myself and a baby. Mom and Dad insisted I move back to Arizona. My sister made it clear I should probably put the baby up for adoption. My friends all thought not going through with the pregnancy would be the best way forward. All valid choices, but not for me.

Not one single person thought I could do this. But here I am, fucking doing it. Making a better life for the baby I love from the very moment I saw that pink line. I understand why everyone felt the way they did, but no one seemed to understand that I wanted Mica more than I have ever wanted anything in my life. He isn't a mistake I'm stuck with. He's the manifestation of my hopes and dream walking, or crawling, in the real world.

So I don't appreciate my hot as hell neighbor inserting himself into my life uninvited. As annoyed as I am at him, I am equally annoyed at myself for not being able to go more than five minutes without wondering about the over-eager, too hot for his own good man. Even knowing I should distance myself from him, the possibility of his presence on the other side of the rippling water pulls my gaze.

Has he finished his shift at the cafe?

What does he do over there all alone? Just him and a three-legged dog.

Ready to go inside, to stop my brain from going down a rabbit hole I have no business exploring, I start to turn, but a ripple slightly bigger than the others catches my eye. An arm arcs over the water's surface before scooping beneath for the opposite arm to follow the same path. Light catches in the wet grooves of the muscles along his back and legs.

A twist in my lower belly forces me to stumble forward grabbing the porch railing as he nears the end of the pond closest to where I am. Orion executes a nearly perfect flip as he completes the lap, starting across to the opposite side of the pond. His swim shorts are brightly colored in a godawful floral design. But they sculpt to his ass like their only purpose in life is to make perfectly sane women have thoughts like *what would it feel like to bite him there?*

Every other stroke his head twists, his face coming into view for a split second as he sucks in a breath of air before disappearing beneath the water again. Even swimming at a fairly fast pace, the man is nothing less than stunning.

A groan of protest beneath my hands cuts through the lust-induced fog my lizard brain has succumbed to. As Orion's swim takes him farther away, my body involuntarily leans out over the railing, trying to see around the corner of the cabin to watch his progress as long as possible.

What am I doing?

Before I can right myself, the railing about two decades past needing to be replaced gives way, and my body flails in mid-air. I pitch forward, arms windmilling, reaching for the cabin wall just a few inches too far for me to reach. Stupid short arms! My toes slip forward and my desperate attempt to catch myself fails miserably as I fall.

A loud screech echoes off the surrounding trees and mountains, boomeranging back to my ears. Part of me hopes they are sounds from a nearby bird or creature, but the rest of me knows it was my scream of surprise and terror as I toppled forward.

In the space of a breath, or a scream, I land on top of the shattered shrapnel of the former porch railing, now no more than a pile of ragged toothpicks on the ground beneath. Thankfully, the porch is little more than a foot or two above the ground, and the weeds and overgrown grass do a lot to cushion my fall. Still, my palms and knees smart where I tried to catch myself.

As soon as the adrenaline coursing through my body starts to abate, a series of loud barks vibrates through the air. Between each loud boom of my neighbor's dog, I hear splashing water, and I know. He saw.

If I stay here with my face buried in the grass, would it be possible he'd forget he witnessed yet another of my most embarrassing moments?

"Hey!" His voice is closer than I want it to be. "Are you okay?"

"Yup, fine!" I shout, my face still planted firmly against the ground so the words come out muffled.

"Then why aren't you moving?" The splashes of water slow in their frequency.

I pick up one hand and I fling it about as if to say *see, I'm moving, go about your business.*

Resigned to my fate, I push up onto my knees, then up to my feet. I'm met with an eyeful of ripped, wet man.

God damn.

That is not fair. Suddenly I relate all too much to Emma Stone's character in *Crazy, Stupid, Love* when she sees Ryan Gosling shirtless for the first time. Orion looks Photoshopped. Or sculpted by loving hands out of stone. Created by the gods and goddesses themselves to body shame the rest of the human race. Huffs of breath make Orion's abs collapse in and out, changing from eight pack to twelve pack as the muscles relax and contract. In, Out. Eight, Twelve. The movement is hypnotizing.

"Seriously, are you okay? You seem a little out of it." He takes another step forward and I hold up a hand, palm facing him in the universal sign for stop. Thankfully, he recognizes the not at all official sign and stops where he is on the muddy shores of the pond, still a good six feet from where I stand.

"I'm fine." The edge of annoyance in my voice might be a little sharper than the situation strictly calls for, but how many more ways can I embarrass myself in front of this man that I don't like? Or more accurately, that I don't want to like. "I need to get back in to Mica. I was just bringing something out to the porch and tripped into the railing."

One eyebrow arches up as if to say *so that's the story you're going with*. But he nods, letting my half-assed lie slide.

Across the pond, his dog lets out a single mournful bark. The sound breaks the silent staredown we've lapsed into.

"Looks like someone else needs you."

Orion chuckles and twists back to look at his dog. "He's terrified of the water. Hates that I swim nearly every day." He cups his hands around his mouth and yells to his companion. "It's okay, Spruce, relax."

Focus finally off me, my limbs regain feeling and the ability to move. I turn back, clambering up onto the side of the porch where the railing used to be. Safely on my feet once again, I glance over my shoulder to find Orion once again staring at my ass. That low twist of arousal in my belly rears to life, stronger than before. What woman wouldn't react to a man dripping wet with tiny swim trunks? Tiny swim trunks that are a little more tented than before. Or am I imagining things?

Orion ducks down until the water is lapping around his waist, hiding what seemed to be a growing problem beneath the surface of the water.

"Thanks for checking on me."

He just nods and walks backward a few steps until the water rises up over his stomach, then chest, almost up to his shoulders

I break yet another stareoff first, turning to the cabin and forcing my feet to move forward. As I reach the door, I hear the rhythmic slapping of skin hitting water and know that Orion has resumed his swim.

I refuse to go to my bedroom window and watch, no matter how strong the invisible string I feel tugging at me insists that is exactly what I should do.

Chapter 11

Orion

The hum of the lathe is barely audible over the music playing through my headphones. The soundtrack for tonight's work is a Folk Rock playlist that I've been growing for years, adding songs as I find new bands I like or my standard favorites release new albums. At this point I think I could leave the list on for twenty-four hours and never have to repeat a song.

Some people are mood readers; I'm a mood listener. Spotify has become a museum to curate my feelings into beats and chords. Genre, generation, artist, nothing is off the table if it puts me in the mood for whatever task is at hand.

Woodworking usually requires something wistful. Melodic and earthy. Something to inspire.

Driving calls for the best songs to sing along with. Bubbly pop and belting standards.

Workouts need metal or rap. Heavy beats, lots of bass, the kind of cussing that motivates you to push that little bit harder.

R&B and Soul are for cooking and working around the cabin.

No matter where in the world I've been, music and books have been my constant companions. But music is the great equalizer. I could always connect with a perfect stranger over a shared love of an artist or song. It's a shame I have not one lick of musical talent. Guitar, piano, and drum lessons were all lost on me. The only place I've ever been able to keep up a steady rhythm is in bed.

As The Lumineers sing about Ophelia, I sink my gouge in a fraction of a centimeter, curls of wood spitting in every direction as I taper the dowel from the wide base to the skinnier tip. I want these spindles to be smooth and clean, no fancy scrolls or turns. A new idea has been knocking around in my head that I haven't been able to shake for the last day or two.

The perfect project for a huge black cherry I brought down more than a year ago and has been sitting drying in my workshop waiting for a strike of inspiration. Turns out my muse for this piece was a curvy, dark-haired stranger.

Satisfied with the shape I've achieved, I turn off the lathe and let it slow to a stop before removing it and adding it to the pile of other dowels I've turned.

My spine pops and cracks as I stretch from my hunched position over the lathe, an involuntary groan rumbling from my chest after finally moving after hours of work. An all too familiar ache spreads in the muscles and bones. My ass is getting older every day.

Eyes adjusting from the focus they'd been honed into on the project at hand, it dawns on me that while I'd been working, the sun had set, Spruce curled up in his bed snoring away, twitching with the dreams of a pup chasing squirrels.

My stomach growls loud enough that I'm surprised it doesn't wake my faithful companion. I fucking forgot to eat dinner. Again. When the hyper fixation sets in, everything else fades away, for better or worse.

After shutting down my equipment and rousing the dog from his slumber so he can move into the cabin with me, I shut the lights off and make my way to the silent, dark cabin.

Across the pond, a single light shines down onto the dock behind the Lickinbill cabin. It's such a stark change from what I'm used to. There has been no sign of life on that side of the pond for as long as I've lived here, so it's hard not to notice every single one now.

I just replaced all the lightbulbs on the exterior of the house earlier this morning. I felt like an idiot tiptoeing around on Brigid's porch, unscrewing the decades-old lightbulbs and replacing them with new, brighter ones. And also measuring the new gaping hole in the porch railing.

All that work was worth it. Bathed in the warm light falling from the flood lamp precariously perched on the corner of the roof is a single figure, swaying slowly back and forth in a rocking chair. The same rocking chair that I spotted in her cabin that first day if I'm not mistaken.

My feet divert from the well-worn path leading to my front door and instead make their way toward my own dock. It isn't a conscious decision. A force stronger than anything I've felt before is drawing me in like a fish on the end of the line, only I'm not fighting the tug of the hook. I willingly allow myself to be reeled in by the beauty.

Night in the woods is anything but silent. There are crickets, owls, frogs, all making their various mating calls. Wind in the trees rustling. The night is just as alive as day out here.

The echo of my heart pounding inside my chest has to be loud enough to drown out all the sounds around me though. Because across the pond, sitting on a dock I'm half-afraid will fall apart under her feet, is Brigid, the witch next door. Her head is tilted down, the light of an e-reader lighting her face. One leg is thrown over the arm of the rocking chair. The toes of her other foot are pressed into the splintering wood, pushing enough to keep the rocking of the chair going.

The pale curve of her calves, meeting her knees, then up to her thick thighs are bare to anyone that wishes to see. All she wears is a T-shirt about five sizes too big, but her position has pushed the hem high enough that if I were closer, I might be able to see the color of her panties. Probably black, just like when she came crashing into me that first day.

My cock hardens so fast it nearly steals my breath straight from my lungs. I grip the railing surrounding my own dock, thankful I disconnected the motion sensor lights when it proved to be too sensitive last spring and even the toads and frogs finding their way onto the dock would set it off and flood my room with light bright enough to wake me from a dead sleep.

Does my gratitude that the light won't give me away as I watch my neighbor across the pond make me a creep? Probably.

A gasp slices through the night air, and Brigid shifts in her seat, tapping at the edge of her e-reader and switching hands. So focused on whatever she's reading she doesn't know a man is watching her from across the pond. If she looked up, she'd probably be able to see me. The pond isn't that big. Longer than it is wide, the two docks are no more than a dozen yards apart. Close enough that I can see the way Brigid sucks in the corner of her bottom lip. But not so close that I can tell if that gesture is one of anticipation, fear, or excitement.

One hand sweeps up her cheek, then pushes a strand of hair behind her ear, then trails down the side of her neck. Am I imagining the red staining her cheeks? The stutter in her breath? My hyper fixation is back, only instead of being focused on my work, I am entirely tuned into the spitfire across the water.

Slowly, painfully slowly, her hand slides across her collarbone, sweeping back and forth a few times before moving lower. Lower until her fingers brush across her breasts, and another echo ripples across the water to my ears.

Fuck.

Excitement. Whatever she's reading, it is definitely making her excited. My dick pulses in my pants, pressing against the zipper of my jeans so hard I'm a little afraid there will be an imprint of the teeth there later.

Idly, her fingers stroke the top of her chest, rising and falling with her deep breaths.

She shifts again, her hips moving no more than an inch to the side, but that inch causes her legs to open ever so slightly. The shadows cast by the overhead light means I have no prayer of seeing what lies between those thighs, but fuck, I want to.

Part of me considers hopping into the water and swimming as fast as I can to find out exactly what she's reading.

All thought flees from my head when that hand starts going south once again. Over her stomach. Lower. I track every centimeter of progress toward that part of her I haven't been able to stop thinking about since having her panty-covered cunt pressed against me.

Yeah, I'm a fucking bastard for remembering the heat of her center as she clung to me, terrified of a little spider. But fuck if I can stop myself from thinking about it every damn minute for the last forty-eight hours.

Finally, her fingers find their way to the hem of her t-shirt. Toy with it. Weaving it between her fingers, is she thinking about slipping those fingers between her thighs? Easing whatever ache that book is obviously giving her?

As if the strength of my thought spurs her on, her fingers curl around the bottom of the oversized shirt and slowly pulls it up over the apex of her thighs, her pussy covered in a pair of black panties, just as I suspected.

My grip on the railing tightens. I'm a little afraid my much sturdier dock will not be able to withstand how tightly I'm holding on. Teetering on the edge of indecision. Stay here and finish watching the show Brigid has no idea she's about to put on for me. Or do the right fucking thing, turn around and go into my fucking house. Forget that the most beautiful woman I've ever seen is a mere dozen or two feet away slipping her fingers into the waistband of her panties.

Another gasp, and her head falls back, thudding against the back of the rocking chair, her eyes falling shut. I might not be able to see it from here, but I fucking know she touched herself.

How wet is she?

I would quite literally kill to know.

A low growl rises up from my throat. It's a sound I've never made in my life before, something reminiscent of a wolf or bear. I try to choke it back, not wanting Brigid to know that I'm watching her in a very private moment like a complete asshole.

But I don't manage to swallow my reaction in time. Her head pops up, eyes wide open and looking directly at me.

Fuck.

If she hated me before, she's going to fucking despise me after seeing me watching her like a fucking stalker.

"Sorry." The word is so fucking rough, scratching up from my lungs tightened from the strain of the last handful of minutes. I wish I could say I immediately start backing away from the railing. Retreat to the safety of my house and stay there for the remainder of the time Brigid is living in the cabin across the pond.

But I don't.

I stand there for another heartbeat. Two. Still watching Brigid with her hand buried down the front of her panties. And I feel like an asshole for every single one of those heartbeats until I realize she isn't taking her hand away from her pussy.

Hell, I think her fingers might still be moving, but I can't see, so I can't know for sure. More than likely she's so fucking surprised or so scared she's frozen in fear. Like a deer in headlights.

Another beat and she must realize that she's still touching herself. Slowly, almost reluctantly, she takes her hand from her panties, lifts the leg from over the arm of the rocking chair and places it back on the planks of the dock.

Finally, the fucking spell she has me under breaks, and I turn away, stomping up the dock and into my house.

I wish I could say I was a good enough man that I didn't shut myself in my bedroom and jerk off to the memory of those few moments.

But I am not a good man.

Chapter 12

Brigid

Breath stutters inside my lungs and the plate I've been washing slips from my hands, clattering into the sink. I wish I could say this was the only time it's happened this morning, but that would be a complete and total lie.

Every few moments the vision floats to the surface of my thoughts. Orion's tall frame bracing against the railing of his dock, staring at me as I touched myself on the opposite side of the pond. His side of the property was dark, but there was just enough fall off from my own light that I could see his chest rising and falling as if he'd just come in from another of his long swims. Every muscle in his body seemed to be tensed.

I couldn't see his face though. Couldn't see the expression as our eyes met. Also, couldn't see if the show I had been inadvertently giving had made a certain appendage in his pants... grow. Again.

Each time that moment replays in my brain, everything I'm doing stops. Dishes. Folding laundry. Reaching out to customers to let them know I'm a little behind on orders with my move. Nothing else exists as thoughts of Orion watching me crowd everything else out.

I should have been pissed. Should have yelled over at him to go the fuck away. But I didn't. Too late, I tried to call him back. I wanted to invite him to stand there and watch as I finished the job I had just started. Show him that I can do everything myself, including get myself off.

Being a single mom means I almost never get alone time. There is no partner to watch Mica. No custody arrangements. My family, as wonderful as they are, is all on the other side of the country. So, I take whatever stolen moments to myself I can. Including dragging a chair over to the water's edge and reading a book about men that shift into wolves and the kinky ass sex they have with their mates.

Mica was fast asleep in his Pack 'n Play, the window cracked so I could hear if he woke up and needed me.

So yeah, when the book got to a particularly spicy scene, I didn't hesitate to seize the moment and take care of the ache that had been building since I met my sexy, annoying as hell neighbor. His cabin had been dark, not a single light that I could see. So, I figured he was asleep and wouldn't notice me out on the dock. Or maybe, a part of me hoped that he *would* see me.

For the hundredth time today, I shake the thoughts from my head and slip the last of the clean dishes into the drying rack.

It has to stop. Orion is no different from every other man I have ever known. A self-centered creep who judges anyone slightly different from him. He covers it better than most with the helpful neighbor routine, but I know the truth. William hid his narcissistic ass well in the beginning too. I shouldn't be allowing Orion to occupy this much of my brain space.

Across the room Mica continues to squish the banana I had cut up for his snack between his chubby little fingers. At this point we're veering into sensory play more than snack time.

"You are one messy kid."

At the sound of my voice my not-so-little blonde baby peers up with a huge smile and giggles as he slams his banana slime covered hands onto the tray of his highchair.

"Well, if you want to get messy, let's really do the thing." I unstrap him from his highchair and lift him onto my hip, banana getting smeared across my shoulder in the process.

At this point of motherhood, I have accepted the fact that I will never make it through a day without getting some kind of kid-grime on my clothes. I'm glad it's just food this time and not snot, poop, or puke.

"What do you say, should we try and clean up some of the garden beds?"

The kid has no clue what I'm saying, but he claps his hands together all the same and babbles his favorite word: "mama mama."

"I will take that as a yes."

Outside the sun is shining, the air has the slightest hint of a chill, and everything smells of earth and trees. I suck in a deep lungful of the sweet air and tilt my head back to feel the sun on my skin. I loved Pittsburgh, but this is where my soul feels most at ease. Nature surrounding me and the sounds of sirens and traffic nowhere to be found. Since moving east, I have truly fallen head over heels for the novelty of having four seasons. Arizona mostly has summer in different shades of hot. But Pennsylvania's falls have been something I find myself looking forward to year after year.

Involuntarily, my eyes swing over to the other side of the pond. I'm not sure if I'm hoping to catch a glimpse of the man today or desperately wishing to never see him again. I don't embarrass easily, a lifetime of being the weird girl has made me fairly impervious to other people's opinions. But every time I think about Orion catching me in the act it makes me simultaneously wet and want to shrivel up and die.

So, when I see Orion's black truck is gone from where it normally sits beside the cabin, I'm both relieved and a little disappointed.

Curiosity tucked away for the moment, I turn back to the task at hand, letting my kiddo play in the grass while I pull weeds from one of the many overgrown flowerbeds. It's too late in the season to do any planting, but I hate seeing the waist-high weeds each time we come out to play or go on a walk.

It hasn't escaped my notice that there are yet more little changes to the property this morning that are not at all my doing. The shards of wood from where I demolished the porch railing a couple days ago have all magically disappeared overnight. Light bulbs I know weren't working when I left for town the other day were replaced and shining bright when I got back. All things so little I don't think it is worth it to go over and tell my neighbor to cut it the fuck out. I can take care of myself.

No better way to prove I am capable and don't need my neighbor's, or anyone's, help than taking care of things myself.

For the next hour, Mica works at making himself as dirty as humanly possible while I clear the largest of the garden beds. After a while Mica picks up on what I'm doing, and his tiny hands start reaching for leaves to pull. I have a split second to stop him from shoving one in his mouth and decide that is probably enough for the day.

Time to get the kiddo in for a bath, a nap, and hopefully a shower for me while he sleeps.

* * *

The morning chill has burned away, and it's turned into a fairly warm day for mid-October. It's been a few days since our initial foray into town, and though I love the solitude of the mountain, I need to start setting up the life I hope to start in this town.

First stop is the post office. I'll need a P.O. Box and to let them know I tend to get large shipments a few times a month and arrange for them to let me know when I need to come pick them up.

"I heard she's working out at Delia's place," the woman at the counter in front of me whispers loud enough for me to hear, but makes it at least appear like she doesn't want me to know she wants me to hear. She has white-silver hair piled on top of her head in a tight bun that makes my scalp ache just looking at it. A floral dress hangs on her frail form down to her knees where compression socks are pulled up to meet them. The postal worker on the other side of the counter is obviously just barely tolerating the conversation. I think I even catch an eyeroll or two. "I saw them talking at The Bean the other day. Probably an interview."

"Actually, Delia was just inviting me out to take one of her dance classes. I hear they are a great workout." I lean forward, matching the busy-body's dramatic whisper. "Have you ever been? Do you recommend it?"

The woman gasps and quite literally clutches the string of fake pearls around her neck. "I would never go out to that den of sin."

"Oh really, I could have sworn I heard you had to drag your husband out of there a couple weeks ago," the postal worker interjects with a faux innocent tilt of his head.

The old lady's face burns bright red, and she turns with her book of stamps to flounce out of the post office, mumbling about the youth of today having no respect.

"Well, now that our town's one-woman judge and jury is gone, how can I help you?"

The man is tall and thin, with dark silky hair, brown eyes, and olive skin. His expression doesn't seem to ever wander far from bored senseless. As I tell him I'll be getting lots of heavy deliveries, mostly consisting of rocks, crystals, and herbs, he has the same flat expression. The only thing that piques his interest at all is when I warn him I might also get deliveries that say there are medical specimens inside.

"What are you doing up on the mountain? Building Frankenstein's laboratory?"

"Haha, no, I run a metaphysical e-commerce store. Most of my inventory is held at a warehouse a few hours away that covers my bigger orders. But I make beginner spell kits and a few other items, and for those I have everything shipped here, I hand package them, and then ship them out myself. Same with some of my more niche items that aren't worth taking up space in the warehouse or are too fragile to trust the workers there with."

"So, the rumor that you're a witch is true?"

"Exactly how many rumors about me are there? I've been in town less than a week now and this is only my second trip down from the cabin."

"Oh, trust me, that is plenty of time for the imaginations around here to start running wild. I get to hear most theories in their infancy. There have been the stripper rumors, but honestly every young attractive woman that comes to town gets that one. Apparently, the youth today just wants to make a quick buck with their bodies."

I mean fair, if I was more coordinated and wouldn't almost certainly injure myself on the pole, I wouldn't turn my nose up at the money some of those dancers probably make.

"Then there are the rumors that always come with being connected to the Halsted family. Mail order bride is my current favorite." He plants one elbow on the counter and props his chin in his hand. "I would gladly sell myself to marry Orion. The man was always hot, but when he came back from the military he was on another level."

Finally, the guy's face melts from impassive to wistful. Yeah, I know what he means. "I'm sorry, I've totally missed your name."

"Oh, yeah, I'm Lee." He holds his hand out over the counter and for a second, I'm not sure if he means for me to take it and kiss it or shake it. I opt for the latter. "I'm the post-master general here."

"Nice to meet you, Lee. I'm Brigid and this is Mica." I nod down to my little guy happily strapped into the stroller babbling away in the background.

"Nice to meet you both." He glances down at Mica and mimes tilting a hat at my son who has no idea what that means but smiles all the same. "So, I take it since you are opening a P.O. Box you are planning to be in town for a while?"

"Yup, hopefully making this our home. Speaking of which, do you know of any houses or apartments for rent nearby?"

"If there is anything to know in this town, trust me, I will know about it." Lee pulls open a drawer behind the counter and takes out a form for me to fill out as he talks. "Unfortunately, not much comes on the market here for rentals. Usually if people leave town, they just sell their houses. Even then, people either leave right out of school or stay until they die."

The bell over the door rings. When I go to turn and see who is coming in, Lee leans forward and rests his hand on my arm. "But I hope you find a rental. This place could use more new blood. New ideas."

Lee turns to whoever came in the door and taps one finger on my forms. This town loves their paperwork.

The minute I go back to filling out the empty lines on the paper, Mica starts fussing, probably upset we've been stationary too long. He's a kid that likes to be on the move. So, I push the stroller forward then back again over and over, trying to eke out a few more minutes of cooperation so I can finish up this one task. There are far too few things crossed off on my "get settled" to-do list.

"Ms. Bernie, right over here, I can grab the bulbs you ordered while she finishes up the forms." Just like that Lee is back to his flat, expressionless face. His voice also goes a little more monotone. I realize this is his customer service voice.

For some strange reason I am beyond happy that he dropped the unaffected voice with me. I guess I'm already making friends here.

I'm dismayed that once again the thought has visions of Orion staring across the water resurfacing. He is not my friend, no matter how much my body tells me it wants to be more than friends.

Chapter 13

Orion

I manage to avoid seeing Brigid for two days after the dock incident. I've been waking up at damn near the crack of dawn to make my way into town for no other reason than avoiding my too tempting neighbor. Spruce is delighted with the change in routine, happy to be along for the ride every day, riding shotgun in the front seat and getting lots of treats at every stop we make.

I've returned well after dark each night, avoiding the dock or even glancing over at Brigid's house for fear of getting a glimpse of her and losing all the well-honed self-control I've learned in my thirty years.

There were close calls though. I nearly walked right into the post office to pick up my mail, but got warned off by the town church lady complaining under her breath about the sassy new girl in town and not liking the new riff raff. I turned around so fast I almost ran right over Miss Bernie, the local piano teacher and best friend of our illustrious mayor. I had to listen to a lecture about the younger generations moving too fast for a good ten minutes after. The whole time I nervously shot glances at the post office door, afraid Brigid would emerge at any moment.

Later that day I stopped by the cafe to check up on Mom only to have Brigid back into the front door, pushing the door open with her delectable ass and pulling her son in a stroller.

Mom hobbled around the counter to help her, but I turned tail and booked it to the back room before my neighbor could see me.

Spending two days in a row in town means I'm behind on projects. I can't keep spending my days wandering the town where I grew up, trying to fool myself into thinking I'm catching up with friends and errands. I resorted to stopping by Knox's farm to see if he needed help getting the fields ready for winter.

He looked at me like I had lost my mind.

Sure, I help out on the farm during harvest season, sometimes during planting too. But only when Knox asks for the help. The farm has always been his deal. His and Dad's. I'm honestly not sure if I never had any interest in taking over the family business, or if it had just always been so clear that the farm would go to the firstborn that I never bothered to try. Now, when I do help, it's with feigned reluctance so my brother doesn't figure out that I actually love toiling with him in the fields. I never want him to think his inheritance was something that left me wanting.

But now I can't insist on showing up at the farm without it tipping my brother off to something being awry in my world. He would inevitably mention it to Mom or Delia, resulting in a bunch of conversations I'm not interested in having. Like how I don't know where I fit into the family. Or that I spend too much time alone on the mountain.

The excuses for escaping the mountain have run out. There are pieces that need to be finished, consultations to be scheduled, and shipments for the large pieces going several states away.

Not to mention I'm behind on editing and posting videos. The exposure social media provides helps sell some of the pieces, all through a business manager who keeps me anonymous by dealing with the inquiries that come through my website. But the truth is, I don't need the income from my furniture. Revenue from my videos has far exceeded my expectations. So much so that I had to hire a guy to invest for me and an assistant to field emails and appearance requests. I've thought about bringing on someone to edit for me, but this thing has already spiraled further than I ever thought it would. What started out as a funny way to pass the time has turned into a gig so good I have freaking employees.

Despite all that, I spend most of my time trying to ensure my identity stays a secret. I question that decision more and more these days. Each day my following count grows, and the likelihood someone in town finds out increases. Part of it is embarrassment. Making money because I look hot chopping wood is fucking weird. I'd get endless amounts of shit about it from my siblings. The old biddies in town would probably form prayer circles for me.

Part of it is shame. I fucked up my shot to play college football with one impulsive, hotheaded move in high school. Then a week after I found out my scholarship had been pulled, I signed up for the Marines without so much as talking to Ma and Dad about it. They were so fucking pissed, I think mostly out of fear that I'd be in danger. But I insisted it was the smart thing to do. I enlisted as a mechanic, I'd be learning a skill. Then I could use the GI Bill after getting out to pay for college, get an engineering degree or something. None of that happened. Instead I'm making more money a month showing off my body on the internet than my brother makes in one season of the farm. It's not fucking right.

The furniture business may not be the moneymaker, but it gives me legitimacy. Keeps my mind and body busy. Keeps my head from going places it shouldn't.

If I keep following these fucking lines of thought I might never stop. The shame of disappointing my family with one foolish decision has a tendency to consume everything else. Of missing out on my father's final years. By the time I was discharged from the Marines, Dad's cancer had robbed him of who he was. Either literally cut from his brain along with the tumors, or killed by the disease itself. He didn't know who I was, would forget a few moments after I told him. But I sat by his side anyway, telling him the same stories over and over again hoping to see a glimmer of recognition before he was gone. It never came.

But I can't let myself go down that dark train of thought. So instead, I focus on turning trees into furniture.

My plan is to go directly from the front door of my cabin to the workshop I built back in the woods. It is separated enough from the main clearing that I won't be able to see any activity that may or may not be happening on the other side of the pond. Just put my head down and get shit done. Then go straight from the workshop back to the cabin. I won't look around. Won't hope for a single glimpse of the woman I haven't been able to stop thinking about.

That's the plan at least.

Apparently my luck has run out.

A little over forty-eight hours without a single Brigid sighting and the very second I step from my cabin, there she is. The morning light softly peeks through gaps between orange and red leaves still clinging for life to branches as fall marches on. It's cold enough I'm happy I threw on a hoodie over my standard t-shirt and flannel.

But there, across my driveway, the expanse of grass that separates our properties, and the other cabin's driveway, there she is, wearing sweatpants and a t-shirt, both far too big and drowning out any hint of the curves I know for a fact live beneath the billows of fabric.

She stands frozen at the edge of the clearing, staring into the woods. Something about her position has my nerves on end, my instincts rising to the surface. "Spruce, sit. Stay." On command the best boy plops his butt down on my porch and stays there as I cross to where Brigid stands rigid.

"Hey, you okay?" I keep my voice low, calm, all too aware this is the time of year bears will start making their way to their hibernation spots deep in the forest.

Brigid starts a little at my words, a jump in her shoulders. She whips her head around to me and raises her finger to her lips. "Shhhh."

By degrees, my muscles relax, unclenching now that I see she's not frozen in fear. Rather it looks like fascination. I step closer, pulling up beside her to see what has her so fascinated, it takes a moment for my eyes to focus and translate what I'm seeing to my brain.

On nearly every surface, trees, the ground, everywhere just beyond the clearing where the forest begins are hundreds of monarch butterflies.

"Isn't it amazing?" Brigid whispers so low I can barely hear her. "Why are they all here?"

"It's their migration season. Actually it's a little late for them, but it's been so warm they probably got a little mixed up."

"I had no idea butterflies migrated."

"Monarchs are the only ones. They head from north of here and then all the way down to Mexico where they stay for the winter. They'll be back again in the spring. Believe it or not, it will be the great-grandchildren of these butterflies that will start the migration again next fall."

The need to look at her outweighs the sight before me. Brigid stands so still, probably afraid if she moves the butterflies will all go fluttering off. One cheek still has wrinkles from her pillow. Her usually neat black bob is all over the place, the back especially reminiscent of a rat's nest. There's something smudged on her shoulder that I'm ninety percent sure is some bodily fluid from her son.

She's the fucking sexiest thing I've ever seen. Even dressed like Adam Sandler, I want to peel away the voluminous layers of her sleep cloths and see what's beneath. I want to roll over in the morning and see this exact thing on the pillow next to mine.

It's a thought I've never had before. I went from having a couple high school girlfriends to the military, where I was more than a little slutty, to here. My serious relationships start and end with the dog someone dumped in the woods and I took in. I've never felt like I had much to offer a partner.

But looking at Brigid first thing in the morning has a vice squeezing so tight in my chest drawing in a breath becomes nearly painful. It makes me want to earn the privilege of waking up next to her each and every day. Part of me wonders if this is what Dad felt for Ma when he fell in love. I desperately wish he was still here so I could ask him.

Unable to take her eyes from the hordes of butterflies, Brigid tilts her head slightly in my direction, keeping her voice low. "I woke up and there were a few sitting on my window. Mica was still asleep, so I came out to get a closer look, but the minute I stepped out the door I saw them here. I've been standing here ever since." A sheen of unshed tears coat her eyes, emotion muffling her soft voice. "I know you'll think this is silly, that you don't believe in signs, but seeing them all here, it feels like a sign to me."

"A sign of what?" I try to match her volume, the reverence that I swear I can feel radiating from her whole being.

"That this is a safe place," the words are little more than a breath slipping over her lips.

Movement catches my attention from the corner of my eye and I look down to see one of the butterflies has landed on Brigid's bare foot. She must feel it too, because her eyes fall to where its wings slowly open and close.

"Monarchs are a symbol of transformation, of significant changes." Slowly, she folds down, staring at the little creature resting on her foot. "I can't help but feel like this is the world telling me this is where I'm supposed to be as I complete my own transformation."

I could listen to her talk like this all day. "Are you transforming?"

She wraps her arms around her bent legs and tilts her head to look up at me. "Definitely. From a slightly irresponsible kid to a mother. Turns out you don't give birth and automatically change overnight. Everything around you changes, but you are still you. You have to learn how to adapt to this new life that you're responsible for. It wasn't easy. Still isn't. But being here with Mica, it's felt nothing but right."

"I believe in signs." I can't take my eyes from her face.

The blissed-out expression morphs almost instantly to one of doubt.

"I do." I shove my hands deep into my pockets, willing myself to not reach out and touch her no matter how much I want to. "The reason they are here, not flying off yet, is because they need to warm up from the chill of the night. They fly and they fly all day, then find a safe place and land. Their wings get cold overnight, so they'll stay right here, warming their wings in the sun. Opening and closing them until they take off back on their journey." I force my eyes to shift away from her face, afraid they will give away too much.

"That's you. You went through a huge change, found a safe place to land, and you're waiting here until your wings are ready to finish the journey." Some emotion I don't recognize tightens my throat, makes it hard to speak. Because maybe that's what I'm doing here, too. Waiting. I just don't know for what.

We fall into an easy silence, watching the butterflies. There is so much I want to say, apologies that I owe her, but now isn't the time.

I don't know how long we stand there. Long enough that taking her hand in mine doesn't seem like it would be odd. But I know that is just my eternally optimistic side playing tricks on me, so I keep them firmly planted inside my jeans pockets.

Sooner than I want, the moment is broken by a quiet, plaintive cry of *Mama* from inside the house. Brigid sighs, but it isn't the impatient sigh of a mom who has had her peace broken by the cry of a child. It's a contented thing, full of peace and happiness.

As she turns toward her cabin, she places her hand on my arm and I'm suddenly very mad I put on so many layers this morning. "Tonight is a full moon."

I nod.

"On full moons I like to spread my crystals out to be filled with the moon's energy." She gives me a hard look. "Don't judge, I don't care if you think it's silly. But I also like to sit out and recharge myself."

My cheeks burn as they heat with a blush I don't have a chance of hiding from her. She's trying to tell me not to go creeping on her while she's out enjoying the full moon. I keep my eyes firmly focused on the butterflies. "No problem, I'll make sure to make myself scarce."

"Don't." She squeezes my arm once, then again until I turn to look at her. "I wouldn't mind it if you happened to also want to be out with the moon." She lets her fingers slowly trail down my arm before they fall away. "I've been reading out on the dock every night for a few nights now, always hoping to feel the same way I did the other night."

"How did you feel?"

Mica calls for his mama again and she takes a few steps in that direction, calling over her shoulder. "Stop avoiding me and come find out."

As Brigid hits the porch, she spins back around, a finger pointed directly at me. "Oh, and stop with the one-man repair crew. It isn't your job. I can take care of things."

I don't nod, don't acknowledge her words before she turns back to head into the cabin. There is no way in hell I will stop trying to make this place better for her and Mica.

Chapter 14

Brigid

The muffled tinkle of crystals clanking together in velvet pouches as I carry them out to the dock mixes with the sounds of nature at night. Something about how right the sounds meld settles my nerves. But only slightly.

Why did I invite Orion to join me tonight?

It was an impulsive move. I've been reading a book from a new author looking for the opportunity to sell through my site. It is all about harnessing sexual energy to manifest your desires, heal the spirit, and reclaim your strength. Not only is it fascinating, but it is hot as hell, too.

As we stood there together, watching the butterflies and talking about signs, transformations, something in him called to me. Maybe the same thing that called to me when I saw him across the pond that night. Watching me. I might not be able to stand him on a personal level, but there is no denying the physical connection when I'm around him. Like something deep inside me is waking from a long slumber.

That night when he caught me out on the dock, as I traced my hand down my body, the experience was amplified more than any other time I've touched myself. The brush of my fingertips over my usual sleep shirt felt more like the finest lingerie. Every nerve ending came to life, buzzing with need. I could sense the confidence I lost over the years with William building inside me, restoring me to who I once was. Who I should be.

Then, I looked up, and there he was. Orion, gripping the railing along his deck, half hidden in shadow. A noise seeped from his throat, far closer to an animal than human.

The energy from him *wanting* me hung in the air.

What if he had stayed? What if I had snapped to my senses and kept going?

I haven't been able to stop thinking about that moment. The missed opportunity. What it would be like to have all that energy swirling around as I touched myself.

As we stood, gazing at the gathering of butterflies in the forest, the energy crackled around us once again. If we had touched in that moment, I would not have been surprised in the least if there had been an actual electric spark.

So, without thinking about it too much, I put my plans for tonight out there. He can take the invitation and finish what we started, or he can ignore it and neither of us will be any the worse.

I decide not to turn on the dock light tonight, both because I won't be reading and because the moon is casting more than enough light for me to see what I'm doing. It's a cloudless night and the clearing is practically glowing with the Hunter's Moon.

The rough wood of the dock boards digs into my knees as I kneel with my back facing Orion's dock. I don't want to know if he comes out. Afraid he won't show, that he regrets seeing me that night. The pouches come in every color of the rainbow and I spread them in their correct order. White, red, orange, yellow, green, blue, purple, black. Inside each pouch are crystals that correspond to the color of its bag.

Quartz. Scolecite. Selenite.

Red Jasper. Carnelian. Tiger's Eye.

Orange Calcite. Barite Desert Rose. Aragonite.

Citrine. Jasper. Opals.

Leopard Stone. Epidote. Bloodstone.

Amazonite. Azurite. Lazulite.

Amethyst. Fluorite. Lepidolite.

Hematite. Snowflake Obsidian. Black Coral.

Each piece gets laid in order of power and energy, no two pieces touching. The weather should be clear tonight, so I'll leave them sitting out to recharge in the moonlight all night.

As I reach forward to readjust two pieces out of the shadow of the cabin, my skin heats. Pebbles. An invisible weight presses against my back.

He's watching. I don't need to see him to know.

I don't turn. Just continue futzing with the crystals until they're arranged perfectly. Not all practitioners of the craft are this meticulous when charging crystals. One of my mentors would throw all her crystals into a Tupperware bowl and put them on a table by the window. But there is something about a neat little row of crystals that feels right to me.

Orion's eyes on me feel right too. I don't want to examine that thought too closely.

It's been a year and a half since I've been with anyone. Not since the night Mica was conceived, so the memories of what I felt like during sex have faded to a dull shadow. I know I liked sex with my ex. Loved it even. He might be an awful human, but he was a decent lover.

Looking back, I can see now, every encounter with him, sexual or otherwise, seemed to take another tiny piece of my spirit away, until I was nothing but a vessel for him to fill with awe and appreciation for himself. He might have made me come, but it was a selfish act on his part. Making me orgasm was something he accomplished, not something we shared in together.

Tonight isn't about Orion. It's about me, about filling me with energy and positivity. Appreciation for the body I inhabit. I focus in on the desire I want to manifest under tonight's full moon. Healing.

I might be putting on a show for Orion, but really, I'm taking his appreciation for my body and letting that fuel my own confidence. I might not need a man to fulfill me, but knowing that a man who looks like Orion can't keep his eyes off me, even when

I am covered in dirt after making a fool of myself, is a powerful aphrodisiac.

Crystals perfectly in order, I pull salt and rosemary from two other pouches. With three deep breaths, I center myself. Keep the healing of my spirit, picked away by a man not worthy of my thoughts, in my mind's eye. I picture my spirit as colors, swirling around me. Pink and purple at its core. Shocks of orange and yellow dancing at the edges.

Carefully, keeping my goal in mind, I form a large circle around myself using rosemary and salt, both strong protective forces. Where the dock ends, I sprinkle the mixture into the water, imaging the protective herbs infusing the pond with their properties, completing my ritual space.

I turn my eyes to the opposite side of the pond, heart pounding in my chest. The moon is so bright I have no trouble picking out Orion's imposing frame in the exact position he'd been three nights ago.

Both hands grip the wood railing that surrounds the dock. I wish I could see if his knuckles were white from the hard grip. Or are they simply resting there, waiting to move. Wish I could see his eyes, are they heated? Curious? Angry?

Unlike that first night, I'm wearing something I picked out in case he did show. Lingerie isn't something I invest a lot of money in. Give me comfy sweats and I'm a happy girl. But I did pick up a beautiful, crimson velvet robe at the Renaissance Faire a few years ago. It is soft, warm, and sexy with its hem slightly shorter than I would ever wear in public. I haven't worn it in years but couldn't part with it when I was cleaning out my closet before the move. Now I know why. I needed it for tonight

Keeping my gaze focused on Orion, I untie the belt holding my robe closed, and let it slither against my skin, off my shoulders to my arms. I catch it in both hands and toss it to the side, away from the circle and crystals.

Slowly, I lower myself to sit right on the edge of the dock, my feet dangling in the cool water. The platform is tall enough that the water laps around my ankles with my feet swirling just below the inky black surface.

I place my hands on the dock behind me, let my head fall back, press my chest up toward the sky. I invite the moon to cast its light on me. To infuse me with its energy.

Orion might be across the pond, but I can hear the groan that claws up his throat. If I didn't know it was him, I'd be afraid there was a bear nearby.

I invite his energy in, too. Let the heat of his gaze on my naked body warm the parts of me that are already pulsing with need. The Hunter's Moon is good for new beginnings. For opening new doors and closing ones that don't serve you anymore. To invite new experiences. This is definitely a new experience.

I turn my mind to this place. To feeling the transformational essence of these woods. Think about the butterflies stopping in this safe space on their way to warmth.

My legs spread, opening to the man across the way. The moon's rays caress my skin like a lover's touch. I desperately want that touch to be real. To feel Orion's rough skin from years of working with tools and trees as it traces over my own softer flesh.

Sitting up straight, I start at my hair, let the silky smooth strands shift through my fingers. Trail the tips of those fingers down over my neck, trace along my collarbone. Each touch of my own hand sends sparks crackling under the surface of my skin. Idly, I wonder if he can see the light from those sparks at his place in the shadows.

Beneath the cool mountain air, my nipples gather to a point. An invisible line connects them to the space between my thighs, and as my fingers trail down to graze over the sensitive tips, that string twists tighter. Taunt arousal pulls at every nerve. I grow slick between my legs, my thighs spreading of their own accord. Almost as if they are making room for Orion's hulking body. Welcoming him.

I don't rush. Savor the pressure of his gaze. A weighted blanket of lust pushing down on me at every point he focuses on. My breasts. My face. My pussy. I don't need to see him to know when he looks at each. That invisible string connecting each erogenous zone connects him too. I wish I could pull it tighter. Pull him to me like a boat tied to an anchor.

Rustling on his side of the dock pulls my attention and I look at just the right moment to see him throw his shirt behind him. The moonlight casts his body into stark relief, each muscle casting a shadow below where it swells with tension. The light and dark warring for space on his skin as his breaths rise and lower his chest and belly.

He's beautiful normally. Half naked in the moonlight he's a god. I've never seen his long, red hair out of his trademark ponytail, but he's freed it tonight and the strands fall in waves down his back.

With my eyes trained on him, I skate my palm down over my stomach, to the space between my thighs, cupping myself. Warming that delicate part of me. "Fuck." The strangled word echoes over the water and I can't help but smile a little knowing I've affected him enough to make him break the silence.

The insistent throbbing between my legs won't be ignored any longer. Lying back, I arch my back, offering myself to the moon, the sky, the stars. To Orion.

For a moment I consider what his view must be. My legs spread, pussy in full view. Does it glisten in the moonlight?

Just thinking about him over there watching me has that invisible sting twisting, tugging at every sensitive inch of me. I bring my feet up to prop on the edge of the dock, spread far enough apart there is nothing hidden.

My fingers dip between my folds. A harsh gasp slips past my lips as I graze the swollen bundle of nerves. It's the lightest touch, but it feels like an electric wire pressed to my flesh. My back arches off the dock, head tipping back. It won't take much to make me come. But I don't want this to end; I want to stretch out this decadence as long as I can stand. Instead of centering my attention on my clit, I move to my opening, dipping one finger inside and then spread the wetness up to circle my clit again without directly touching it.

Through the fog of my arousal, of the inevitable end to this scene, the tinny crinkle of a zipper floats to me. How is it possible to hear the rustle of his jeans being shed from so far away? It's that invisible string again. Like kids talking through tin cans, I can hear everything he does because there is something tying us together.

If I listen hard enough, will I be able to pick up the sounds of his palm shuttling up and down his shaft?

I desperately want to sit back up and watch him just like he is watching me, but equally I want to keep wondering. The mystery of what he's doing winding the spring tighter and tighter. Every sensation getting closer to the surface, harder to fight off.

Splash

His body hitting the water makes me spring up to a sitting position, hand still moving between my thighs because at this point I can't possibly stop. Not until I reach that finish line. Every swing of his arm over the surface of the water brings both himself and my orgasm closer and closer.

What is he doing? Is he going to touch me? Just the idea has a moan slipping out and my fingers sweeping over my clit.

Five feet away he stops, his head and shoulders bobbing in the water as he treads water. The moonlight sparkles on water dripping down the sharp planes of his face to disappear in his thick beard. "Don't stop."

The desperation in his voice almost does me in. Honestly, I hadn't realized I'd stopped my ministrations until he told me to keep going. He's so fucking beautiful, how can you not stop everything to admire it?

"Brigid. Don't. Stop."

Holy shit. The pain in his voice. The pure need emanating from his eyes, his tensed jaw.

Experimentally I sweep the pads of my finger over my clit, once, twice, three times until I'm panting and my hips move of their own accord.

Water ripples around him in circles and I realize he's moving. Not closer. His arm works below the surface, pumping himself beneath the water. Watching me. It's all so delicious. So salacious. I spread my legs wider. Push two fingers into my cunt and sweep my thumb up over my clit.

"So fucking beautiful."

I let his words, his outright awe at me spread out before him, bolster my confidence. That invisible string is stitching together the spirit I thought might be so broken and battered from being tossed aside it might not be reparable. But the moon, and Orion's energy and the pleasure building to a crescendo inside me piece the edges together until something inside me feels whole again.

I try to slow it down. To stop my orgasm from knocking me flat out and ending this unforgettable moment, the strength rushing through my body. But even taking my hands away to stroke at my thighs, my belly, my breasts, it all makes the edge creep closer and closer.

Sounds I've never heard escape me before filling the clearing, overpowering the sounds of nature around us.

"Let me see you come." His voice drifts closer, I don't know if he realizes he's moved to just barely out of reach, but there he is, no more than three feet away. Each detail of his face clear as a bell in the bright moonlight.

I obey, gladly moving my hand back between my thighs, sitting a little higher, spreading my legs a little wider.

Everything between my thighs is so fucking slippery, my fingers skate and skip over my sex. Within seconds I'm giving him what he asked, *begged*, for.

The orgasm washes over me in a torrent, as if the moon has worked its magic and sent waves of pleasure to Earth just for me. Involuntarily my hips pulse, my legs snap shut, trying to hold on to the pleasure, to not let it all seep out yet.

"Open, Brigid," he growls.

With effort, I pry my knees open, the climax still ravaging my body, buffeting against me again and again. My body curling in on itself then relaxing before everything twists tighter again.

It's a confusing ebb and flow that makes it impossible to catch my breath.

I can't keep my legs open as another orgasm builds with my fingers frantically rubbing at the insistent bundle of nerves that demand more.

"I won't tell you again." God, the warning, the threat there is so fucking hot. But I can't obey; my body is trying to condense down to the few inches of real estate at the center of me.

The next growl is so close my eyes fly open in surprise and Orion's hands are on me. His elbows planted on the edge of the dock and palms spreading me apart as I continue to masturbate right before his face.

His eyes hold a question, *Is this okay?*

I nod, but say nothing. Afraid if I say anything else it will turn into begging him to climb from the water and fuck me here under the moonlight. As much as that sounds like everything I need right now, I want to finish this moment how I started it. Him watching, me letting him.

I lay back again, no longer able to hold myself up. Both hands now free, I let one wander over my breasts, tweaking my nipples and then soothing the pain away before repeating the process. My other hand is focused entirely on my clit, drawing a third, stronger orgasm from my body. One of Orion's hands disappears from my legs beneath the dock, into the water.

I wish I could see him touching himself. The other hand keeps one leg pinned open, no longer able to hide from him. Every muscle in his shoulder and arm is tensed with the struggle to keep himself propped up on the dock. His whole body shakes with the effort, but the look of determination on his face tells me he would do this all night if it meant he got a front row seat to the show I'm putting on.

Why does his discomfort make me so fucking hot? The lengths he'll go to just to bear witness to my pleasure is like nothing I've experienced.

I don't know how long we stay like that, wringing orgasm after orgasm from my body until I'm shaking with my own effort. Time ceases to exist. Outside this pool of moonlight doesn't matter.

Eventually I can't manage another single ounce of pleasure. My body is wrung tight, like a towel twisted to expel every drop of water.

My hands fall away. I'm honestly not sure I can move.

The dock dips and sways as Orion climbs up onto the boards. If he asked to fuck me right now, I would let him. I'm not sure where I would get the energy, but I would. I'd welcome it. That's not what he does though. Instead, he scoops me up into his arms, pressed against his wet, cool skin. He carries me up the dock, around the too tall grass and onto my porch. At the door he stops, seeming to instinctually know he can't come in.

There were a lot of lines crossed tonight, but entering the cabin where my son sleeps is one we both know is off limits.

"I've got it."

Reluctantly, he places me on my feet. I sway for a second but find my equilibrium.

The tension in the air envelopes us. I can feel how badly he wants to kiss me. After what I just did in front of him, a kiss should be nothing. But fear rips through me stronger than any of the orgasms. Strange as it may sound, I do believe this little sexual ritual tonight has gone a long way to healing what I thought was lost. But my spirit is far from good as new. It might be stitched back together into a messy quilt, but each seam is still delicate, too easily ripped apart again. I refuse to let the work I've been doing on myself be unraveled by another man.

Orion helped me restore some of my confidence tonight. But I need to do the rest.

Chapter 15

Orion

Is there anything more awkward than having to walk naked around your neighbor's yard back to your own property to pick up all the clothes you discarded before jumping in the pond? Yes, walking around her dock and picking up the clothes she had shed but was too tired to put back on.

Totally in the buff, I tiptoe around the creaking boards, taking note of the ones my foot almost goes through so I can replace them later, grabbing the velvety robe from where she dropped it on the dock.

I will not smell it. I will not smell it.

I give in and hold the fabric to my nose, inhaling the spicy citrus scent I've come to associate with my little storm cloud.

I had every intention of staying on *my* fucking side of the water tonight. She wanted to be watched, or that's what she insinuated, and I was all too happy to oblige. I never thought the pond in my backyard was all that big, but standing on the dock, watching as Brigid played with herself, it was too damn far. Hell, the six inches separating us at the end was too much.

Watching as she wrung each second of pleasure from herself was the sweetest torture I have ever experienced in my life. So sweet that not even jumping into the freezing cold water dampened my need. I mean, sure, my manhood tried to retreat into my body for a minute there, but by the time I swam to her side of the pond, he was back to full strength.

Now, standing on her dock, I fold the robe into a neat little pile. A shift of light catches my attention from the corner of my eye. Through her windows, only covered by thin gauzy fabric, I watch as Brigid enters her room and bends over Mica's crib, probably checking to make sure he's okay. Quite literally on the outside looking in while Brigid gets ready for bed, turns off the lights, and then from the sound of the springs in her mattress squeaking in protest, collapses into bed.

All I want is to be in that tiny, shitty shack with Brigid.

Holding her in my arms, carrying her when she was too exhausted to move, it was the greatest honor of my life. How can I make it happen again? And again?

It is a bone deep need that springs up from a well somewhere inside me. The attraction was immediate and insistent. But since I've gotten to interact with Brigid, seen her care for her son with a fierce love, watched as she stubbornly marched toward her goals, intent on achieving them alone, something quieter but just as strong has developed. Respect. Affection. Another word I'm scared to even whisper in my own mind.

I watch like a creep as the lights turn off. The need to touch her during the throes of her orgasm is nothing compared to the absolute desperation of wanting to tuck her into my side in a warm bed.

I need to *earn* that privilege.

* * *

Operation Win-Over Brigid comes together overnight. After returning to my own cabin after the hottest hour of my life I was so keyed up I couldn't settle down and sleep. So instead I started organizing.

Step one—become someone who makes her life easier—is already underway.

I might not have been raised by a single mother, but come harvest time and Ma might as well have been solo parenting us. Those weeks in late summer Dad would be out in the fields from sunup to sundown. We barely saw him except in the distance on the tractor or in the fields. Everything fell to Mom and she never batted an eyelash. She somehow made it look easy when I know it was anything but.

If it was hard for Ma a few weeks out of the year, I know it has to be exponentially harder for Brigid who has no help what-so-ever.

I gotta keep it small though, or my storm cloud is going to get spooked. She's like a stray dog that's been kicked one too many times, a single wrong move and I'll either chase her off or get my nuts ripped off. She's already noticed the little fixes I've been making around the place, and shown her disdain for them. So I gotta go smaller.

My first official act for Step One of Operation Win-Over Brigid is something I know she will be desperate for this morning.

Caffeine.

I don't imagine a nine-month-old baby cares all that much that his mom was up till at least one in the morning.

Thankfully, having a mom that owns her own coffee shop has spoiled me when it comes to coffee. No regular drip machine would do after living off Mom's concoctions the first few months after coming home from the Marines. One of my first big, frivolous purchases for the cabin had been a state-of-the-art espresso machine.

Brigid seems like a salted caramel kind of girl to me. As soon as the sun peeks over the horizon, I doctor up a latte and put it in one of the many travel mugs I've accumulated over the years. I also throw a couple muffins into a paper bag, shove my feet into my sneakers and set off for my daily morning trail run with Spruce.

My good boy is so used to our morning routine he gets confused when instead of turning right out the front door to head onto the trail I've spent years carving through the woods, I turn left to head around the short side of the pond.

I'll just leave the breakfast on the porch for her to find. The travel mug should keep the coffee warm for a while, and if it does get cold I know from experience it will still be delicious.

That's the plan at least, but as soon as I step foot onto Brigid's porch the door flies open and the woman herself is standing there, baby on hip, those cute-as-fuck creases from her pillow still etched into the side of her face.

The moment she sees me—one foot on her porch, dog panting happily at my side—she freezes in her tracks, confusion and maybe concern painted on her fucking adorable morning face.

"Good morning, Sunshine."

She grumbles in return and shifts Mica on her hip, the voluminous T-shirt she probably slept in inching higher on her thigh.

Do not get a chubby. Your running shorts will do fuck all to hide it.

"Coffee?" I hold out the plastic travel mug.

"What is this?" She examines the cup as if it might bite her.

"This is Step One."

Mica flashes a huge gummy smile at me, his face also still covered in sleep lines, and I take that as his approval of my plan.

"Huh?"

"I mean it's a salted caramel latte." I take the tiniest step closer. "And in here are two homemade blueberry muffins."

"You made muffins?"

I shrug, cheeks heating a little. "Mom insisted both her boys learn how to cook and bake. I was going to leave them on the porch, I was hoping you'd still be asleep."

Finally, she reaches out and takes the coffee cup. "Not with my very own human alarm clock." She kisses the side of Mica's head.

For his part, Mica finally notices Spruce sitting by my side. "Pupupup," he says in that breathing baby talk way.

Spruce's tail starts going double-time against the weed covered walkway.

"This wasn't necessary." She says right before tilting the coffee at her lips and taking a sip.

Eyes slipping closed, Brigid moans. The sound of paper crinkling has her eyes flying open to stare at the death grip I have on the bag of muffins.

"Listen, about last night." She shifts her focus to my face. "I don't want you to get the wrong idea."

"The only idea I got is that you are sexy as hell and I would very much like that, and more, to happen again." The truth, but also not. Yeah, I want a repeat, but the *more* goes beyond fucking her until she's shaking. I want to bring her breakfast in bed. Mow her fucking grass for her. Help her with anything and everything she asks of me. I want to get to know the little guy in her arms who is obviously so central to everything she does in life.

"That probably isn't a good idea."

For a second I think she means me getting to know Mica, but it only takes a second to realize she means anything physical happening between us again.

"We're neighbors. And while I'm used to sharing walls with my neighbors back in Pittsburgh, all alone up here on the mountain, we're more tied together than any other neighbor I've ever had." She takes another sip of the coffee, and I watch as she struggles to hold back another moan. "This could get complicated. I don't know how long it will take me to find an apartment in town that will work for us. How long we'll be here practically right on top of you."

Do not get a chubby. Do not get a chubby.

"So, let's just chalk last night up to an incredible night and agree to be friendly neighbors."

I can't outright lie to her and say I agree to the friends plan. But there is no way in hell I will *just* be friends with this woman.

"I promise I won't try for a repeat of last night." I pause, considering if that is close enough to the truth, but decide it isn't. "Not until you give me the green light at least."

"I hate to break it to you, Orion, but the only man I plan on being a part of my life is the one I'm raising." She squeezes her son tighter to her, both in affection and because he has grown tired of the adults talking and is now attempting to throw himself from her arms to get closer to Spruce. With a sigh, Brigid crotches down and plants her son on the porch where he promptly crawls over to my dog.

To my knowledge Spruce has never been around kids before, other than passing the town kids now and then when we come down from the mountain. But as soon as Mica gets within reaching distance, Spruce splats down onto his side and lets the baby tug at his ears and fur.

"Gentle, Mica."

"Judging by Spruce's smile and tail wagging I'm thinking he's okay. Plus, he will get up and walk away if he doesn't like anything. Trust me, he does it every time I get the nail trimmer out of the drawer."

Even with my reassurance, Brigid hovers nearby, ready to pull back her son if the dog shows the slightest sign of annoyance or aggression.

Without taking her eyes off the two guys playing on the ground, Brigid continues our conversation. "Seriously though, last night was not the norm for me. It was the butterflies and the moon and the book and I'm ovulating and it's been a long time. It was the perfect storm of circumstances and hormones. Please don't read too much into it."

"Okay." To be honest, everything after saying she's ovulating is a bit of a blur. What is it about knowing that that makes me want to scoop her up and carry her to the bedroom? To make a little friend for Mica?

It's just stupid biologically programmed male ego bullshit.

Right?

Chapter 16

Brigid

I should not be disappointed that Orion has agreed that he won't read too much into our... interlude. But the moment he says *okay* something in my stomach sinks and twists in an unpleasant way.

With one hand still on Mica's back, ready to pull him back if I need to get him away from the dog, I glance up to Orion. But instead of seeing him nodding in agreement, his eyes look hazy and he's staring at me as if he doesn't really see me. Like he's far away.

"Are you grossed out that I talked about ovulation?"

That snaps him out of whatever fugue he'd slipped into and he zones back into the moment.

"Not grossed out, at all."

I believe him; his eyes heat, and even though it had been the middle of the night, I recognize the look on his face from the night before.

"I'm well aware of all the phases of the menstrual cycle and how they can affect a woman."

"Oh, right, I forgot. You're a feminist."

Orion huffs a laugh and places the bag of muffins next to me on the porch. "Never gonna let me live that down, are you?"

This has to stop. I can't sit here on my porch flirting with my neighbor. Especially when that neighbor got a front row seat to my one-woman show last night.

I scoop Mica back up, him trying to nosedive back down to the dog who has apparently surpassed me as Mica's favorite being on Earth in less than twenty-four hours.

"I gotta get us moving. We're going into town for a bit this morning." I try to shift Mica to the other hip, hoping that a little more distance from Spruce will stop his fussing. When he wants something he becomes harder to hold than a fistful of sand. "We just came out to clean up from..."

I should not finish that sentence. *Last night* is what I was going to say. No need to bring it up. Again. The gentle pressure of Orion's eyes on me has me feeling restless. My eyes shift to various points around the yard, the trees, the porch. Anywhere but at him. Which is when I see my robe folded in a neat little pile next to the door. Right where Orion said he was going to leave my homemade breakfast.

Like a magnet has flipped, my gaze swings back to Orion who obviously knows where I was looking.

"I went back and got them for you last night." He shoves his hands down into his pockets, something I notice he does a lot around me. What is that about? "I wasn't sure if I should clean up the crystals. Decided to leave them alone so I didn't mess with the energies."

He manages to get the sentence out without rolling his eyes or making a face.

"Thanks." Suddenly, everything is too much. The tension in the air, the wriggling child in my arms, the way Orion seems to be holding himself back from saying or doing something. The energy that I found so restorative last night overwhelms me this morning.

Rather than confront any of it I quickly bend down to scoop up the coffee, bag of muffins and pile of clothes from the porch.

"Let me help..."

"No, I got it." I respond a little too loudly, at the same time as coffee comes spouting out of the sipping hole in the travel mug. I'm barely keeping my grip on Mica, my arm wrapped around under his armpits as he twists and kicks his legs trying to get back down. "Okay, thanks again for the coffee. Bye, neighbor!"

I rush awkwardly into the cabin, kicking the door behind me and slithering a now crying Mica down the side of my legs to crumble in a tantruming puddle on the floor.

Real smooth, Brig.

* * *

The text I got from Roxy this morning was suspect to say the least. I knew this woman was a little out there from the minute I met her at the cafe. It might be part of the reason I immediately liked her so much. The minute I walked into the back room she got this smile like we were the oldest of friends and said, "Well hello stranger, welcome to the Love-Library."

We sat and talked about books, Mica, the town, it was amazing. Within two minutes we were trading titles of our favorite books and I was telling her all about Mica. I don't trust many people, but within seconds I knew this woman was something special. A kind soul who had lived many lives.

So when I got a text this morning that said *Meet me at the cafe at 10 a.m. Bring that adorable baby and don't tell anyone.* Instead of immediately shutting that shit down, I laughed and responded that I would see her there.

The hours on the door tell me the cafe is normally closed Mondays, so I'm not sure if I should walk in or knock. As I'm raising my hand to knock another text buzzes through on my phone.

Come to the back.

What is with all the cloak and dagger stuff? We're meeting for coffee, not organizing a drug deal.

But I do as she says and follow the wraparound porch to the back of the house. There is a fire escape that goes up to the second then third floors of the house-turned cafe. Beyond the porch is a small gravel parking lot with only one car occupying a space.

The back door opens and Roxy pokes her head out, looking left and right as if checking to make sure no one else is around. "Hurry, in here."

She waves her hand at me as if to urge me to go faster.

The woman who has to be in her sixties has a deceiving amount of strength as she grabs me by the wrist and pulls me the rest of the way into the building.

"Did you tell anyone you were coming here?" Roxy asks as she closes and locks the door behind me.

"I mentioned to Orion that we were coming into town but didn't say why."

With a relieved sigh she turns and crosses what I now see is a decent sized kitchen. "That should be fine, he almost never comes to town on Mondays."

Mica and I stand awkwardly by the door, not entirely sure what to do. The kitchen is beautiful but also a bit of a mess. There is a large island in the middle of the space topped with butcher block counters. Along the walls are cabinets that I have a feeling are original to the house but have been painted a bright turquoise, a huge six-burner stove, and gigantic industrial refrigerator that is most definitely not original.

Every surface is covered in what I can only describe as an apple murder scene. Peels are piled high in the corners of the counters, the cores are flung around, some on the floor, and the apples themselves are sliced haphazardly in bowls. On the stove is a huge pot with something boiling inside. The air is thick with the sweet scent of tart apple cider and something sweeter.

"Ignore the mess, I'm working on a new recipe. I'm thinking about calling it the *Fallin' Fast Latte.*" Roxy stirs the pot of bubbling liquid, then takes a clean spoon from a drawer and dips it into the pot. "Come taste the syrup. It is an apple cinnamon brown sugar syrup."

I close the space between us and Roxy holds her hand under the spoon to catch any drips from falling on Mica's head since I'm wearing him today. The moment the warm liquid hits my tongue it's like fall wrapping around me. It's crisp air and crackling fires. Leaves snapping underfoot and a pie baking in the oven. "Holy shit."

"Good?"

"That is an understatement. I would drink that straight from the bottle, forget the coffee."

Roxy laughs and places the spoon into the sink a few feet away. "While I appreciate the compliment, I would advise you to not drink a whole bottle of this. You'll go into a sugar coma within seconds. Oh!" She spins to the fridge and muscles the heavy door open. "I forgot, I also made some fresh apple sauce for Mr. Mica."

Arms loaded with huge Mason jars of apple sauce, she kicks the fridge closed again and places them on the counter. "All sugar free, though I did put the tiniest bit of cinnamon."

"Roxy, it is going to take me months to get through all that."

She glances down at the abundance of applesauce and waves me off. "Don't worry, it's not only for you. I'll give a few jars to Sam and Paula; they own the local hardware store and hair salon. They have five kids under seven."

My eyes widen with just the thought of that many young kids. Mica is a pretty easy baby, but even he has his moments that make me want to rip my hair out. I can't imagine that times five.

"The rest of the jars will go to the community pantry for whoever needs it." She pops one of the jars open and pours some of the smooth apple sauce into a bowl. "Now, why don't I take this little guy and I'll feed him a snack while you get to work."

I trail behind Roxy as she leads the way into the front rooms of the cafe. I'm starting to see where Orion gets his energy. His mother is incapable of sitting still. "I'm sorry, Roxy, did you offer me a job here and I forgot? What exactly am I here to work on?"

Much to my surprise, we are not alone in the café. Sitting at one of the small tables is a tall, lean man. He has thick dark brown hair that's just a touch too long so it hangs haphazardly across his forehead. Black, square-framed glasses sit on a nose with the slightest arch in the middle and a slight hook at the tip. His face is angular, jaw clean-shaven.

As Roxy and I cross the room, he stands a little too quickly, his long legs bumping the table causing his cup of coffee to slosh over the rim of the mug.

He wears a pair of tans slacks and a checked button-down shirt with the sleeves rolled up to just below the elbow. Both look like they've been ironed within an inch of their lives. He is that ever-elusive mix of incredibly handsome and complete nerd.

"This—" Roxy swings the hand holding the bowl of applesauce toward the man, nearly spilling half the contents on the floor "—is Wesley Smith, my secret friend."

I raise my eyebrows, eyes darting back and forth between the two. Roxy has at least thirty years on him, so if she's saying what I think she's saying, I mean, go girl.

"Secret friend as in…"

"Oh! No!" Wesley's hand flies to the back of his neck, trying to hide an embarrassed smile.

"Sorry." Roxy laughs with her whole body, the bowl of apple sauce in her hand nearly flying as she rocks back and forth with the mirth rocking her. "That did not come out right. We are friends, *just* friends, but no one in town can know." Roxy's voice goes a little hard, her face losing some of the light that naturally radiates from her. "I really mean it has to stay a secret that we are friends, because of who his family is."

"You related to the Hoffas or something?" I swear, this town gets weirder and weirder every time I learn more about the local lore.

"Worse, I'm a Lickinbill," he says with an apologetic smile.

"Wait, Lickinbill? As in the mayor that refused to come out of his office and talk to me?"

Wesley nods, cringing at my words. "That would be him. Please don't judge me by him."

"Wesley is nothing like that old prude." Thankfully, Roxy puts the bowl of apple sauce on one of the many empty tables near us, so I can stop wondering if it will end up all over the walls. "He is the town librarian. We struck up a friendship a few years ago thanks to our mutual love of books. But if his uncle, or my children, knew we were friends it would cause quite a bit of drama." She turns to Wesley, giving him a classic mother who thinks she knows best glare. "Though I think it is long past time we let the people of Amoresville in on the secret that Wesley is a perfectly nice young man and not at all like his uncle." It is almost as if she means the words to convince him, not me. Her face softens and she pats Wesley on the shoulder. "But, he keeps insisting it is for the best. So I would appreciate it if you kept this to yourself."

"Oh, okay, no problem." What a strange little town this is. "So, what exactly are we doing here?"

"Wesley here is going to help get you your business license." Roxy plants her hands on her hips and beams, obviously proud of this clandestine meeting.

"Roxy, I told you, and your son, that I am fine taking care of this on my own. I started and grew this business on my own. I prefer to handle these things myself." I rub Mica's back as he cranes his head around from where he is tucked against my chest, trying to see what is going on with the voices behind him. "I appreciate the thought, but I will pass on the offer."

"Listen, I may not be quite as Type A as you obviously are, but I understand the desire to handle things yourself. Us mothers love to think we can handle everything ourselves all the time. But trust me when I say you will need help with this." Roxy nods her head in Wesley's direction. "This young man is the only way you have any shot of getting that business license and opening your store. Please trust me when I tell you to at least listen to his advice."

I eye him with trepidation. Why would the mayor's nephew want to go behind the back of his uncle to help a stranger? "So you know the trick to getting a business license approved in town?"

"Well, I know how to appeal to my uncle's quirks."

Roxy scoffs as she turns to go behind the long coffee bar. "That's a nice way of saying he knows how to stroke the old idiot's ego."

Wesley shrugs, but nods in agreement.

"So why would you want to help me? You don't know me."

Wesley pushes one hand through his hair, pushes the glasses up the bridge of his nose, then crosses his arms casually across his chest. "First, Roxy can be very persuasive, and she insisted."

Roxy rolls her eyes and leans down to coo at Mica.

"Second, I believe this town desperately needs new businesses. We are seeing increased foot traffic thanks to June's work with the town's events and social media efforts. But most people only spend a handful of hours in town because there isn't much going on. The empty storefronts in the town square aren't a good look either." Wesley rocks back on his heels, and something about his whole aura screams professor in his element. "I have an obligation to this town, and I want to help it grow where I can. Third, I like a challenge. Getting Burt to allow a Pagan shop in town could be a fun one." A spark of mischief I did not expect to see lights up the man's eyes. "I don't mean this as an insult, but if this application isn't worded very precisely, there is no way Burt lets a store like yours open its doors."

I admit, his little speech has me curious. Could his uncle really be that bad? Is my own stubborn pride worth risking my dreams?

"Well, working on the application might be hard. I didn't bring it with me since I didn't know this was why Roxy wanted me to come over."

Wesley smiles and bends to pull something from the briefcase on the floor. He hefts a familiar stack of papers up and slaps it on the table, causing his coffee to slosh dangerously close to the rim of his mug.

"I brought an extra. I figured we would need to start over anyway."

With a sigh of resignation, I give in. "Okay, I guess it can't hurt to at least listen to your advice."

As Roxy heads to get a drink for me, I unstrap Mica and pull up one of the highchairs. I arrange various toys and books onto the tray hoping they will keep him occupied for at least a little while.

Wesley has the application spread out into a few stacks on the table, with a neat line of pens to one side. "Believe it or not, this is the slimmed down version of the application. I convinced him to edit it last year, and this was the best I could do."

Roxy hobbles over to us, her skirt fluttering around her walking cast as she carries two mugs. "Which is why I never bothered filling one of those asinine things out."

"What? You don't have a business license?"

"No. I have all the food and safety certificates required by the state and county. I'd like to see that old asshole try and shut me down." She says it as if Burt might be standing right outside and she was daring him to come in and try right at that second.

"So, are you telling me this is a speakeasy coffeehouse?"

Roxy's smile widens across her face, pure joy radiating from her every pore. "You bet. Wait until I tell you about the years it was a whore house."

Wesley plants his face in his palms and chuckles. "Don't let her start, we'll never actually get any work done."

Roxy waves him off and pulls up a chair to sit next to Mica, picking up a book from his tray and reading the simple words to him.

Making a mental note to revisit this conversation with Roxy later, I turn to Wesley and shrug. "All right, Teach, where do we start?"

Chapter 17

Orion

I had to go to town anyway. Delia tattled on Mom, who apparently hasn't been wearing her walking cast half the time. Of course as a good son, I should go down to the cafe and make sure she's actually taking care of herself. And I have a present that I think will make the whole walking cast thing a little more palatable for my mother.

Plus, Spruce needs his nails cut and the only one that can ever do it is Paula at Cuts and Mutts. Granted, every place in town is closed on Mondays, but I know Paula will open for one of her husband's oldest friends.

My impromptu trip to town has nothing to do with hoping to run into Brigid.

It would just be a nice fringe benefit.

I repeat the lie to myself during the whole drive to town. Windows down so Spruce can stick his head out into the rushing air, Whitney Houston blasting on the radio as I belt right along about wanting someone to dance with. Granted, I can't quite hit the high notes she could.

My heart seems to add an extra little hitch each time I think about Brigid and her tired face when she came to the door. Something else twitches in my nether regions each time I remember watching her last night.

But I can't go there again. If I tug it one more time to that memory I'm going to start chaffing.

The streets of my hometown are quiet as I slow to the polar icecap speed limits the mayor has imposed downtown. I swear, it is not physically possible to drive fifteen miles per hour.

The man is insane.

Speaking of which, as I reach the square, the man himself comes strolling out from Town Hall, his briefcase in hand. Before I have time to consider what I'm doing, I jerk the truck to the right and pull up to the curb slightly askew, and throw it into park. In the next breath I'm jumping from the truck, not bothering to close the door behind me. "Spruce, stay." I swear the dog huffs in protest behind me, but he keeps his butt in the seat.

"Mister Halsted, what do you think you are doing driving like that on our busy streets?" Something about Burt's nasally voice and shitty comb-over make me want to do violence that I would never contemplate normally.

I glance around us with exaggerated movements. "Burt, it's Monday during a school day. Literally no one is around but the two of us."

"As if that is an excuse for breaking traffic laws." The aging mayor puffs up his chest, trying to get another inch on his hunched frame.

"You're one to be talkin' about breaking laws. I'm fairly certain renting out that shit hole of a cabin has to be breaking some state fair housing laws." Anger isn't something I'm super familiar with. I pride myself on keeping a cool head in tough situations. It was necessary when you lived in a bunker with fifty testosterone fueled dudes who could only be called adults in the legal sense of the word.

Watching as our town's miserable fucking mayor puts on a haughty expression and scans me from head to toe like I'm less than mud under his shoe makes a rage I have never felt rise quickly from my toes to my head.

"There is nothing wrong with the cabin, and the tenant hasn't once complained." Burt adjusts the glasses perched on the end of his nose.

"Because you wouldn't come out of your office to hear her complaints. And I'm guessing you aren't listening to the voicemails she left. Or read the emails she has sent." How dare he put anyone in danger, but especially a single mother and her child. "When they got there the water and electricity weren't even turned on. Not to mention how filthy the place was. She's got a fucking baby for god's sake."

"Interesting. The woman I spoke with never mentioned anything about another occupant. She said she would be staying there alone." Burt's thin lips tilt slightly at the corners. "That omission is reason enough for me to cancel our contract."

I cannot punch a man half my size and twice my age.

"You wouldn't dare."

"I would. I take my contracts seriously. They are ironclad. There were no other occupants listed on the rental agreement. It also stated very clearly in Section Four, Article F that the structure came strictly as-is."

What is the next level past rage? Fury? Wrath? Apoplectic? That's where I am. If we weren't standing in the middle of the town square I would very seriously consider taking this man out of this world.

"If you are so concerned with the condition of my family's property you should have taken me up on the offers I have made to sell it back to you."

Suddenly everything inside me goes still. Calm.

"I'll buy it now."

Burt's smirk wavers. I've surprised him. Something about that gives me an immense amount of satisfaction.

Every time I've asked him to send someone up to work on his side of the property he's offered to sell it back to me. Always at twice the price it would be worth. Saying I was never tempted would be a lie. I looked into the financing once. But I never went through with it because I didn't want to give Burt the satisfaction of giving him a single cent for the land that should rightfully belong to my family.

But now? None of that matters. Pay twice the price? Hell, three times would still be worth it to know I could get that cabin in working order and safe for Brigid and Mica. And maybe they would stay a little longer. Maybe she wouldn't start looking for houses in town quite yet.

"I don't think you could afford my price. That's why you've been resisting all these years."

I shake my head. "See, that is where you are wrong. I just didn't want to give you the satisfaction. Give me a number."

Burt lifts his chin, and I swear if his nose gets much higher in the air he might tip over backward. "Four hundred thousand."

The number is absurd. I still own the majority of the land around the clearing. His property is just the one acre parcel the cabin sits on. It's literally surrounded by my land. One acre and a shitty cabin up in the woods, not even all that close to the state park, shouldn't go for more than one hundred thousand.

"Two hundred. That's still twice the amount it is actually worth. Plus you won't have to worry about the property taxes anymore. Or the possible lawsuit when the roof caves in on the occupants."

For a man I have always considered soulless, I see the emotions play out behind his eyes. At first it's annoyance that I'm haggling with him, something he considers low-class. Then intrigue at the thought of not having to pay the tax bill. Finally, fear at the mention of a lawsuit. For someone that is known to be quite litigious, Burt would be mortified to be on the receiving end of a lawsuit.

"Three hundred," he shoots out.

"Two fifty, I get to start on improvements before the sale closes—" no reason he needs to know I have already been putting in work on the place "—and it stays between us."

Slowly, he nods his head, a devious gleam creeping to those beady little eyes. "Two seventy-five. I'll have my lawyer draw up the papers."

I stick my hand out between us and it hangs in the air for a moment before Burt slips his sweaty palm into mine and we shake on the deal. "Since you are such a stickler for contracts, you realize this is a verbal agreement and will hold up in court if you try to pull something."

"I'm aware."

And just in case, I pull out my phone, turn on the camera and flip it into selfie mode, pressing record. "On this day, October tenth, Burt Lickinbill here has agreed to sell the property adjacent to mine to me, Orion Halsted, for two hundred and seventy-five thousand dollars. We shook on it and everything." I hold up our joined hands and point the camera to Burt. "Correct?"

"Yes," he grumbles petulantly.

As soon as he confirms, I put the phone away.

"That wasn't necessary. I am a man of my word."

"Burt, I would say I don't trust you as far as I can throw you, but I'm fairly certain I could throw you a good distance if I tried."

Burt sneers at me like the little rat he is. "Now that we have an agreement, I hope you know that I am getting the far better end of this deal. The rent checks from the tenant won't come close to paying your mortgage."

I lean in close to Burt, savoring the moment I drop this little tidbit of knowledge into his lap. "Who says I'm getting a mortgage? I'll have a letter with proof of funds to you in the morning."

The look of shock on his face is worth every cent I'm paying for the cabin.

*　*　*

After leaving Burt to get things going with the paperwork for the sale, I head to the Cuts and Mutts to drop off Spruce for his mini-spa day. Paula has all five of her kids with her and they take turns brushing the dog, who looks like he has died and gone to heaven with all the attention.

I also pull Sam aside to get started on the order from The Nail and Bail for everything I'll need to get started fixing the cabin's roof. Not to mention repairing the broken porch railing and rotting floorboards. I'll also need to find out if I can tie the electricity to my solar panels or if we'll need to install an all-new system for the cabin.

Getting a line of credit might not be such a bad idea so I don't have to worry about moving funds around to pay for all the projects piling up in my mind.

A new project, a way to make Brigid and her son safer, and managing to one-up Burt have me in the mood to hoof it down to the cafe. The brisk fall air elevates my mood even more. October has always been my favorite month. Not only does it have the best holiday, Halloween, but toward the end of the month was always when things would start to wrap for the year on the farm and we would have more time with Pop.

He was always so proud of the work he did and the way he both provided for the family and continued his family's legacy. I never totally understood that pride, never understood the farming mindset. It was never something I wanted to be a part of, not like Knox who was practically born to carry on the agricultural life.

But as the plans to make the cabin better for Brigid and Mica come together in my mind, the thought of making my family's land whole again takes root, and I think I understand at least a part of what drove my father. The need to do something tangible that made the lives of the people I care about better. It's a heady feeling.

Knowing Mom will probably be holed up in the cafe's kitchen, working on some new recipe for the month's themed drinks, I head around to that side of the old house and let myself in.

To my surprise, the kitchen is empty, and in its usual state of disarray. Mom has always used Mondays as her experimenting days since the cafe is closed. It's odd seeing the kitchen with no sign of her whirling about stirring and chopping practically simultaneously.

Laughter out in the dining room pulls my attention. That must be why Mom isn't in her usual spot. She's probably got some of her friends holding court over some tidbit of town gossip.

The kitchen doors swing behind me as I push through, squeaking on the hinges that I make a mental note need to be greased. The smile that hasn't faded one bit since my parting shot at the mayor slips incrementally at the scene laid out before me.

On the floor is my mother cross-legged with her walking cast not on her leg, but off to the side sitting under a table. In front of her is Mica, who is happily beating on upside down pots and pans.

Behind them, huddled together at a table, chairs pulled far too close for my liking, are Brigid and Wesley fucking Lickinbill. True, that isn't really his last name since his mother left town and ditched it as soon as she could when she graduated from high school. Or at least that was always the story that went around the town when they talked about the deceased daughter of our town's second most famous family.

But still, call a spade a spade. Wesley is a fucking Lickinbill through and through. Right down to how he lets his uncle dictate what books the library and schools can and can't keep in their stacks. And he's making *MY* Brigid laugh as they pour over the far too thick business license application.

"What the fuck is going on here?"

Chapter 18

Brigid

My whole body jerks in an automatic fight or flight response when Orion's voice booms through the cafe. In the next breath I'm up from the table and grabbing Mica from the floor.

Roxy's face goes white as a sheet.

Wesley slouches down in his chair, letting his unruly hair slip over his forehead to hide his eyes.

"Seriously, anyone want to explain what the hell a Lickinbill is doing here when I know damn well they've been banned from The Bean for years?"

"Listen, Orion, I'm just trying to help." Wesley stands from his chair, and I realize the two men are more similar than I had originally clocked. They are both tall. Both obviously in good shape. And both have a stubborn set to their jaws that speaks volumes of the history between the men and their families.

"Oh, I'm sure. It makes complete sense that the nephew of our illustrious mayor would be trying to help someone get around his insane rules." Fists balled tightly at his side, I see the muscles along Orion's forearms tense to the point I'm afraid he might pop a tendon where they disappear in the rolled-up sleeves of his flannel. "Mom, I can't believe you would let this asshole in here."

Finally, Roxy snaps from her state of shock and slowly climbs to her feet, listing to the side with her injured ankle. "Orrie, I can explain everything."

"You can explain why the nephew of your sworn enemy is being served, off hours, in the cafe you have literally chased his uncle out of with one of those pots on the floor?"

The history between these two families is obviously long and complicated, but this is insane.

"What would Delia say if she knew he was here?"

I swear, the breath rushes from Wesley's lungs beside me. I can feel the conflicted energies wafting off him. Anger, longing, confusion, resolve. They are practically tangible layers covering his aura. What is that about?

"There is no reason for you to tell your sister about Wesley being here." Roxy has found her voice again and it gets stronger as the seconds tick by. "This young man has been helping town members with the ridiculous paperwork the mayor's office keeps instituting for years. How do you think Theo got approval for an expansion of the deli? Or Dolly was able to replace all her old signage?" Roxy is whipping up a good head of steam. "Your siblings and you are so wrapped up in crap that happened in high school that none of you can look past the ends of your noses.

Okay, as pissed as I am about the way Orion came barging in here, I want to know what the hell went down in high school that has the Halsted siblings icing out Wesley.

"Yes, Burt is an asshole, but Wesley is nothing like him. Neither was Wesley's mom and you know that." Roxy points her finger in her son's face. "Just because there is one bad egg in the basket doesn't mean you throw them all out."

"You going to explain that to Delia?" Damn, Orion isn't letting this go. "This better not be more of that match making bullshit you love to pull around town. Delia is not June and Wesley sure as shit isn't Knox."

"Excuse me, but you do not get to say who I am or am not set up with." I turn to Roxy because I instantly recognize the names June and Knox from the Instagram page for *Happy Accidents Farm.* "You set up June and Knox from the farm?"

Roxy's face softens. "Of course I did. Knox is my son after all. I have a sixth sense for when two people belong together and I could see it between them from the very second I met June."

"There is no connection between Wesley and Brigid," Orion growls out between clenched teeth.

"Like I said, it is none of your business if there is." I pull Mica closer to my side as he begins to fidget, wanting back on the floor to continue the drum session he'd been so enjoying. Despite the obvious anger floating around the room, everyone's voice has stayed at a relatively normal level, which I appreciate. Still I'm not loving the tension around my son. It brings up too many bad memories of shitty men past.

"Oh, really? Because after last night I would think I have at least a little skin in the game." Orion looks smug as the words slip from his mouth. But the anger rising up through my veins like boiling water must show on my expression, because that smug smile slips from his face as he realizes his mistake.

"What happened last night?" Roxy pipes up from behind me.

Orion's eyes slip closed and regret is painted all over his body as the fight drains from his muscles.

"Nothing. A mistake." Being able to mask my emotions from my voice is something I am endlessly proud of, and is coming in extremely handy right now.

His eyes snap open and I can see the argument he's holding back play out there. But he is apparently smarter than I have given him credit for, because he keeps the words to himself.

"Brigid, I think we had most everything covered. I should probably go." Wesley packs up the leather satchel he had pulled his own copies of the application from. What was supposed to be a little advice turned into him nearly dictating answers verbatim as I wrote them in. Each answer is filled with half-truths and ego stroking that he ensured me would help the process go much smoother. "If you have any questions, here is my card."

As he holds out the small rectangular piece of card stock in my direction, Orion takes a step forward as if he might try to intercept my accepting it. But one scathing glance from me and he freezes.

For the first time, I take in his appearance. Unlike this morning when he was dressed for a run with his long, red hair pulled up into a man bun, he is dressed in slightly wrinkly khakis, a hunter green flannel with a bright white t-shirt peeking out at the open collar. His hair is down around his shoulders, flowing freely. Before last night, I had never seen his hair outside of a ponytail, braid, or messy bun. The perfection of his locks, because there is no other word to describe it, has my breath hitching in my throat. It also stirs that needling feeling that I absolutely know this man from somewhere. Maybe we knew each other in a previous life? As infuriating as the man is, he is painfully beautiful. Actually, that might contribute to his infuriating-ness. If we had met in this life I would remember it.

I push my attraction aside and turn back to Wesley, someone I desperately wish I was attracted to. "Thanks for the help, truly. If I manage to get the shop open it will be thanks to you."

We all ignore the sound of popping knuckles coming from Orion's pockets.

Wesley ducks his head in acknowledgment and silently walks through the kitchen to leave through the back door. A wave of empathy washes over me for this man that I have a distinct feeling just wants to serve his town and for people to like him. But because of who his family is, he has to do it in secret.

"I should go, too." I turn and hand Mica to Roxy so I can pile up the papers still spread over the table. "I can finish the last of the essays back at home."

A wide, veined hand reaches in to help by taking the empty mugs and crumb covered plates from the table. "Brigid, can we talk?"

"I don't think that is a good idea."

"Mica and I are going to put these pans away," Roxy mumbles while already hobbling across the room with Mica on one hip and a couple pans dangling from the other.

"She should put her boot back on," I mumble.

"That was why I was coming down here, Delia said she's been resisting the doctor's instructions."

Orion holds up a beautifully carved wooden cane gripped in one hand. "I made this for her to try and get her to warm up to the idea of wearing the boot. Thought a pimp cane seemed her style. But I might have hoped to run into you while I was down here." He takes a deep breath, and I watch as he gathers courage into an armor around his chest. "I like you, Brigid. I want to get to know you and show you that I am not the asshole I have somehow slipped into twice now around you."

My head is shaking in the negative before he finishes the sentiment. "Like I said, that isn't a good idea. We're neighbors. Men are not a priority of mine. Now or ever again."

"Brigid, I promise, I am a good man. There is a lot of history between my family and Wesley." He pushes his long hair back from his face. "Seeing you sitting here with him, laughing, letting him help you when I've been trying like hell to get you to like me hit a particularly sore spot in my ego. I'm sorry."

"If there is anything I've learned from my past with Mica's dad, it's that when a tiger shows you his stripes, don't insist it's actually a zebra. Some women might be turned on by the whole caveman she's mine act, but I'm not. Those stripes are a warning and I'm going to listen to them."

With everything properly in its place, I grab the diaper bag and stand from the table. Orion steps back and I slide past, keeping my eyes resolutely glued to the floor. The truth is, as much as I want to believe Orion is like every other man in a parade of douchebags back through the years, culminating in the grand master of douchebags, William, something about him makes me want to give him a second, third, and fourth chance.

It is critical that I ignore that urge.

Roxy has Mica in the kitchen, music playing low in the background as she sways around the space with his head on her shoulder. He's not asleep yet, but the slow blinks and the way he reaches for me with one noodle-like arm makes his imminent nap obvious.

"Come here, my sweet boy."

Roxy hands him over and I pray to all the goddesses I know that she will just let everything go unsaid.

She opens her mouth and I brace for the words of a protective mother. But she closes them again and smiles a little sadly at me. "If you need anything, you know where I am."

I'm not a crier. I didn't even cry when Mica's dad rejected us. But for some reason the day crashes down on me the minute I get Mica buckled into his car seat, his eyes already slipping closed.

The tears manage to stay put, held at bay behind my eyelids with nothing but a stubbornness famous in my family. But as soon as I pull away from the cafe in my shitty little Honda I have to blink away the blur of the tears and let them fall unchecked down my cheeks.

I don't try to read too much into the emotions rioting inside my heart and brain. Simply let them come in and out like travelers passing through a rest stop. I acknowledge them and let them go. Just as I think the tears are starting to dry up, when we're more than halfway up the mountain but still several miles from the cabin, the steering wheel jerks under my hands.

My first thought is the old girl's alignment is finally crapping out after the trips up and down a road that hasn't been paved in most likely decades. But then another jerk of the steering wheel and the car goes silent. No engine knocking. No music on the radio. No air coming through the vents. The car gradually slows and I have just enough time to pull over before it coasts to a stop.

"What the fuck now?" There are those tears again, burning insistently behind my eyes. And as I look at the dashboard it dawns on me. I was supposed to get gas before heading home. The one and only gas station in town is four blocks past the cafe. The opposite way of how I get home.

Over the years I've been diligent about getting the car fixed as soon as something went wrong. Except the warning light that tells me when the gas is low.

Chapter 19

Orion

"Son, we need to talk." Brigid hadn't been gone more than thirty seconds when Ma walked back in carrying two cups of tea and that look on her face that meant I wasn't getting away.

No point in fighting it.

"Sure, why not. I'd love to know why you've been secretly hanging out with a person that I thought we all hated as a matter of principle." There is no heat in my words. I am genuinely curious.

"Well, hate rarely has anything to do with principles." She sits at the same table Brigid and Wesley had been occupying a few minutes ago. "Sit."

I do as she says. Roxanne Halsted isn't someone you say no to. Or at least her kids don't.

"That boy has been saddled with more heartache than most people twice his age. Something I would think you and your siblings would understand."

The crappy thing about small towns? Everyone knows all about your past whether you like it or not. Stories spread, and sometimes morph, faster than a forest fire during a drought.

Just because Wesley didn't step in this town until he was sixteen doesn't mean he escaped that small town fate. In fact, he might have had it worse because everyone was curious about the newcomer. His story made it through the gossip network faster than most, and it never needed embellishing because it was tragic enough on its own.

The short version is his mom had left town the very second she could after graduating from high school. Went to NYU, became a mid-level theater actress on Broadway, married another actress. They had Wesley in their thirties. When he was a teenager, his parents were driving from a weekend away and got in a horrible crash on the New Jersey turnpike. They both died. Wesley came to live with his only living relative, Burt Lickinbill.

"Listen, I felt bad for him in high school, we all tried to make friends with him, you know that. But you know what happened with him and Delia. Having a shitty childhood and losing a parent doesn't excuse being a total dick." The seething anger from all those years ago still sits brewing in the bottom of my stomach, but I don't let it boil over again.

"They were teenagers, Orion. You all act as if all three of you weren't assholes at some point as teens. It has been almost a decade, you all need to get over it." Mom calmly sips her tea, but the fire in her eyes lets me know she's barely hanging on to her own temper. "You lost your father just a few years later. Can you imagine going through that then in addition being carted off to live with a complete stranger. With Burt fucking Lickinbill?"

Staring at the mug in front of me, I pick at the rough texture of the hand-thrown clay with my thumbnail. Losing Dad was the hardest thing I've ever been through. Harder still because I couldn't be here for the years he was sick. The military kept denying my request for extended leave saying Dad wasn't sick enough, so I had to make do with a few days or weeks here and there when I could manage it and I wasn't deployed.

I completed my four years in the military and got discharged three months before Dad died and I spent every second after returning home sitting by his side as he slowly declined. A sharp, searing pain singes up my back, a wispy reminder of the real pain I had been in back then, sitting hour after hour in a shitty hospital chair for days on end.

But as hard as that time had been, I am thankful that I got time at the end to say goodbye to the man that raised me.

Wesley didn't have that. He had parents one day and then didn't the next. Then he had to go live with the man that all but disowned his mother.

Shame seeps through me. Mom must see that I have taken her point to heart, because she picks my hand up from around the mug and holds it in both of hers. The heat from her own mug lingers on her skin and I let that warmth ease some of the emotions that have been simmering.

"I made my peace with Wesley years ago. I won't go into all that because it isn't entirely my story to tell. But trust me when

I tell you he is a good man and he does not deserve your vitriol. He is *not* his uncle." She pats my hand and draws away, curiosity now replacing the heat in her eyes. "What I really want to know is what happened between you and the new girl in town."

"Not entirely my story to tell either, Ma." Not that I would anyway. I may have an incredibly cool mom who raised us to be sex positive, but that doesn't mean I want her knowing the details of what we did. "And please, no meddling like you did with Knox. I'd like to figure this out on my own."

She gasps in feigned shock. "I would never. I stay in my own lane these days."

I fight the urge to roll my eyes at my meddling mother. "Yeah, okay."

* * *

By the time I leave the cafe and pick up Spruce to head home, it is getting late into the afternoon. The sun is making its slow descent in the sky, but if I'm lucky I'll have at least a couple hours to do some videos before the sun goes down. I know there is a whole pile of wood I need to chop, and those videos always do well for me. Plus I could use something to help burn off the lingering hurt and anger at seeing Wesley. Not to mention the guilt after talking with Mom.

"What the hell?"

As I crest a hill in the road, I see a figure dressed in black and pushing a stroller on the road ahead. There is no mistaking Brigid as she trudges toward me looking miserable.

Back at the cafe, I hadn't fully taken in what she had been wearing because I was being such a fucking asshole. But it is hard to ignore the way her flowy black dress catches in the fall breeze. It cinches in at the waist with some ties that look like a corset, and the neckline is low enough to show more than a hint of her generous assets. She must have put on makeup for her excursion into town, because as I draw closer I see that there is now mascara tracking down her cheeks.

Her head snaps up at the sound of my truck approaching and for a moment pure relief paints her beautiful face. I slow the truck, pulling to a stop a few feet in front of her, not bothering to pull off to the side of the road. Parking in the middle of the street is becoming a habit for me today.

As I open the door and hop out, she appears to remember how we left things and her expression goes hard. Damn, that fucking sucks.

"What happened?"

I walk quickly up to her, and since I forgot to tell Spruce to stay in the truck, he follows quickly behind like my little shadow. He runs ahead to poke his head in the stroller as if to check the baby is okay. I'm relieved to see Mica is smiling and clapping at the dog.

Brigid stops walking, letting me close the three-foot gap between us. She leans both arms across the handlebar of the stroller, engaging the wheel brake with on foot so it doesn't go flying.

"I ran out of gas. Car stalled." She's breathing hard, her chest rising and falling with the effort of sucking in oxygen. "I tried calling your mom but the reception..." She waves her hand around as if to indicate that we are in the middle of absolutely nowhere.

She tried to call Mom. But not me. I know she has my card. She has Wesley's too, did she try him? As much as I hate that idea, I push it aside. It's not important now.

"How long have you been walking?"

She shrugs. "No idea. I waited for a while in the car, hoping someone would pass, but well, I've never actually seen another car on this road." Her breathing slows now that we are standing still. "But the longer we waited the more I worried it would get dark soon and then I'd be well and truly screwed. So, we started walking. Good thing Mica loves a good walk in the stroller. He's been loving my suffering."

"Good news, someone else does drive this road."

But she shakes her head. "I don't have his car seat. I think I'm closer to town at this point and should keep going."

A click at the ground when the break disengages and Brigid starts walking again, which is when I notice she's limping. I glance down to her feet and she's wearing black knee-high boots that would be fucking sexy as hell in any other context.

"Brigid, we're a good ten miles from town, there is no way I'm letting you walk that." I plant myself right in front of the stroller so she can't take another step and Mica reaches out to give a handful of my khakis a tug. "Hey buddy, don't worry, we'll get you home in no time."

"I am not letting you drive him in the truck without a car seat. It isn't safe." Jaw set, Brigid gives me a hard stare, as if that stubborn streak is going to do anything to change my mind.

"Yeah, neither is walking on the side of a road with no fucking sidewalk. Not to mention those aren't exactly hiking boots." I nod to her feet. "I tell you what. You get in the truck and sit Mica on your lap, I'll buckle you both in and drive so slow it will be like we're walking back to your car. We can put the seat in and then get home nice and safe."

Brigid bites her bottom lip, looking like she is actually considering my proposal. "What if you drive up to the car, get the seat, then come back and get us. It's probably only a mile up."

I can't help it, I roll my eyes. Dad used to drive us around in the same fucking truck when we were kids. Hell, he sat us on his lap and let us steer around the dirt roads between pastures.

But I can see this is a sticking point for the overly protective mother. "Stay here."

I run back to the truck and open the back. Thankfully, I still have my camping gear back here from a trip I took a few weeks ago with Murphy. Including a collapsible chair. I grab it and a bottle of water that has probably been in the truck for a few days but should be perfectly drinkable. I jog the supplies back and set them up in the tall grasses just off the shoulder of the road. "Okay, sit your butt down and don't move until I get back." I wedge myself in between her and the handlebars of the stroller. She reluctantly hobbles over to the chair and practically collapses into it as I position Mica in his stroller beside her.

"Spruce, stay. Watch." At my command, the dog sits his butt down in front of the two people he will now protect with his own life. An adoring look over his shoulder, back at the little boy in the stroller tells me he would have done that without the command too.

I jog back to the truck and don't bother buckling in before I'm off down the road in search of her shitty little car. She was wrong though; it wasn't a mile up the road. It was three fucking miles. I can't believe she made it that far in those fucking shoes pushing a baby in a stroller.

I wasted so much time talking with Mom. Then chatting with Paula when I picked up Spruce and paid for his spa day. All that time and the woman I can't stop thinking about was stranded on the side of the road. Did she actually think she would be able to walk the fifteen miles back to town? The woman is as equally infuriating as she is impressive.

Coming to a stop behind her car, I open the back to find the car seat buckled into the back. I take a minute to inspect how the thing is attached, then unbuckle and carry it to the truck, trying to replicate the setup in the small back seat. It's a tight fit, but with some twisting and more than a few cramps in my back, I manage to get the thing hooked in.

It takes me a total of ten minutes before I am pulling back up to where the little motley crew of stranded travelers is still sitting on the side of the road. Spruce is sitting between Brigid's chair and Mica's stroller. Brigid absently strokes at his short white fur and Mica is reaching over patting him with a little more force than is probably necessary. But I don't think babies know how to control that sort of thing yet. Spruce looks like he is in absolute heaven, his tongue lolling out the side of his mouth and head tipped back.

Something about seeing the three of them sitting there on the side of the road has my heart contracting in a way that is both uncomfortable and amazing. *My girl, my kid, and my dog.* The words parade across my mind before I can stop them. Only one of those things is true, but damn do I want to earn the other two as well.

"Alright, let's get home." As I stroll over to where they are all sitting, I notice Brigid's feet are now bare, her boots and socks lying on the ground beneath her chair. Even from a few feet away I can see the bright red blisters already starting to form.

As she stands from the seat, I catch the brief gasp and cringe of pain. Before she can take a single step, I'm at her side, scooping her up into my arms.

"What the hell?" She slaps at my chest. "Put me down."

"Your feet are so torn up I'm shocked you could stand at all." I hold her tight to my chest as she squirms trying to get down. "Will you stay still."

"I need to get Mica."

"I'm not going to leave him. I'm walking you the two feet to the truck, and then I'll get him."

That appeases her and her body relaxes in my arms. "I'm only allowing this because I think I would have started crying again if I had to walk anymore."

A zap of satisfaction that she is allowing me to do this for her zings through my body. "Yes, ma'am."

Chapter 20

Brigid

Every single part of me hurts. From my very swollen and bruised toes to my brain where I am pretty sure a dehydration headache is ripping through behind my eyes. I'm so exhausted I can barely hold my head up as Orion carries me to the truck. I lay the side of my face against his shoulder, enjoying his fresh, clean air smell.

Behind him, Mica is reaching out for me repeating his favorite chant. "Mamamamama."

Orion settles me into the front seat, setting me down with such care it brings tears to my eyes that I need to shove down. Two hours ago, I wanted to throat punch this man. Now I am sending a thank you to every higher power that has ever existed for helping him find us. Once I'm buckled in, Orion turns back to grab Mica.

I turn to look at the car seat wedged into the back seat of the truck and am fairly shocked to find he got it buckled in right.

I give the back of it a wiggle and am satisfied that it is secured enough to last the drive back to the cabin.

"Did I do it right?"

I jump a little at Orion's voice. Every nerve is still on edge. "Yeah, looks good. I'm impressed. It took me an embarrassingly long time, a few YouTube videos, and lots of cussing the first time I had to install this thing."

A blush creeps up his cheeks, and I realize Orion might not be very good at taking compliments. "This guy has quite the grip."

My eyes shift to Mica, who has both hands wrapped in Orion's hair, tugging at the thick red strands. Orion's eyes are watering from how much it hurts, but he just laughs and makes faces at my kid.

Something twists in my chest. The only other man who has ever held Mica is my dad, and he was only here for a few weeks after he was born before having to fly back home to Arizona. My parents are amazing. Despite their initial doubts about my choice to take on parenting alone, they came and stayed with me for a month after Mica made his way into the world. But they still had jobs and lives they had to get back to eventually. We do weekly video calls and text like crazy, but it isn't the same as being here in a physical sense.

"Am I doing this right?" Orion is trying his best to get the squirming kid buckled, but can't quite get the two sides lined up right.

"Here, I can get it." I unbuckle, twisting and bending until I'm wedged back between the two front seats enough so I can grip the two buckles. I show him how they fit together, but when I glance up I see Orion isn't looking at the car seat tutorial I'm giving him.

Instead his eyes are zeroed in on my chest. I look down and realize all my maneuvering to get half in the back seat has pulled the stretchy neckline of my peasant top style dress down so far my boobs are nearly falling out.

I tug the dress up and Orion glances up to meet my eyes. It only lasts for a fraction of a second, but I can see all the incredibly dirty things he is thinking as if there was a projector displaying them across his face.

"I'll go get everything else."

I unwedge myself from the back seat and settle back into the passenger seat, concentrating way more than is necessary on buckling myself back in.

Within a few minutes Orion figures out how the stroller folds and carries it and the collapsible chair to the back of the truck. Spruce jumps in as soon as the driver's side door opens and goes right to the back seat. The sweet dog lays down right beside the car seat, resting his solid head across Mica's legs, who is delighted with this development and promptly starts tugging at the dog's ears.

Leaning against the door, I press my forehead against the cool glass of the window. I can see Orion's reflection in the side mirror. He has both hands firmly at ten and two, his face focused entirely on the road ahead. The truck rocks side to side over the uneven pavement.

The exhaustion seeps into my skin, muscles, bones, and eventually I can't fight the tug of my eyelids as they slowly close.

On some level I'm aware of being carried into the cabin and placed onto the bed, but no matter how hard I try to wake up fully, the exhaustion drags me down again.

* * *

Waking from a sleep so deep it feels like wading through cement to make it back to consciousness is disconcerting. The first thing I become aware of is the soft mattress beneath me.

Then the warmth of the quilt wrapped around my body.

A rich scent of cologne and pine on the pillows.

No squeaky mattress as I stretch out my limbs. Strange.

The sweet giggle of Mica is what has me bolting upright in bed. *Shit, how could I pass out when I have a baby to care for?*

Stumbling from the bed, I sprint into the main living room area to a strange sight. Mica sitting in a highchair I've never seen before, little bits of spaghetti dotting his face, tray, and the floor around him. Spruce doing his best to catch every piece of noodle the kid dropped over the edge of the tray.

"Shhh, dude, you gotta be quiet. Don't want to wake your mama," Orion chuckles as he rubs Mica's blonde head. "Are you going to eat any of your dinner or just spoil my dog for his kibble?"

In response, Mica's chubby fingers grabbed another handful of the saucy noodles and chucks them toward Spruce, who I can now see has red splotches all over his fur from where the pasta was landing on him.

"Oops, too late." Orion smiles across the room at me and tosses an unfamiliar kitchen towel over his shoulder. "Hey Sunshine, how was your nap?"

It was like I fell asleep in one world where I begrudgingly accepted the help of a man I didn't like and then woke up in an alternative reality. Actually, in this reality apparently my shitty cabin is gorgeous and huge.

"Wait, where are we?"

"My place. I wasn't sure if you would want Spruce coming into your cabin now that it is all clean and I didn't think these two would accept being separated."

Orion crosses to a huge stove set against the wall and I take the moment to look around the space. Much like my own cabin, the living area is all open concept, just times a hundred. There are vaulted ceilings with roughhewn beams stretching across the width of the room. A huge gray sectional couch sits facing an equally sizeable TV. In front of a stone fireplace there is a dining room table that could seat at least a dozen people and mismatched chairs that somehow all work together.

Besides the couch, almost every piece of furniture is wood and appears to be handmade. I'm guessing by Orion. The place is warm and inviting and has most definitely never seen the touch of a woman or decorator. No art on the walls. Photos propped up against random surfaces but none in frames. Books literally everywhere. On shelves, stacked on the floor. Sitting open face down on side tables.

It's clean, but not neat. Boots and shoes are in a pile by the door. Dog toys, leashes, and bones are scattered about the floor. There are dishes drying in a rack by the sink. And on the stove something sizzles. A large island with a butcher block countertop has various ingredients waiting to be cleaned up from dinner prep.

"I wasn't sure if babies could have garlic or onions, I know dogs can't, so I just sautéed some tomatoes and mashed them up. I cut up the noodles real small, too, because I didn't want him to choke."

Laughter claws at my throat to be freed, but I hold it back. "Well that would be why he's feeding it to the dog. He's wondering why you gave him bland-ass noodles."

Seeming to agree with me, Mica throws another handful of noodles on the floor and blows raspberries at the tray.

"Well then, he can have some of ours." Orion pulls two mismatched colorful plates from the cabinet and starts dishing up noodles, not cut up for us, sauce and what I now see are meatballs in the pan on the stove. "Are meatballs okay? They're turkey."

"Yeah that's fine. I can cut up the meatballs for him."

"I got it, you sit. How are your feet?"

Now that he mentions it I realize they ache and burn. "They don't feel great." I slide onto the stool closest to where Mica is set up in the highchair, relieved to be off my feet again. "By the way, why do you happen to have a highchair hanging around?"

"That is something I made a few months ago and the client ghosted me on it. Paid the deposit and then just never picked it up or paid the balance."

"It's gorgeous. I almost feel bad my son is making such a mess of it."

Orion chuckles and shrugs. "Well, now I'll know how to make them easier to clean. I can already tell I'm going to need to find a way to seal the joints so gunk won't get stuck in there."

"You make lots of baby furniture?"

"Yeah, it is a pretty good chunk of my orders. Cribs, high-chairs, rocking chairs. I also do a lot of tables, bookcases."

My stomach rumbles as he places the plate of food in front of me and I duck my head in embarrassment.

"Dig in." A fork and knife appear beside the plate. Orion dumps the cut-up meatballs on Mica's tray. They are cut into nearly perfect little cubes for him to grasp and shove in his face.

I wait to see if Mica is actually going to eat the new round of food or if Spruce is going to have a very good night. Thankfully, my kiddo picks one piece up with a perfect little pincher grasp that makes my heart swell. He concentrates so hard when he tries something new, it is the cutest damn thing. The meatball piece gets shoved into his mouth along with half his fist and Mica's eyes literally light up. Eyes go wide, and he smiles big showing off his four teeth, two on top and two on bottom.

"Well I guess the meatballs pass muster," Orion chuckles while grabbing his own plate. Instead of taking the seat next to me, he turns and leans back against the counter so that we are facing each other with the island between us. "Now I need to know your verdict."

Okay, eating someone's food while they are literally staring at you is a little awkward. But he went through all the trouble and not even I am a big enough bitch to brush off a homemade meal not made by me.

I twirl some pasta onto my fork, then stab the meatball and cut off a slice. The moment the food touches my tongue it's like an explosion of flavor. Garlic, onions, basil, tomatoes— it's amazing. My eyes slip closed and I try my best to hold back from shoveling the entire plate into my mouth at once.

"I'm going to interpret that expression as a second approval. Third if you count the dog." Orion digs into his own serving, not bothering to cut anything since he's standing. He just takes giant honking bites out of his meatballs and pasta.

We eat in silence for a while, or as much silence as is possible when there's a nine-month-old squealing in delight each time the dog licks his lips hoping for a bite.

Sitting in his house. Eating his food. Knowing he took care of my kid while I slept. It all makes it really hard to hate him. I try to hang on to the annoyance I felt at the coffee shop. But it's like trying to hold onto a dream after waking up. Just shifts farther and farther away.

Chapter 21

Orion

Brigid sitting in my house is about the most terrifying thing I've ever experienced. But also the best.

While she napped, the boys and I walked around the property. Grabbed the highchair from the shop. Played with some toys I found in the gigantic diaper bag she had stuffed in the bottom of the stroller. Mostly Mica and Spruce continued their journey to best friends and I was just there to make sure neither of them got hurt.

It's nice having other people in the cabin. Visitors aren't common on the mountain. Occasionally Mom will come up for dinner. Knox is too busy with the farm and being totally in love. Sometimes Delia will come up to hang out, but since the club has gained popularity over the last few years, those drop-ins have become less and less frequent.

About once a year a few of the guys I served with will come up and we spend a week fishing, cutting trees down, and trying to outdo one another lifting weights.

Otherwise, if I want company, I need to make the trip down the mountain and into town.

So having Brigid and Mica in my space is a welcome treat. Watching my neighbor not just eat a meal I made but love it, well, it's giving me ideas that I shouldn't have considering she is always five seconds away from ripping my balls off.

Watching what I say has never been one of my strengths. Something that got me in a good bit of trouble as a Marine. Thoughts have always popped into my head and out my mouth at the same moment. But if I make one more wrong step here, my shot will be blown before I can even make it.

"What's with the tripod? And is that a ring light?" Brigid's questions pull me from my silent spiraling about saying or doing the wrong thing and straight into a different spiral about how to explain the equipment I totally forgot is leaning by the front door.

"Furniture." The word plops out from my mouth as if it will answer all her questions.

She tilts her head and arches her eyebrows, obviously thrown by my outburst.

"I mean I was shooting photos of the highchair earlier to put on the website. I was going to list it for sale since the customer never picked it up."

Not a total lie, I've been meaning to list it for sale on my website for months now. But the equipment in question is all for what has turned from the silly side-project I worked on occasionally to something that has taken over my life.

Being a content creator is a weird world to live in. It's a constant choice between what to film and post and what can just be mine. Not to mention I have the added challenge of trying to keep it all a secret from my loved ones and the town. Thankfully, Amoresville has an aging population and very few people are on social media. The ones that are frequent community Facebook groups where they fight about how close a fence can be to the property line, not looking for a shirtless guy cutting down trees and making furniture.

I went so far as to steal the phones of my sister, Mom, and a few of my closer friends in town to see if they have the app and then block my account. I also blocked them on mine. Not a fool proof method, but it has worked so far.

"Huh, you really need a better setup for product images than a ring light and tripod." Brigid accepts the explanation and moves on. "So, are you going to tell me about the history with you, Wesley, and apparently your sister?"

The question takes me by surprise, so much so I almost drop a meatball on my shirt, but just manage to catch it on the plate. "Most of it isn't my story to tell. I know my sister pretty well and she would hate it if I told her business to people in town."

"To be fair, we aren't in town."

I shake my head; no way I'm giving her the full story. But after the way I acted at the cafe, I do feel like she is owed a little bit of an explanation. "I'll tell you this. Wesley and Delia were sophomores when I was a senior. I got wind of some shit that didn't sit right with me and confronted Wes. Confronted him with a cross straight to his nose."

At some point during the very condensed version of the story, Brigid laid her fork down to give me her full attention. But there is a crinkle between her eyebrows and question in her eyes. "Okay, you got in a fight as teenagers? How does that translate to still icing him out to the point he is banned from any of your family's businesses a decade later?"

Well, that part of the story is mine, but it's one I try not to dwell on much.

"That one punch changed my life. I played football in high school. Was pretty good. I got recruited to play for Penn State. Full ride since my grades were pretty good too. But breaking Wesley's nose changed all that. His uncle pressured the school board to throw the book at me. With a violent incident on my record, the scholarship got rescinded and no other schools would touch me." I let out a sardonic laugh that holds no real humor. "Burt tried to get State Police to press charges, but thankfully I was seventeen and they had more important things to deal with than a school fight. My whole future was dependent on that scholarship. I had no clue what to do with my life. Hated the idea of working the farm with Dad and Knox, or spending the rest of my life in this small town and never seeing the world. So, without talking to anyone about it first, I signed up for the Marines."

"Wow." Brigid peers at me with no judgment, only understanding. "I can see how that would color your relationship with Wesley."

Now that gets a laugh out of me. "There is no relationship there. I think we've said maybe five words to each other since that punch, and you saw most of them today. I'm actually shocked he came back here after college."

"Thank you for telling me that. It does put things from earlier into a little more perspective."

An awkward silence descends between us. I'm not sure how to keep the conversation going when it feels like I've fileted myself open for her to inspect.

"Have you read all these books?" Brigid picks up her fork and takes another bite of the food I made as she glances around the cabin. Her lips enveloping the fork and then sliding it out captures every bit of my attention, eclipsing the awkwardness. There is a speck of sauce still on her cheek that I desperately want to wipe away. And then maybe taste it myself. Taste her.

Her eyes finish their perusal of my collection of books and land back on me, which snaps me from the weird journey I had taken to wondering what she tastes like.

"Um, not all, I definitely have a heck of a TBR pile." I take the change in conversation and run with it. "But I would say I've read about seventy percent of them."

Brigid smiles down at her plate, obviously trying to hide her reaction to my book collection. To hide that she actually does like something I've done or said. "Your organization system is shit."

"That would be because I don't have one other than find a space and fill it." I can think of something else I'd like to fill. Thank god I managed to keep that thought to myself.

I glance over to Mica who is still doing his best to pick up little bits of food and shove them in his mouth, all under the close watch of Spruce. The kid hasn't so much gotten the hang of the whole hand eye coordination thing and occasionally smooshes the sauce-covered meatballs against his chin before pushing them up to his mouth.

I shouldn't be thinking all these dirty things about his mother while he is sitting right there. If he knew how to throw a punch yet he'd definitely slug me for what I'm thinking.

"This is why I usually stick to e-readers. Easier to organize and the books don't gather dust." Brigid places her fork down and pushes the plate away. "Also easier to read at night without the lights on so a certain someone stays asleep."

"I can't do the e-reader thing. I need the weight of a good book in my hand. The smell of the paper. The trophy of my latest kill prominently displayed on a shelf."

She looks around again. "Or a table, a chair arm, the floor."

Heat sweeps up my neck to my face and I know I'm blushing from the embarrassment. "Yeah, I guess it is a bit chaotic in here."

"It's not that bad." She's still looking around, squinting as if to read some of the titles from across the room.

At the same moment my eyes zero in on the book I've been making my way through that is draped across the arm of the couch, spine side up, Brigid rises from her seat and makes her way to the same spot.

"Wait, are you reading this?"

The plate thuds on the counter behind me as I discard it in my rush to snatch the book up before she can get a look at it.

Too late. She's looking at the dark cover with gold leaf lettering and scrollwork and flipping it over to where I had marked the spot last night.

"Why are you reading *A Modern History of Witchcraft and Paganism*? My store literally sells this book."

Yeah, I'm aware. I don't mention that I did in fact buy it from her shop and paid an extra fee to have it overnighted.

"I like learning about things I don't know much about." The words come out quietly, not sure where this might go and treading carefully around the unpredictable woman. "It occurred to me after that first day that I might have judged you a little bit based off something I knew very little about and the thought didn't sit right with me."

Witnessing someone run through an entire spectrum of emotions is an interesting thing. In seconds I watch as anger, confusion, curiosity, apprehension, hope and finally panic scroll through Brigid's eyes like a digital billboard advertising her thoughts. The display only lasts for moments before something inside her shutters closed.

Gently she places the book back in the exact position she found it, her eyes lingering on the cover for a moment before she brushes past me, careful to avoid actually touching me.

I stifle a frustrated sigh. As soon as I thought I was making some headway, I once again did something to unknowingly upset that progress and stumble back several steps.

"Thank you so much for dinner." She starts unbuckling Mica from the highchair and he smears pasta remnants all over her shoulders as he holds onto her. "And for the nap. And watching Mica." I can't figure out why her breathing seems to be picking up pace, as if she's struggling to keep up in a marathon and not simply holding her baby. "And the roadside rescue."

"Brigid, listen, if I put my foot in my mouth again, I'm sorry." I scroll back through everything we'd said since she woke up from her nap and honestly couldn't pinpoint what could have set her off. Was picking up a book about witchcraft so bad? "You don't have to leave."

The smile on Brigid's face is brittle as if it might break at any moment and turn into tears. "No, it's getting late and I need to get Mica into the tub and winding down for bed."

Not wanting to push any more, I shove my hands deep into the pockets of my slacks, feeling a little foolish now for dressing up to accidentally run into my neighbor in town. "Okay, have a good night. If you need anything let me know."

She nods and slips through the door, leaving Spruce and me standing in the middle of my now empty cabin that seems too quiet without them.

Chapter 22

Brigid

I go into autopilot.

Put Mica in the tub. Wash off the detritus from spaghetti night at Orion's.

Don't think about Orion.

Dry Mica and get him into a warm pair of footie jammies since it's getting colder at night and the furnace is old and frankly scares me a little.

Snuggle up with my little man and read books on the bed. Remember the piles of books in the cabin across the lake.

Don't think about Orion.

Once Mica's eyes begin to droop and finally close just after eight, I carefully transfer him to the Pack 'n Play I'm still using as his crib. Realize for the first time that Orion must have carried me in from the car. Regret being asleep when I was in his arms.

Don't think about Orion.

Turn to work as a distraction. Take care of questions from the warehouse on shipments. Go through orders from the past two weeks and reconcile them with the inventory lists.

Notice there was exactly one copy of *A Modern History and Witchcraft and Paganism* sold the day after I moved in.

There is no way. I've never told him the name of my shop. He would have had to do some serious sleuthing to figure out which of the literal hundreds of metaphysical stores online was mine.

I click into the order to see the delivery address. It's a P.O. Box in Amoresville, Pennsylvania.

What the hell?

I'm on my feet before I can think better of it. Storming out onto the porch ready to go give my neighbor a piece of my mind.

But the son of a bitch is already there, on my side of the yard, dragging the mouse infested couch in the direction of his side of the property. I had yet to figure out how to dispose of it way up here on the mountain. In Pittsburgh, I would have paid a couple college kids to drag it down to the street and then someone would have either picked it off the curb to do Goddess knows what with it, or the trash guys would have grabbed it during bulk pickup.

"What the hell are you doing?" I charge toward him, not caring that I am barefoot and only wearing the oversized T-shirt I threw on after Mica's bath.

Orion drops the couch and raises his hands like I'm a cop yelling freeze. He's shirtless, wearing just a pair of mesh shorts.

They aren't the long basketball kind. Many inches shy of his knees, showing off the sculpted thighs I have no right noticing right now.

"Sorry. I was walking Spruce one last time before bed and I saw that it was still sitting out here so I figured I'd break it up and burn it for you."

Damn it. There he was again, doing something nice for me. Doing things I had every intention of doing myself. "You don't have to do that. I would have figured out a way to get rid of it."

He nods, puts his hands down and goes to push them into his pockets before he realizes the shorts he is wearing don't have any. Instead, he rests them on his trim hips.

"I also don't need you to watch my son. Or make us dinner. Or repair shit around the property. Don't think I haven't noticed the shutters are somehow magically straight and the boards on the dock have been replaced. I know damn well it wasn't the asshole that owns this place."

Orion stares at the grass under his feet, and even in the waning light of the evening with only the perimeter lights shining on us from his house illuminating us, I can still see the blush racing furiously up his neck to his cheeks.

"I also don't need you ordering books from my store. How the hell did you even find it? Were you cyber-stalking me?"

He doesn't look up, just keeps his eyes planted on the ground. "You gave your card to Mom. She left it by the register."

"Are you reading it to try and get into my pants?"

His head snaps up and I see the slightest ember of anger there. Good. For some reason I want him to feel just as mad as I do. Irrationally mad. Everything inside me feels like it's jumped the track. Like I'm a train barreling through cars and buildings with no end in sight since there is nothing guiding it where to go.

"No. I wanted to understand you. To understand something I had never put a lot of thought into." He pauses, but I can see there is more he wants to see.

An impatient huff slips past my lips and I cross my arms in front of my chest, waiting for him to continue.

"And I am getting rid of this fucking couch because if it stays out here it's going to attract more pests who will eventually figure out the cabin is warmer. And because it will make your life easier, which is all I think about lately. How can I make things better for my neighbor who hates me?" He steps around the couch, his chest heaving up and down as he sucks in a few breaths and charges on. "I would literally rebuild this whole cabin just to have you smile at me. To have you breathe on me. Read a book to get in your pants? Fuck no. I would burn the world down to have you even consider for a second letting me touch you. You don't want to know what I would be willing to do for a taste of your mouth. *I* don't want to know the lengths I would go to be able to sink my cock..."

He doesn't finish the sentence because I can't hold myself back for another second. The space between us disappears as I leap into his arms, somehow knowing he'll catch me. I'm right. His arms wrap around me and my lips land on his. It takes a second for him to process what is happening, but once he does it's like a dam bursts and he rushes forward in a flood of lips and tongue.

Orion grips my ass with both hands and moves further up my body, I wrap my legs around his waist and the shorts he's wearing do nothing to suppress the hard length trapped by our bodies.

The kiss is frantic, heated. My hands are everywhere. Running over the stubble covering his jaw. His shoulders. His chest. It's all so solid. Steel covered in molten skin. I reach up and pull the tie holding his hair in a messy bun, rake my fingers through the messy waves of copper air. It's so soft.

A groan fills my mouth and I'm not sure if it's his or mine. I start writhing against the bulge making itself very known, rubbing my throbbing clit against him chasing a feeling that can't compare to my own hand or the toys I've come to rely on.

We're moving. Orion breaks the kiss, apparently needing to see where he is going. He climbs the stairs to my porch and the sounds of his sneakers hitting the floorboards snaps the slightest bit of reason into me.

"Not in there. Mica's sleeping."

Orion growls against my neck, but redirects us to the exterior wall just outside the door. He presses me against the rough, stacked logs that make up the exterior of the cabin and returns his mouth to mine, sweeping his tongue over mine in a slower, more controlled taste.

"I do anything you don't like, you tell me. You want to stop, say it and I will. No questions."

As soon as I nod in agreement he drops me to my feet, a moment of disappointment that he might be changing his mind striking right through my lust.

But in the next second he's falling to his knees in front of me. He's so tall and I'm so short in comparison that his head is even with my chest. Rough hands skate up the outsides of my thighs, pushing the shirt up over my hips, stomach and chest until I'm lost in the soft cotton for a moment then it's gone, thrown to the other side of the porch.

Orion sucks in a breath, his hands wandering over my naked form. "So fucking beautiful."

Then his mouth is everywhere. Covering my nipple with a sharp suck. Trailing kisses across to the other breast while his fingers play with the first. My fingers fist in his hair; not directing him, simply holding on for the ride.

He works his way lower, nips and kisses along my sides to my hip bones. As he gets closer and closer to where I need him most, he skips over it all together. I whine, actually whine like a petulant child instead of the grown independent woman I am. His responding chuckle frustrates and thrills me. A swift tug of his hair and he gazes up at me from his kneeling position.

Oh boy. Seeing the man look up at me, over the curves and valleys of my body, with a devilish smile makes my insides melt into a puddle of want and need. "If you don't get to the point real soon I might burn down the world. Just fair warning."

Those gorgeous blue eyes sparkle, the joy blatant on his face causing my world to flip upside down.

"I don't want to miss an inch of you, and once I get to what's between these thighs—" He picks one of my legs up and drapes it over his shoulder, biting my inner thigh just hard enough to make a zing of pleasure and pain careen through every nerve ending "—I won't be able to concentrate on anything else. But if you are very patient, I promise there will be a very happy ending in it for you, Sunshine."

Well, okay then. I loosen my grip on his hair, not entirely letting go, and Orion continues his absolute worship of my body. His hands caress and grip my calves, thighs, ass, tongue and lips following in their path.

Thankfully he skips my feet which are probably coated in wet grass and blisters. What feels like several blissful ages later, he runs his nose up the inside of my leg, from knee all the way to the junction of my thighs, pressing his face against the now soaked cotton of my panties and inhaling deeply.

It's so fucking simple, so primal and filthy, it takes me by surprise. For a moment my body goes limp, and I slump back against the cabin.

"God, you smell good. You always smell so fucking good. Like oranges and cinnamon and something else I can't place."

"Sandalwood," I pant out, so fucking turned on I can barely speak. "Orange, sandalwood, and cinnamon. It's a protection essential oil roller I make."

"I fucking love it." Apparently done with the slow introduction to my body, Orion dives in now, pushing my panties to the side and swiping his tongue over my slit. "Need more of you."

He grabs the leg that had still been planted on the ground and lifts it up and over his shoulder. I squeal and laugh, a little off balance and afraid he might drop me.

"I got you, neighbor." He winks up at me from between my thighs. Spreading me open with his fingers, he goes in for the kill, sucking and licking at my clit like a man starved.

My hands grab at his long hair, holding on for dear life as he brings me to the edge of an orgasm so fast it makes me dizzy. "Holy shit."

He backs off the direct contact, leaving me right there at the edge, hovering but not yet able to slip over into ecstasy. His mouth moves lower, to my entrance, where he licks around the perimeter, pressing his tongue inside. The feeling is amazing, not enough to get me to where I desperately want to go, but wet and slippery in a way that makes me want so much more.

I grip his hair in one hand, my hips pulsing in time with the pumps of his tongue. He moves back up to my clit, using the same circular path to tease it until I'm whimpering and moaning.

"Please, Orion, please. Help me come."

"Oh, so you *can* ask for help." He smirks up at me from between my thighs.

Smart ass.

My fist tightens in his hair, pulling back slightly until he flinches slightly in pain, but his eyes light up with pleasure. "Yes, I can. Can you follow directions?"

He nods, wincing as the movement causes me to pull harder on his hair. The second my grip loosens, he goes to work.

No more skirting around the edges; Orion goes for the kill, licking at my clit until I'm right there on the edge of oblivion again. Somehow he manages to wedge one of his huge hands between my thick thighs and presses one finger inside me.

Before he had been dragging out the slow climb to my orgasm, now he's racing toward that finish line like he has something to prove. The orgasm crashes over me so fast I go a little dizzy, the world spinning around me while fireworks explode inside me. My screams and moans echo around us, reverberating off the neighboring peaks and valleys of the mountains.

My hands search for something to hold onto and find one of the curved logs that make up the exterior walls of the cabin. My nails sink into the grain of the wood, holding on for dear life as Orion adds another finger inside my pulsing cunt.

"Holy shit, Oh God, Orion."

I whimper a little when his mouth disappears from between my legs and the pumping of his fingers slows slightly. "How am I doing on those directions?"

"So, *so*, fucking good," I pant as I nod frantically. "Now get up here and fuck me hard."

"Yes ma'am." He climbs to his feet, somehow rearranging me so my feet never meet the floor.

I push at the waist of his sweatpants, and thankfully they are loose enough that they drop to the floor immediately. He grips his shaft in one hand and notches the head of his cock against my entrance.

I hold my breath, bracing for that first thrust, so ready to be filled by him. But it doesn't come. I try to focus through the absolute flood of lust and pleasure still racing wildly through my veins.

"There you go not listening to directions, again."

"Fuck, Brigid, I am so sorry."

Chapter 23

Orion

"Sunshine, I don't have a condom." I'm right there, so fucking close to being able to slide inside her. It'd be so easy, one thrust and I could be stuffing her so full of my cock.

She's still gasping after the orgasm I gave her with my mouth. That inner caveman I've tried to deny for so long rears to life inside, wanting to pound his chest and proudly declare he made his woman feel so damn good.

Brigid looks about as desperate as I feel to have us joined in the most essential of ways. "I want to feel you so bad," she sobs out. The desperation in her voice is so fucking hot. Like the world might collapse around us if she doesn't get me inside her. "Maybe, j-just the tip. Just a little, just to feel it."

"Just the tip? That's a dangerous game to play, Sunshine." I can do it though. I can hold onto my willpower and give her what she needs. To feel full if only for a second.

"Please," she begs, grinding her pussy down on the underside of my cock, making it slip closer to where she wants it.

"You have to stay still, Brigid."

"Please, Orion, please. I need to feel you."

My hips move at the same moment I've made up my mind. "Hold on and don't move."

She wraps her legs around me even tighter, hands gripping my shoulders. With one of my palms firmly planted against the cabin, I reach between us and notch my cock at her entrance. I will time to stand still. To let the next few seconds last a fucking lifetime. A lifetime of being inside Brigid sounds like the absolute best way to spend my days and nights.

Slowly, so painfully slowly, I press in until just the head of my cock fills her tight cunt. Every inch of me wants to slam home, to fill her to the very brim. I fight the instinct. Hold as still as possible as she moans and squeezes my traps with her fingers.

Every breath is a fucking battle. I press my forehead against hers and we both stare between us where we are connected, but only just.

"A little more," Brigid whispers. She circles her hips, and another inch slips in. She gasps, her mouth falling open. "You feel so good, Orion."

"Sunshine, you're playing with fire." I take her mouth in a delicious, slow, wet kiss. Make sure to keep us exactly where we are in this in between space fucking, yet not. "I'm already fighting every cell of my body telling me to bury myself so deep inside you you'll feel me there for an eternity."

She whimpers, squeezes her thighs around my waist trying to pull in more inside her. "I want to feel all of you. Please. It's been so long."

"For me too, Sunshine. But I don't know if this is truly you begging for my cock, or the need pent up inside us. If I fill you, are you going to regret it tomorrow? Because I couldn't take that. When I take you, really take you, I want it to be because you are so fucking sure of me."

My words must penetrate the fog of lust that's descended between us because she tips her head back looking me in the eye with the embers of regret already simmering there.

I start to pull back, to do the most painful thing I've ever done and leave the warmth of her body.

"No, don't, please," she cries out, tightening her grip on my shoulders and waist. "Don't leave. I need you to come. If you don't I know I will wake up tomorrow and regret it. I'll wish for it so much I won't be able to think about anything else."

I hear the truth in her words. But I also can't fuck her knowing there is a chance she'll wish we hadn't.

"Sweet Sunshine, I'm so close to coming right now I don't need to be inside you to do that. You have no idea how many times I had to stop myself from coming while I ate that sweet cunt."

This seems to perplex her, a little line forming between her eyebrows as she looks at me with awe. "You could come from making me come?"

"Easily."

Brigid reaches down between our bodies and grips my cock in her soft hand, freeing me from her. I see the moment we both mourn the loss, but it quickly fades as she presses my length flat against my lower stomach. She arches her back, lining her pussy up so it can slide up and down my shaft. I grab her waist, afraid she'll slip as she works herself up and down my cock.

"Can you support me like this?"

I nod, unable to speak through the tension building low in my gut. Mesmerized by the motion of her body as she undulates against me, the wet tip of my dick appearing from between her puffy lower lips and then disappearing between them again as she grinds up and down.

Brigid's breathing picks up a little with each bump of my head against her clit. She makes sure not to let me come too close to her entrance; we both know that if we were to play that particular brand of Russian roulette again it would not be nearly as easy to stop.

"Holy shit, I'm going to come again. I can't believe I'm going to come again." She moans, the sounds reverberating straight down to my balls.

"Fuck, Brigid, where do you want me to come?"

"Anywhere. Everywhere," she pants.

I'm holding on by a thread, but I hold on because I will be damned if I come before Brigid. She's so fucking slippery, easing the glide of my cock up and down through her slit. My eyes switch between her face and where we are rutting against each other, trying to take it all in just in case I don't get another chance at this.

Finally Brigid's body tenses, every muscle in her body contracting in that moment right before she detonates. The sounds coming from her echo around us in the clearing, probably scaring any animals that might have been hanging around in the early evening.

I don't know how long we've been at it, but the sun has completely set now, and I find myself wishing I could see her face more clearly as she orgasms for the third time tonight. The security lights on my side of the property do next to nothing to light her porch.

As the pleasure surges through her body, those muscles that had tensed moments ago turn to jelly and we begin to slip. Her eyes fly open, fear and pleasure warring. Forget the projects around the cabin, the first task on my win Brigid over mission should be make sure she knows she never needs to fear I'll drop her.

With one hand behind her neck and one around her ass, I pull her close against me, continuing to grind my cock against her as she moans and pleads in my ear to please come on her.

I'm already there, deep, guttural sounds bursting through my lips as my cock pulses where it is trapped between our bodies. She must feel it, because Brigid leans back with her arms still wrapped around my shoulders and watches as I spill everything inside me onto her soft belly.

I'm sure it's quite the sight, but that isn't where my focus is. Her face, that's where I can't look away from. The expression of awe and joy as I come all over not just her, but myself as well is something I am captivated by.

Is this what every time would be with her? True, we didn't have sex in the traditional sense, but it felt like more than any quick fuck from my past.

After a few more spurts, I'm tapped, and frankly a little light-headed from the strength of my orgasm. When Brigid reaches down between us with one hand and swirls her fingers in the sticky cum coating her stomach, my dick twitches.

"Don't even think about it." I swear she's talking to the beast between us that is trying valiantly to come back to life. It makes me laugh.

"I promise, he'll behave."

Sweat drips down my back, cooling in the night air. Brigid's bangs are plastered to her forehead, mascara smeared slightly beneath her eyes. We're a fucking mess and I love it. I suddenly wish we were still at my cabin. That I could carry her straight into my shower then to bed where she would sleep in my arms, cheek pressed against my chest. A vision of her stretching sleepily in the morning with the lines on her face not from the pillows but from being pressed against me nearly takes my breath away.

"I should get cleaned up." Slowly she drops her feet down until they dangle a few inches above the floorboards since I haven't released my hold on her yet.

"You need anything, a cup of sugar, a light bulb changed, to feel good—" I grip her tighter, pressing our bodies together from chest to knees "—call me. Come knock on my door. Promise."

A shy smile spreads across her lips, something so unexpected from this spitfire of a woman it makes my heart thump double time in my chest.

"Okay. I will." She leans in for the kiss first, not frantic like when this whole thing started. Slow. Sweet.

I don't want it to end, but I know it has to, so I lower her down till her toes touch the floor. We pull apart and she turns, walking into the cabin naked, a single glance over her shoulder at me as she closes the door.

Pulling up my pants from where they still sit around my ankles, I wonder if she will wake up tomorrow and regret everything that happened tonight. Once all the dopamine and oxytocin levels in her brain go back to normal, will she go back to hating me? I hope not.

I gather her discarded clothes and head back to my place to throw them in the wash. Then I head back out to where the couch is still sitting in the far too tall grass and finish the job I started.

Chapter 24

Brigid

The next morning, my car is sitting in its usual spot next to the cabin with a full tank of gas. I woke up feeling refreshed after a great night of sleep and ready to finish up the last of the business license application.

Which was still in the car.

The car I thought was halfway down the mountain.

I'd been debating going over to Orion's later in the day to ask him to drive me down to get gas and retrieve the car when I remembered my clothes were probably still scattered around the porch from the night before. With Mica, who woke up extra clingy, propped on one hip, we ventured outside to gather my pajamas and underwear and bring them in. Which is when I noticed the car.

My clothes from the night before are folded in a neat little pile on top of a beautiful wooden table that was definitely not there before. There is also a travel mug with a caramel latte and a muffin on a plate with plastic wrap keeping the bugs away. There's also a rocking chair sitting where the one from the dock had been before.

I don't need to look out at the yard to know the couch is probably gone, too. Does the man ever sleep?

The real estate between my thighs has that pleasantly sore, used feeling that lets you know something amazing happened the night before.

Just the tip. Yeah, that was insane. I lost my mind for a minute there. But Orion held strong as I begged him to fuck me against the wall of my cabin. We hadn't even talked about birth control or STDs or any of the things responsible adults are supposed to talk about before they jump headfirst into unprotected sex.

That wasn't like me. Not at all. Sure, Mica is proof enough that I am nowhere near perfect, but he had been the result of antibiotics interfering with birth control and the sperm donor insisting he could pull out in time because he hated condoms. It was the best oops ever and I don't regret how any of it happened since I have my son with me now.

I also don't regret what Orion and I did last night. If anything, I regret not doing more. Considering how amazing my neighbor had been at everything we did do, I can't imagine sex with Orion Halsted would be anything but amazing.

A high-pitched bark has my head swinging around to the more well-maintained property across the pond. There is Orion, in workout shorts and a tank top that looks like it must have been cut with a machete rather than bought off the rack. He's got a rope of some kind in one hand and is swinging it around over his head like a helicopter before sending it sailing across the yard. Spruce bounds after it, snatching the toy from the ground as he runs full speed past it then takes a turn a little too tight considering he is missing a leg, stumbling a little.

At first, I'm concerned the dog might be hurt, but he's up in the next second rushing toward his owner. The dog comes up short, right in front of his owner and lowers his chest to the ground with his tail high in the air wagging back and forth. Instead of dropping the rope for another throw, the dog takes off with the rope in his mouth and Orion follows.

"I'm gonna get it, you can run but I always catch you, you mongrel." They circle around each other a few times, Orion continuing the playful shit-talking. Finally, he gets the edge of the rope in one hand and a quick game of tug-o-war ensues before Orion wins and starts waving the rope around again just out of the dog's reach.

Watching them play makes my heart do that extra little kick that surely can't be healthy. I wonder how close the nearest cardiologist is? There is also something so incredibly familiar about it. As if I have seen this whole scene play out before. Recognition dances just outside my grip; if I could just concentrate a little more I would be able to place why I keep getting this sense of familiarity.

The sharp, loud ring of a call coming in on my phone echoes out from the cabin, and apparently across the yard, because both Orion and Spruce turn in our direction.

Caught ogling the neighbor, again. Is there anything more embarrassing?

Orion waves and Spruce starts running in our direction. I can hear Orion call after his dog as I rush into the cabin to grab my cell phone from the island and answer the call. "Hello?"

"Brigid, good morning!" Roxy's warm voice filters through the phone and I suddenly hope very much she doesn't have some sort of sixth sense for when women are thinking dirty thoughts about her son. "I hope I'm not calling too early."

"No of course not, Mica and I have been awake for a while."

"Oh good. Sometimes I forget not everyone is used to waking up at the crack of dawn. Doesn't matter that I haven't lived on the farm in years, the early mornings are ingrained in me as deeply as my DNA at this point." I can hear shuffling on the other side of the line and I wonder if she is in the cafe getting things ready for a morning rush. "I was calling because I asked around yesterday after you left and found a house for rent that might work for you and Mica a little closer to town. You mentioned yesterday you wouldn't be able to stay up at the cabin for too long because of its condition."

I had said that, hadn't I? Yesterday I had been so eager to get away from the tiny cabin and big neighbor. Twenty-four hours shouldn't have changed that much. If I want to own a business in town I can't live forty-five minutes up the mountain. What would I do in the winter? If a tree fell across the one and only road leading to town?

"That's amazing, Roxy. Thank you so much." My tone says I'm excited, but inside I'm a knot of confusion.

"You are so welcome. You should act fast, though. I heard Marty's son has been looking to move out from her basement, and I refuse to rent the room at the Bean to him because the man only showers once a month." A loud hissing, the steaming wand on the espresso machine I think, nearly drowns out Roxy's voice as she continues the tale of Marty's son and his poor hygiene. "Anyway, I'll text you the address and the owner's phone number so you can check it out."

"Thanks so much, Roxy. I'll look at the place on Google Maps and see what I think."

From behind me I hear loud panting. I turn and see Spruce sitting on the porch outside the open door, practically begging if Mica can come out and play.

Orion is right beside him, a concerned look on his face.

As soon as I hang up with his mom, Orion takes a small step forward. I have a feeling he wouldn't come in unless I explicitly asked him to. Almost like a less violent vampire.

"Was that my mom?" He braces one arm on the top of the front door's frame. The position has his shirt riding up slightly to expose a strip of his toned abs and the trail of hair I know leads to a very happy place.

"Yeah, I had mentioned yesterday that I needed to find some-place closer to town to live before the winter. She asked around and apparently already found a prospect."

His disappointment is instantaneous and obvious. "Right, that makes sense."

"This place is so run-down. Between the roof and the heater, I'm not sure a winter in here would be safe." There is no reason I should be explaining all this to him. The things that happened between us the past two nights don't mean anything. I owe him nothing. Yet I can't stop. "Plus, if I manage to actually get a shop up and running, I'll need to be more accessible to town."

Orion is nodding along, agreeing with everything I say, but behind his eyes I see the desire to resist. But he keeps the words to himself.

"Mom is the best at working the town for these things. If she says it's a good place I'm sure it is."

Why is this so fucking awkward? I knew the cabin was just a stop on the journey to making Amoresville our home. That was true before we got here, and even more so after I saw the state of the place.

Silence fills the cabin, neither of us knowing what to say, not able to voice the hesitations both of us are obviously thinking. Mica helps the situation by reaching out suddenly for the dog until I almost drop him.

"You can come in. So can Spruce"

Orion simply nods and steps across the threshold, tapping his outer thigh in a sign to the dog that he could follow.

Mica squeals in excitement and waves his arms around wildly as if to say *put me down so I can play*. With a chuckle, I put Mica down in his giant baby jail-slash-play area, who immediately grabs onto the side of the fence to pull himself up and reach between the gaps for the dog.

"Whoa dude, you're going to knock this thing over." I hold the plastic walls as they begin to wobble. "Do you think Spruce would be okay in there with him? I don't like him to have free rein of the cabin because some of the floorboards are pretty rough or have nails sticking out. In there I at least have a bunch of blankets cushioning his hands and knees."

Orion studies the cabin's flooring, seeming annoyed or dismayed, I'm not sure which. "Yeah of course." He lifts the dog, who has to weigh at least fifty pounds if not more, and places him inside the large playpen. Spruce immediately flops onto his side in the middle of the space and Mica crawls over to pat and pull at him.

"That has to be the world's most patient dog."

Orion chuckles and nods. "Yeah, he's a good boy. Whoever was idiot enough to dump him in the middle of the woods is missing out."

"People are idiots." The silence returns like a fifth person in the house standing between the adults while the kids play. "Oh, I almost forgot, I have something for you."

Happy to have something to do other than stand around awkwardly staring at Mica and Spruce, I cross the small space to our bedroom. Just inside the door is the dresser I have yet to open, too afraid what creepy crawlies I might find lurking inside the ancient drawers. Sitting on top is a book with a well-worn cover.

"So I don't keep physical copies of many books, but this is one I've always carried with me." I hand it over to Orion.

"*Crafting Balance,*" he reads the title of the book, then flips it over to look at the description.

"Yeah, it was self-published by a woman I took a seminar with a few years ago. It's a good overview of modern witchcraft. The one you have is okay too, but I've always thought it placed too much emphasis on Wicca. This one is also a little more digestible." A sudden rush of shyness washes over me. "Not that I think you wouldn't understand the other one, obviously you can. When I read it I felt like I was trudging through a history lesson. This one is more narrative, less history professor talking from his pulpit."

The stoic expression melts off Orion's face to be replaced by a genuine smile. "Thanks, I can't wait to start in on it. So, you aren't Wiccan then?"

"Nope, I consider myself a general garden variety magic practitioner. Atheopagan, if you want to get super technical about it."

"I thought all witches were Wiccan." Orion flips through the book, checking out some of the illustrations and chapter titles.

"Look at it this way, all Wiccans are Witches, not all witches are Wiccan. In fact, not all people who believe in witchcraft call themselves witches."

"My family didn't grow up in any sort of religion or any belief system that we talked about. In small town rural Pennsylvania, my parents were judged a lot for not going to church." Orion picks his eyes up from the book, pinning me with a serious look that instantly has my skin prickling. "I'm sorry if that first day it seemed like I judged you for your beliefs. Actually, not seemed like. I did. I was judging you and I shouldn't have. I know better as someone who has been on the receiving end of this town's judgment. Don't get me wrong, I love Amoresville and can't imagine ever leaving it again for any real amount of time, but it has its downfalls, too." He holds up the book. "Thank you for sharing this and for not holding the first impression I gave off against me." He considers that and then chuckles a little. "Or at least not holding it against me too much."

I can't help but smile, because yes, I absolutely held my first impression against him. But every interaction has made me begrudgingly reconsider how I see him. He rocked my world last night, while holding us both back from doing something stupid like have sex without a condom. My history has proven that most men would have surged forward without a thought. He has been silently fixing things around the cabin's exterior without asking for any acknowledgment. Is obviously close with his family and helps them whenever possible. Now he is giving me a real apology. Not some half-assed apology that actually blames me for his reaction.

I turn to face him head on instead of awkwardly hovering next to him while Mica and Spruce play. "How about we leave first impressions behind? I might have been a little hasty and let past experiences color my vision of you. I'd like to learn about who you are beyond that first conversation. Do you think you can get past thinking I am some flighty Pagan who moves her son about on a whim? Maybe be friends?"

"Friends?" He says it like he thinks it will be impossible. "Yeah, friends."

We both stick our hands out and shake on it, then turn back to watch as Mica and Spruce continue their bonding on the floor. Inexplicably, I have the overwhelming desire to reach out and take hold of Orion's hand. To entwine our fingers in a completely non-sexual way. Just to be connected physically in some small way.

But right behind that instinct is the small, dark voice that reminds me my taste in men is infamously horrible and I can't trust this feeling of safety that comes so easily around my neighbor. Plus, friends don't hold hands. Right?

So, I keep my hands to myself.

Chapter 25

Orion

Friends? Yeah, I don't think I can settle for anything so simple as friends with Brigid. But it is a good place to start. A good foundation to build what I think could be so much more.

Earlier, when she stepped out of her house, my gut feeling was relief at finally seeing her again, even though it had only been a few hours since our... encounter. Then pure panic as I realized she would see all my equipment as I filmed in the yard. I thought I had gotten up early enough that she and Mica would still be fast asleep. It is getting harder and harder to both get content for my channels and hide what I do from my neighbor.

Play sessions with Spruce always do great on TikTok. Sometimes I think people watch my videos more for him than me. At least once a week I post a video that is nothing but Spruce and I rough housing in the yard and without fail it does absolutely stupid high numbers.

Added bonus: they require next to no editing.

But when I saw her standing on the porch with Mica on her hip, I froze. Thankfully, the tripod had been placed just far enough back that it must not have been immediately obvious.

Part of me wonders why I'm keeping the secret from her. After our talk it is more than obvious that she isn't a judgmental person. She was the one who suggested putting first impressions aside and being friends. Logically I know she would most likely not care one bit how I make a living. But humans aren't always logical, so I can't help but wonder if thirst traps being my main source of income would cause her to hold back, or worse, back away altogether. I know I would be jealous as hell if men were looking at her and saying the things my followers say in my comments every day.

She literally just crashed into my life. I can't lose her just as fast.

I always thought my brother was exaggerating when he said he immediately felt something for his fiancée when she literally came crashing into his life. But I suddenly understand the sentiment.

Love at first sight isn't something I've ever bought into, and I still don't. But lust at first sight? Interest at first sight? Connection? Yeah, those all seem much more likely post-Brigid.

After I stowed my equipment against the house where it would definitely be out of sight, I had to sprint after Spruce to make sure he didn't go running into her cabin without permission. Caught up to him right as he sat his butt on the porch like the gentleman he is. And just in time to hear the end of her conversation with Mom.

Why the hell is Mom helping her find a new place to live?

Because Brigid asked for her help and my mother loves nothing more than making a new friend.

They can't leave yet.

I've never thought of the mountain as lonely until the prospect of no longer having my dark cloud of a neighbor became a reality.

There is nothing that can be done about her need to be closer to town. But I can make the cabin, the cabin that in a few days I will officially own, safer for Brigid and Mica. Maybe if she is sure the roof won't cave in on top of them, she might be willing to stay longer.

Which is why I put in a call to not just my brother, but also Sam at the hardware store, and my best friend Murphy and ask them all for something I never have before.

Help.

* * *

Much to my surprise, the guys all arrive bright and early the next morning. I shouldn't be surprised when I also see June hop out of Knox's truck. Followed closely by Paula piling out of the absolute tank of a van she and Sam got when baby number five made its arrival. Three of their five kiddos are also in tow.

"This isn't a party guys, what's with the caravan?"

"You thought you could call and say you needed help replacing your hot neighbor's roof and expect the girls to stay away?" My brother flicks at my forehead as he passes by to give Spruce ear scratches. "You're an even bigger idiot than I thought you were."

"June, it's not too late, you could leave this guy. I'm sure you can do better."

My brother grabs the bun sticking out from the back of my head and gives a good hard yank. "Get a haircut, hippy."

My soon-to-be sister-in-law laughs at our antics. "If I leave him then who is going to take care of all those women he has locked in the basement?"

"Um, I'm sorry, why are there a bunch of people in my yard talking about taking women hostage?" Brigid strolls up to our little group with Mica perched on her hip and a curious look on her face. She has one of her trademark oversized shirts on that hangs down to mid-thigh. She's completely covered, not at all indecent, and yet I have the overwhelming desire to put my body in front of hers, blocking the eyes of my brother and one of my oldest friends.

June whips around to glare at me. "Orion Halsted, did you not tell this woman that we were all descending on her house at eight in the morning?"

"He most definitely did not." An edge of the icy voice that had thawed after the past few days makes another appearance.

"Surprise! The guys are going to help me replace the roof today. There's supposed to be a cold snap this weekend and I don't want you or Mica getting sick."

"You're going to replace the roof of a cabin that doesn't belong to you? You're basically doing something nice for a man that from what I understand your family hates."

"No, I'm doing something to help you. Burt is a non-issue." Quite literally soon. I got an email from his lawyer this morning with some of the initial paperwork that could be e-signed. One step closer to the land that used to all belong to my family once again being ours.

The more I've thought about it since making the arrangement with Burt, the better I feel about it. True, I mostly did it to make sure Brigid and Mica have a safe place to stay as long as they want to. But I'm also righting a wrong my great-uncle made almost a hundred years ago.

"These Halsted men, I'm telling you they are too sweet and too dumb for their own good." June ambles up to us and stretches her hand out. "Hi, I'm June, Knox's fiancée. Knox is Orion's brother."

Brigid looks a little bit starstruck for a moment, which is when I remember she mentioned being a follower of June's Instagram account when we first met. "It's nice to meet you. I'm Brigid. I've actually followed you on social media for a couple years now. Your posts about moving here are part of why I started looking to relocate."

"Awww, really? That's so cool. Amoresville is a great place to call home." June leans into Mica and waves her fingers at him. "And who is this little guy?"

"This is Mica." The little guy nuzzles his face into his Mom's shoulder, looking a little shier than normal. "You'll have to forgive him, we had a rough night last night. I think he's popping another tooth. He always gets a little cranky."

"Oh boy, do I know that story." Paula joins us as well with her oldest daughter Molly right at her side. "I'm Paula, I own the salon in town. That is my husband Sam—" she points to the man himself as he begins unloading the trailer loaded with all the supplies we'll need to totally replace the cabin's roof "—helping him is our eight-year-old Max. This is Molly—she just turned ten. And Henry is probably looking for Spruce to play fetch. He's six. We left the four-year-old, two-year-old, and baby at home with my parents."

Brigid looks understandably shell-shocked at the barrage of new faces. "Wow, and I thought my one was a handful."

Paula laughs and scans the kids scattered across the yard. "Yeah, after every one I say we're done and then magically a year later I get the itch again."

"Can I play with your baby?" Molly, who might be the politest kid I have ever met, asks.

Brigid appears a little nervous at first but relaxes after a moment. "Actually, that would be great, maybe you could come inside and play with him while I get dressed and make us some breakfast? I'll even pay you for being a mother's helper today."

The little girl lights up at the mention of a little extra cash, and they head into the house.

"Wow little brother, I never thought I'd see the day." Knox bumps his shoulder into mine, making me sway to the side slightly.

"What are you rambling on about, old man?"

"Never thought I'd see the day you looked at something other than a piece of wood like that."

"Shut up, asshole."

A half an hour later, as Sam, Knox and I are starting to tear off the disintegrating old shingles from the roof, a jeep an offensive shade of lime green comes rumbling up the driveway. My old bunkmate from Iraq, Murphy, practically falls out of the driver's side door looking like he's on the tail end of a bender.

"Hey dickwad, I was starting to wonder if you were going to show up," I call down from the roof, throwing another handful of roofing onto the tarp below.

"Sorry, dude, I had to stop in at Delia's last night when I got in and Harley might have gotten me a little drunker than I planned."

"Yeah, well, Harley knows a sucker when she sees one. How much did she get out of you?"

"I don't want to talk about it," he grumbles. The three of us on the roof break out into laughter, knowing that means he probably has just enough in his bank account to get back home tonight.

"That's what you get for going to our sister's club when Harley's working," Knox chimes in.

"Oh, is someone talking about my favorite stripper?" June walks up with Brigid behind her from my side of the property, both carrying a couple thermoses of coffee and water along with several mugs. "I'm taking her class this week now that state fair season is over and we have a weekend free."

"So, classes at the local strip club are seriously a thing people do around here?" Brigid seems perplexed by this little detail, which I don't blame her for. I've been to strip clubs on a couple different continents thanks to my time in the military and I've never heard of another one that offered classes to the locals.

"Yup, and they are an amazing workout. You should come sometime, it's actually really fun. Sometimes they serve mimosas after class. Just be careful, Harley loves to make newbies the volunteer for demonstrations and will probably end up giving you a lap dance."

My brain isn't quite sure what to do with that mental image. On the one hand, hot girls dancing together—good. On the other, I've known Harley since we were kids and that is just fucking weird.

Mom dragged Knox and I to the club exactly once to support our sister in her new business venture, but we both had to tap out when the girl that used to run around the farm chasing chickens with our sister got on stage.

"You know what, I would actually love that, but I haven't found a babysitter around here yet, so it might have to wait."

"I'll watch him." The words are out of my mouth before I can think better of it. Why would Brigid want to leave her one and only child with the man next door that she's hooked up with a couple times? Even if we are *friends* now.

Every single set of eyes both on the roof and on the ground swing my way with varying levels of disbelief.

"What? We hung out the other day and he's a cool kid." I focus in on Brigid, because the rest of these guys don't matter in this conversation. "If it makes you feel better Mica and I can hang out at the cafe, so an experienced parent is there to supervise us bachelors."

Brigid rubs her lips together and shifts her gaze away from me, seemingly considering my offer. "Okay, I'll think about it."

"Give me some of that coffee," Murphy steps between June and Brigid, throwing his arm over both women. "I must still be hungover because I could have sworn the man that used to fart on my face in bootcamp just sounded like a responsible adult."

Knox saves me from having to leap off the roof and remove Murphy's arm from Brigid. "Get your hand off my fiancé, or I will rip your arm from your body."

June shakes her head and playfully pushes Murphy away. "Come on, take a break guys."

My gaze swings to Brigid who watches me with curiosity. Apparently, she didn't miss my flash of possessiveness.

Chapter 26

Brigid

"Okay, tell me absolutely everything about yourself. We don't get newcomers all that often." Paula leans in to stage whisper loud enough for June to hear across the room. "The last one is getting a little stale."

"Hey! I'm going to remember you said that when I tip you after my next color," June laughs good-naturedly. "But I agree, I want the life story."

I forgot how much I love being around women chatting over coffee and pastries. Soon after the work at my cabin started, the three of us packed up the kids and headed over to Orion's cabin to escape the noise. Molly and Mica are happily playing with some of his more portable toys in the living room area. I had great intentions of taking advantage of my little helper and finishing the application I've been picking away at, but June and Paula had other ideas.

"Okay let's see, my life story. Well, I was born on May ninth in Arizona, my mom still says I am her favorite because I didn't make her suffer through pregnancy in Tucson during the hottest months, unlike my sister."

"Okay, maybe not *every* detail of your life." Paula is quite possibly one of the nicest women I've ever met. She has infinite patience with her kids each time they come running up with a rock to show her or a booboo to kiss. I kinda want to sit at her feet and ask her to teach me her ways. "But you're from Arizona, noted. When did you make your way east?"

"Well, that is a long story."

Both women give me their full attention.

"Does it look like we're going anywhere?" Paula asks.

"Good point. Okay, I was nineteen, a sophomore in college. I had this professor and we started seeing each other. He got a job at the Pittsburgh Art Institute. At the time I thought it was incredibly romantic that he asked me to go with him, promised he would help me get a place there the following year. My parents tried to talk me out of it, but I am nothing if not stubborn. Classic Taurus." I pause, looking everywhere but at these two women that seem to have their shit together. "Turned out he just liked having a woman half his age fawning all over him and serving as his live-in housekeeper while he cheated on me with a new batch of coeds each year."

"Why do men have to suck so much?" Paula sounds truly pissed off, and I'm surprised to see fire in her eyes when I get the courage to turn back in her direction. "I swear, if I weren't raising three of them myself I would say we should get rid of all of them."

"Well, your husband doesn't seem too bad either," I remind her.

"True, I somehow managed to find a great one on my first try in high school." A smile softens her expression.

"Knox is pretty great, too. Can we spare him?" June chimes in.

"Okay, my kids, Sam, and Knox. Every other man is on my shit list though." Paula jokingly pounds her fist on the island counter.

"I am going to have to insist you add in my son and my dad," I add.

"Not Orion?" June waggles her eyebrows up and down.

I roll my eyes in response and try not to blush. "I guess he can stay, too."

"Okay, fine, but I draw the line there." Paula tilts her head and gives me a look I can only describe as understanding mom. "I take it that asshole is Mica's dad?"

I roll my lips between my teeth and nod, looking over at the kid in question. "Truth be told, I would go through all the pain of my relationship with William all over again just to get Mica. The lying, the cheating, the gaslighting; worth it for that kid."

All three of us sit in silence for a moment, seeming to be deep in our own thoughts.

"I heard a rumor you're looking to start a business in town. Any truth to that?" June sits on one of the stools at the island, picking at a muffin Orion apparently made last night. I'm starting to wonder if the man has insomnia or something.

"Indeed I am. I'm opening a metaphysical store."

Paula tilts her head to the side, her tight curls shifting at the movement. "Wait, metaphysical, what is that? Like something science-y."

"No, something witchy."

Paula's eyes widen in surprise. "Oh my gosh, the rumors were true for once."

"Rumors?" I'm surprised there are already rumors swirling about me in town since I've only been here two weeks and have been in town no more than a handful of times.

"Oh yeah, the Amoresville rumor mill is something else. Hence the joke earlier about women being held in Knox's basement." June leans forward and whispers so the young ears nearby can't hear. "When I first got to town, they said I was a prostitute Knox picked up on the side of the road."

"Prostitution big out here?" I can't help but laugh at the absolutely ridiculous prospect.

"Oh yeah, totally." June rolls her eyes.

"The rumor mill has been working overtime with you, Miss Brigid," Paula interjects. "I think it is the mystery of having you up here and not being in town much. Your proximity to a Halsted doesn't hurt, either. But the rumor I heard was you are a witch hiding out on the mountain. You have Orion under a mind control spell and you do animal sacrifices to the old gods."

I burst out laughing, totally taken back by the insanity of what the town apparently thinks of me. "Well, I am a witch, but no human sacrifices. No mind control spells. Mostly crystals, herbs, and the occasional chanting under a full moon in the nude."

"Bet Orion loves that," June winks at me, I think to reassure that she isn't serious.

If only she knew what did happen during the full moon.

"So, you are opening an occult shop in town? Is that, like, what you're listing on the application." June shoots one of those looks over to Paula that says *we both know that is a bad idea but how do we tell this girl we barely know.*

"No, thankfully I got some help with the application from someone in town and they were nice enough to tell me that I should call it *a store selling gems, minerals, and other natural specimens that appeal to the educated among the town.*" I make sure to keep Wesley's name out of the conversation. He and Roxy had been so insistent no one know about their friendship or his part in helping with my store, I don't plan on betraying my word to them.

"Oh my god, that is actually brilliant." Paula glances over at her daughter and Mica to make sure the loud squeals that just broke out are laughter and not tears. "Thank God I opened the salon before Burt was in office or it never would have happened. A salon for humans and dogs? No way, he would have said it was frivolous and weird."

"How long has he been mayor?" I'm honestly kind of fascinated with my dead-beat landlord. Everyone I have run into so far can't stand him, yet he's been elected several times it sounds like.

"Twelve years. Thankfully, he can't run again next year. He never had any children, so unless his nephew runs, we might be looking at the very last Lickinbill mayor ever." Paula picks a piece of lint from her sweater and drops it next to her on the floor. "Good Riddance."

"Oh, he's not that bad." June pipes up.

"No, he is, you are just too nice. Just because he's your boss doesn't mean you have to be nice to him."

"Wait, I thought you're an influencer. You work for the town too?"

"I'm a freelancer. I do events and things for the town. Advise on how to attract more visitors, I've even convinced him to redo the website and get some social media accounts." June talks about the man in a far kinder tone than anyone else I've met. I wonder if it's because she didn't grow up here. "He has a pretty sad story actually. Lost his wife to breast cancer when they were young, never remarried, then his estranged sister passed away and he got custody of her teenage son, Wesley." "Okay that is true," Paula interjects. "But just because he's been through a lot doesn't mean he can rule over the town like it's his own personal sandbox."

"You're absolutely right. It's a minor miracle Wes and I convinced him to edit the business license application last year.

There's a reason so many shops in the town square are empty. And it's not a good look from the tourist side of things. Once we pointed out there had been less businesses opened during his time in office than any previous mayor, he did actually listen. I think the man really believes he's doing what's best for the town. He's just going about it all wrong."

"I can't believe that application is the pared down version. I literally had two people helping with it and it still took nearly a week to finish the first half."

"Is it finished?" June nudges my shoulder a little. "I can hand it in for you if you like. Try to work my magic on Burt. I think he has a soft spot for me."

Before I can answer, the door to the cabin flings open, making the three of us jump in surprise. A pack of sweaty, sexy men stumble inside, all talking over each other with what sounds like not-so-gentle ribbing. Orion has Murphy in a headlock and is literally giving him a noogie.

"Women, the men have come in for sustenance. Feed us!" Sam saunters up to his wife and slaps her on the butt, pulling her in for a hug.

"Ewww, get your grody, sweaty hands off me." The words have no heat behind them. In fact, Paula's eyes have a sparkle that says she very much does not mind her husband's antics. No wonder they have six kids.

"Don't you even think about trying that on me, sir." June points her finger at Knox, who is smiling big and stalking toward her like a lion in the pride.

"What? You never mind when I'm coming in from the fields."

June blushes a deep red and Knox rushes up, picking her up off the stool and kissing her so passionately I feel like I should be paying admission.

Orion has finally let his friend go and crosses to the fridge, brushing his knuckles against the back of my hand as he passes me. The small touch has about the same effect as Sam and Knox's overt PDA with their wives. I'm instantly wet and ready to drag him to the nearest flat surface. But that's not what we are, we're friends who made out a couple times, so I brush the thought away.

"Brigid, if you're feeling left out, I'm happy to take one for the team and stick my tongue down your throat." Murphy slides up next to me at the island, but keeps a respectful two feet between us.

The slam of the pantry door a few feet away draws our attention. Orion's previously playful expression has been replaced with what can only be described as a murderous look pointed directly at his best friend.

"On second thought, I'm going to sit at the dining table and keep my mouth shut." Murphy turns his back to Orion, facing me directly, and gives me a dramatic wink.

"Good idea," Orion draws in a deep breath to collect himself, letting go of the sudden surge of anger. Gathered in his arms are several bags of chips and a few loaves of bread, which he dumps on the counter. "I got a bunch of stuff for sandwiches for lunch.

You hooligans know where everything is, grab some plates and utensils and dig in."

The tension breaks as soon as everyone starts moving. Knox grabs a stack of plates from one cabinet. Sam pulls open a draw and grabs knives, spoons, and forks. June gathers the meats, cheeses, and veggies from the refrigerator. Murphy sits silently at the table with a knowing little smile.

The cabin is full of so much life, laughter, and conversation it makes me realize I've missed having a community around me. All my family is clear on the other side of the country. The few friends I had made in Pittsburgh slowly drifted away once I had Mica. They checked in, brought gifts, and we still text on occasion. But my life changed drastically after giving birth. I had no support, no one to watch the baby so I could go grab coffee or drinks with the girls. No desire to go on the dating apps and try to find yet another loser that wasn't worth the time away from Mica. So I slowly became more and more isolated.

But just a few weeks in Amoresville and I suddenly have people helping me start a business. Fixing my roof so I won't be cold. Talking to me like we've been friends for far longer than a few minutes.

And an annoying neighbor turned friend who I can't help but think might be worth my time. As hard as I've fought my attraction, my interest in him, I can't deny it any longer.

Chapter 27

Orion

By the time the sun starts dipping below the treeline, Brigid's cabin has a brand-new roof, as well as a newly weed-free garden thanks to Paula and June helping her clean it out all afternoon. Spruce got in on the fun too, biting down on some of the bigger tree saplings that had started growing and pulling the stubborn roots from the ground.

All seven of us are covered in dirt, sweat, and huge, exhausted smiles. Sam and Paula's kids have hit that point where they have had too much fun and are starting to break down into whiny tears. They'll probably be passed out by the time they get down the mountain road.

Knox and June lean into each other, his arm around her shoulders and her arm around his waist as they amble to his truck to head home.

Murphy climbs into his jeep to head to the shitty motel near the club. I had tried to get him to stay with me, but he just looked toward Brigid and declined, claiming he was going to try and get Harley to come home with him. That will never happen.

Within the span of minutes, the group goes from nearly a dozen to Brigid, Mica asleep on her shoulder, and me. Even Spruce is so wiped out from the day that he collapsed into his dog bed on the porch a few minutes ago.

"Your friends are incredible." Brigid waves her free hand over her head as the last of the cars disappear through the trees down the driveway. "I can't believe they would all show up to fix a stranger's roof."

I should tell her. She needs to know that they didn't fix a stranger's roof, technically they fixed my roof. But for some reason I continue to keep the information to myself. Things could still fall through. Burt is a little weasel, and it wouldn't surprise me one bit if he backed out of the deal at the very last second to fuck with me.

"I'm pretty sure none of them think you are a stranger now."

Brigid looks over at me with a sweet smile. "You might be right. Paula wants to have coffee with me next week. They both asked for my phone number. There is a little part of the painfully nerdy, goth girl I was in high school that can't believe those two beautiful women want to hang out with me."

"I bet you were just as cute in high school as you are now." I desperately want to reach out and touch her. Run my thumb along her cheek. Give her a soft kiss on her pouty mouth. Put my arm around her and watch the sun disappear.

Instead, I stuff my hands down into my pockets.

She clocks the movement immediately, her eyes flicking down to where my fists are balled in the stiff denim of my jeans, then back up to my face where I swear she sees straight through to my soul.

"I bet you were the most popular guy in your high school. I know you played football, you were the quarterback, right?"

"Being popular in a class of a hundred students isn't the accomplishment you think it is."

She takes a step closer, tilting her head back to meet my gaze. Mica shifts his head, changing from one cheek pressed against his mother's shoulder to the other cheek. "I'm going to go put him down."

I nod, a little disappointed it's time for us to part ways for the night. I want her to come over to my place. I want to set up the crib I've been working on for two weeks in my guest room and turn it into Mica's room. I want to have sweaty, frantic sex with my hand over her mouth to keep her from screaming and waking up the baby in the middle of the night.

But I can't have any of that tonight and I know it. Not yet.

"I made some fresh sun tea the other day. Why don't you go take a shower and come back for a glass?" There's a shyness to her words, as if there is a version of this moment where I might say no to any invitation she extends.

Spoiler alert: that world doesn't exist.

"I'd love to." Before I can stop myself, I lean in and brush a kiss against her cheek. Then I turn and rush home, her chuckling behind as she watches me practically sprint to my house.

Spruce's head pops up when I land on the porch. He follows me into the cabin and collapses onto yet another dog bed, watching as I shed my clothes in record time, take the fastest shower possible while also getting clean enough that I won't be worried if Brigid wants to get close. Then re-dress in a pair of comfy gray sweatpants and nearly threadbare black t-shirt.

For a solid two minutes I stare at the stash of condoms in my nightstand, debating if I should bring one. Or ten. Is that too presumptuous? She asked me over for a glass of tea, not a fuck. But if I don't come prepared and miss another opportunity to be inside her, I will absolutely kick myself. I grab two and shove them into the deep pockets of my sweatpants, hoping the square packets aren't too obvious through the thin fabric.

Within fifteen minutes I'm slipping on my sandals while my very confused dog ambles over, looking at me as if to say *this is when we get in bed and read*. The good boy is used to our routine.

Try as I might to get him to stay in the cabin, he follows me out the door and trots behind me as I speed walk around the short end of the pond to Brigid's cabin.

Softly, I knock on the door. Brigid answers in a robe, her hair still twisted in a towel on top of her head. "Did you even use soap?"

"I promise I did. I'm just more efficient than you, apparently."

She holds the door open, silently telling me to come in. Spruce sits at the front door, I've given him vampire rules: he doesn't enter a door unless he's invited. "You too, boy. Come on."

Spruce happily ambles in, going directly to the bedroom. I open my mouth to stop him, but Brigid places her hand on my arm stopping me.

"It's fine, really."

We both follow him and I watch with a lump of emotion stuck in my throat as he curls up right next to Mica's crib and closes his eyes. Through the netting side of the portable crib, I see Mica sprawled out like a starfish, his chest rising and falling slightly with each breath.

"Those two," I whisper. "I'm starting to get a little jealous that your son has obviously taken my place as number one on the Spruce's favorite people list."

"I'm sure he remembers you are number one when it's dinner time." Brigid steps inside the room, looking back over her shoulder. "Let me finish my post-shower routine and I'll be right there. Tea is on the table."

She closes the door behind her and I take a step back, desperately wishing I were still in there so I could see exactly what her post-shower ritual entails.

Not wanting to be caught standing there staring at her door like a creeper, I turn and survey the small room. I've been in here a handful of times since they moved in, but I still can't believe how she's turned the place from a hovel to a home.

There isn't much furniture still, a little table with two chairs on either side by the front window, a extensive playpen gated area with layers of blankets acting as floor covering and various toys scattered around. The rocking chair and side table I had left on her porch the other morning are sitting next to the fireplace. Sitting on the table is a laptop covered in stickers.

There are fresh flowers and herbs in mason jars on almost every flat surface, including the kitchen counters, island, tables, and fireplace mantel. Bunches of dried herbs hang upside down in a few spots around the kitchen. In addition to the flowers, there are literally dozens of framed pictures sitting over the fireplace.

Curiosity gets the better of me and I amble that way to inspect them. They are all in golden frames with an intricate scroll look. No two are exactly alike though, they seem like something she's collected over time maybe from garage or estate sales. Thrift shops. I can picture her shifting through piles of crappy, broken frames looking for the perfect one to add to her collection and the image makes me smile.

Several of the frames have images of her and Mica during various stages of his nine months. There is an older couple, maybe in their sixties, holding Mica when he was just a tiny thing, I assume those are her parents. A group picture of Brigid with two other girls that look like her but in different fonts, sisters I'm assuming. A picture of Brigid with four women in stereotypical witch outfits complete with pointy hats, all mid-laugh.

But the one I keep coming back to is Brigid looking exhausted in a hospital bed with Micah wrapped tight in a blanket so the only part of him visible is a bright red face with his eyes closed.

I've always thought newborns all looked the same. Winston Churchill in various shades and sizes. But the toddler I am getting to know is visible in that tiny baby's face. I see the way his nose and chin developed into the kid he is now.

Brigid's life before Amoresville is sitting there on an ugly, chipping mantle and I know nothing about it. It doesn't sit right with me. I should know the stories behind each of the photos.

The bedroom door squeaks behind me, breaking me from my perusal of Brigid's life in photos. I'm almost afraid to look over my shoulder, afraid she'll see the little bit of sadness inside that is disappointment I don't know much about her. Yet.

Quietly she pads over next to me. She points to the photo of the older couple and Mica. "My parents, Suzanne and Jim. They came to stay with me for Mica's birth and a few weeks after. They live in Arizona, along with my older sister Siobhan—" she points to the girl on her right in the photo of herself and two similar looking girls "—the other one is my cousin, but we all lived on the same street, and Marcy might as well have been the third sister."

She continues down the line, telling me about all the people in the pictures, filling me in on inside jokes and gossip without me ever having to ask. I struggle to keep my eyes focused on the pictures, because she's so fucking beautiful with her hair still damp, a giant T-shirt covering her curvy body, and the scent of the body oil I now know is the source of her unique scent.

"Maybe there is something to this witch thing. How did you know I was standing here wishing I already knew all the stories behind your photos?"

Brigid laughs, and we finally turn to look at each other. "Hate to burst your bubble, but witchcraft has nothing to do with it. You wear your heart on your sleeve. I could practically feel you over here brooding about not knowing much about me. As if knowing each other three weeks and making out twice means you should know my life story."

"I think we did a little more than make out, Sunshine."

She shrugs and blushes slightly, something so fucking cute it takes everything I have not to pull her to me.

The silence between us is both comfortable and tense. I don't feel the need to fill it with meaningless talk. But an electricity hangs in the air, like a static charge waiting for you to touch your finger to a surface to release the spark.

"So, you want some tea?"

I place my hand on her hip and pull her tight against me. "No, but I'll take you."

Chapter 28

Brigid

His lips find mine and it's like my whole body exhales in relief.

His lips are a soft contrast to the bristling stubble of his beard. This is different from the other night. Not frantic and needy. Gentle, searching. It's a question and an answer.

"I dream about kissing you." He switches to kissing down my neck. "Fantasize about it. I swear, I lose time thinking about all the ways I want to kiss you."

Some mysterious muscle low in my belly squeezes, twists, a pressure building just behind my belly button pushing down, begging for release already after a few kisses.

"I wake up disappointed but hard after dreaming you're asleep in my arms."

My breath catches in my throat, an audible gasp that he immediately swallows with his mouth.

"Take myself into my hand and jerk off thinking about you out on that dock. You on the porch. But you know what it is every time that finishes me off—" he kisses across my cheek to my ear, whispering the words that are simultaneously sweet and filthy "—what it is that makes me fucking moan and spill my cum all over my sheets?"

"What?" He's stolen my breath so that the word is little more than a wisp of air across my coal chords.

"It's this. Kissing you. Holding you. All the filthy things I want to do to you, with you, and the thing that has me losing control like a teenager is the thought of having free access to kiss you whenever I want."

Holy shit. I'm done fighting this pull between us. Fuck my history and baggage. Fuck our differences and every inconsequential reason I've kept him at arm's length since moving in. The connection here is undeniable.

"Take me. I'm yours."

Orion pulls away, his moss green eyes searching my face, one hand still gripping my hip while the other cups the back of my head, fingers tangled in my damp hair.

"Don't say that if you don't mean it, Sunshine. I'm already half in love with you. You take off the caution tape and I swear to God I'm not going to be able to stop from falling the rest of the way." His fingers curl into my hair, tugging the strands just enough to sting slightly, but not hurt. I'm not sure he realizes he's doing it, like he's holding on for dear life to the edge of a cliff.

I knew he was developing feelings for me, I'd have to be an idiot not to notice. But love? The thought is thrilling and terrifying all at once. I've proven my judgment when it comes to men is flawed to say the least. William showed me the slightest bit of interest and I practically fell at his feet. It took years and becoming a mother to see all the ways that asshole manipulated me. Yet, something deep inside me says that is not Orion.

Plus, the idea that his man, this beautiful, strong man, could fall for me is incredible. I think I'm beautiful in my own way, but I also realize I'm far from conventionally attractive. Orion could quite literally have anyone he wanted. I wish I knew what it was about me that pulls him in.

"Why do you call me Sunshine? There is nothing about me that's bright." It's something I've wondered about since the first time he used the endearment.

He huffs out a small chuckle and presses his forehead to mine. "When I first met you, I thought of you as a storm cloud determined to hide everything behind a thick wall of darkness. But you made my life so much brighter. It wasn't that you were a storm cloud, it was that everything else was dimmed by your brilliance."

Fuck me. Like literally, I need him to fuck me now.

"I mean it, I'm yours. You're mine. No caution tape."

The words are barely out of my lips when he moves. Both hands grip my legs just under my ass and he lifts me up, my thighs automatically wrapping around his hips.

There are no more words, just our lips pressing together, our hands frantically searching for bare skin. I pull and tug at his shirt until it yanks free from between our bodies.

He puts me down on the Island and helps me pull the shirt off over his head to disappear behind him somewhere.

"I'm making you a couch. Someplace soft I can lay you down and do this properly." He groans as my hands explore the hard planes of his body. I've never been one that cared much about what kind of shape my lovers were in, but I would be lying if I said Orion's body didn't make me fucking crazy. "Or I'm fixing the hole in the floor in the other room so we can set up a room for Mica. Need to have you in a goddamn bed, but for now I am going to fuck your brains out on this ugly ass counter."

The way he kisses me, as if it's not simply a meeting of our lips but our whole lives joining, is enough to make my head spin.

"I fucking love these nightgowns. Hiding everything I want to see; making me imagine that juicy ass and heavy tits." He grips the hem of my sleep shirt and pulls, not up over my head, but apart, ripping it in two until he has to reposition his hands higher and keep ripping until the thin cotton hangs open revealing my body. "I'll replace it, but fuck I needed to do that."

His chest heaves with each breath as he takes me in, no bra or panties. Yeah, I was feeling a little slutty and was hoping this would happen. To be honest I knew it would. Had been thinking about it all day as I watched Orion sweating and laughing with his friends on my roof. He'd stop every once in a while and stretch his back out, probably in pain from hunching over to rip shingles from the room or nail new ones down.

All the men abandoned their shirts pretty early on in the warm fall sun. Tearing my eyes from the flex of Orion's muscles as he worked may have been the hardest thing I've ever done. All day I silently counted the minutes until his friends, as wonderful as they were, would leave.

Now the moment is here and he's just looking at me. "Are you just going to stand there?" I slip the ruined nightgown down my arms, letting it pool beneath me on the counter. "Or are you going to do some of those filthy things you've been fantasizing about?"

With a growl, Orion's pushing between my thighs. His hands cup the back of my head, devouring my mouth. The way this man kisses me is insane, like he's pouring everything, every thought and emotion, into the press of our lips and tangle of our tongues. I can't get enough, want this all the time. It makes me wonder how I've kept him at arm's length for as long as I have.

His hands caress down my back, pulling at my hips to drag me to the edge of the counter. Tight against his body so his cock, covered in gray sweatpants that have no business being that sexy, is nestled right against by aching pussy.

"Fuck, woman, you have no idea how insane you drive me." The slide of his lips down my neck makes me shudder. His warm breath skates across my skin with every word whispered in reverence. "Every day I leave my cabin and tell myself I'm not going to look at your side of the pond. I'm not going to come over and find some excuse to see you. Talk to you. Just be in the same general area as you." Instead of taking the obvious route down to my chest, Orion nips across my shoulder and down my arm. The move is very Gomez and Morticia and I won't lie, that thought makes me swoon a little. "Someday I want you to tell me what every single one of these tattoos means. Why you picked them."

A smile creeps up my face. "I can tell you now. I saw them, thought they were cool, and got them. No deeper meaning except this one." I hold up my wrist to show him the series of black dots and lines. "It says Mica in Morse Code. My parents stayed with us for a few weeks after he was born. The day before they went home, I went and got this."

Gently, Orion takes my hand and kisses the sensitive skin on my wrist.

"Do you have any tattoos? I didn't really get a clear view of your body the other night."

"Let me fix that." Orion backs up one step, dropping his sweatpants. He turns in a circle, seemingly not the least bit shy about his nakedness. Not that he should be. His body is incredible, and that dick. It juts out from his pelvis long and hard and practically begging me to touch it.

"No ink," he says with a smirk.

"A virgin."

He pushes between my thighs again, pressing his hard length against my center. "Not quite."

Talk time is over now. Simultaneously, we move in for a deep, sensual kiss. Not quite as frantic as a few nights ago out on the porch, but no less intense. I pull his hair from the messy bun piled on top of his head. It falls in wavy curtains, still damp in places from his shower. Subtle scents of vanilla and cedar waft to my nose.

"I think I might be obsessed with your hair." I weave my fingers into the strands, palming the back of his head and arching into him so we are chest to chest.

"I'll let you braid it someday."

Even when I'm so wound up, ready to explode, this man manages to make me laugh. Why does that make him sexier?

"I need you inside me. For real this time. Please tell me you have a condom."

In a flash, Orion is pulling away from me and bending to pick up his discarded sweatpants. "I honestly debated about bringing one. Thought it might be too presumptuous. So I brought two."

"Smart man."

I watch in fascination as he tears the wrapper open, pulls the condom out, and rolls it down his thick shaft. I expect him to step between my thighs again, to push his way into me like I desperately want, but instead he drops to his knees before me, kissing his way up from my knee to my thigh, his destination obvious.

"Seriously, Orion, you don't need to do that. I am more than ready."

"Seriously, Brigid, if I don't have a taste of you I am going to lose my mind. Your pussy is a craving I can't deny myself any longer." His mouth meets my center, both his palms press against my inner thighs, spreading me wider. His tongue flicks at my throbbing clit, pleasure immediately coursing through my veins, making my limbs go weak until I fall back against the counter.

All at once I realize I'm about to scream and that is most definitely going to wake the baby, which will cut our fun short. I slap a hand over my mouth, muffling the sounds just in time.

Between my legs, Orion slips a finger inside me, pumping it in and out a few times before adding another. The pleasure is so intense, my legs squeeze closed around his head, yet with my free hand I reach down to fist his hair and pull him closer against me.

Within seconds, I'm coming, my body writhing and twitching as if possessed. Orion rides each wave of my orgasm like a champion rodeo cowboy. As it ebbs away, he gentles his kisses, placing a final kiss against my thigh as he climbs to his feet.

Not wanting to miss a second of what is about to happen, I manage to peel myself from the counter, propping myself up on my elbows to watch as Orion lines himself up at my entrance.

He pauses, and I look up to see him gazing at me. "You're sure?"

I sit up the rest of the way, wrapping my arms around his neck and giving him a slow, deep kiss before pulling back once again. "I'm sure. I'm yours."

My words seem to sooth something inside him. In one strong thrust, he fills me to the brim. "Mine."

Chapter 29

Orion

That single word echoes inside my mind as I bury myself deep inside Brigid's body. That first thrust is like a coming home and an out of body experience all at once. My head spins with the way her cunt squeezes around my cock. But my soul feels at ease for the first time in weeks.

Brigid falls back onto her elbows, giving me room to pull back, only to push forward once again. I can't look away from the image of my dick disappearing into her, then sliding back out glistening with her arousal.

With each thrust, her breaths increase until she's panting. Moans slip out, no matter how hard she's trying to be quiet. "Sunshine, you have to be quiet."

"I know, I'm trying," she whispers around another moan. "I haven't had sex in almost two years. Since I got pregnant." Her head falls back between her shoulders, her thighs tightening around my hips. "I don't remember it feeling this good."

Goddamn. Those words do something primal to my psyche. Satisfies a deep seeded need to make my woman feel good. I'm going to work every day she'll have me to give her everything she needs. Wants.

Falling into a steady rhythm, I let my hands wander over her body. Trace the devastating curves from her hips to her waist to her chest. These fucking tits are going to be the end of me. I gather them in my hands, pressing them together and licking the line where they meet. "Someday I'm going to fuck these. You on your knees in front of me, begging me to come all over your neck and tits."

Brigid writhes beneath me, her volume rising around us.

"Bridge, if you can't keep quiet, I'm going to have to do it for you."

She picks up her head and stares me dead in the eye. "Do it," she moans.

"As you fucking wish." I pull myself from the warmth of her body, pick her up from the counter and set her on her feet. Brigid's eyes go wide with shock, her mouth falling open to protest either the loss of me between her legs or my manhandling her. I don't wait long enough to find out.

In the next second I'm spinning her around and bending her over the counter, chest flat on the wood surface. Only a few seconds have passed since I pulled out, but already it is too long. Plunging back into her sweet pussy has me clenching back my own groan.

"Oh, oh, God. If you were trying to keep me quiet I don't think this was the way to do it, Orion." She gasps and moans through each word.

"No, this is." I bring one hand around to cover her mouth, muffling the next gasp. "What do you think, Sunshine, this work for you?"

She nods enthusiastically and pushes her hips back into me, her silent hint to get going. Not one to disappoint, I grip the edge of the counter by her hip and slam back home, reveling in the vibrations of her muffled sounds on my palm. "Fuck, you feel so good squeezing me. Trying to make me come before I'm ready."

She rotates her hips in little circles as I pump into her and the move nearly takes me out at the knees it's so fucking hot. I pull her up until she has to plant her hands on the counter to hold herself up. "Little tease, do that move again."

She does as she's told and swivels her hips while I fuck her. My gaze is locked on her ass, watching the round globes. Without thinking, I bring the hand that isn't covering her mouth back and let it fly in a light, but not too light, spank. She jumps a little, looking at me back over her shoulder.

The sight of her dark eyes, molten with excitement, my hand covering her mouth, her cheeks flush with excursion nearly does me in. Pretty soon I'm going to need to start reciting the scientific names of every tree in these woods to keep from blowing my load too soon.

"Did you like that, my little tease?"

She grinds back against me, nodding again.

I loosen my hand from around her mouth and slide it from her mouth down to around her neck.

"Let me hear you say it."

"Yes, mmmm, I liked it."

I do it again, a little harder this time and she gasps, then moans, melting down from her palms to her elbows.

"Can't let that mouth go for a second and already getting too loud again." I return my hand to her mouth and start fucking her in earnest. No more talking, I need to get her there because I'm not sure how long I can hold on with the view of her ass and her body splayed out before me.

"Bridge, reach down and play with that needy little clit." Once again she doesn't hesitate. Shifting down so her chest is once again planted on the counter, freeing her hands.

Her fingers slide back, past her clit to circle her opening where I am thrusting in and out. Those curious fingers caressing my shaft before disappearing back up to play with the bundle of nerves I know are begging for her attention.

Within seconds I feel the fluttering of her inner muscles, her panting against my palm picks up speed, and the moans grow in intensity, even behind my hand. "That's right, Sunshine, make yourself come all over my dick."

Beneath me, she bucks and squirms, her body practically convulsing as the pleasure takes over. After a minute, Brigid pulls her hand from between her legs and grips the edge of the counter, but her orgasm continues to rage as I thrust in and out of her like a man with a mission. One mission: ring every ounce of pleasure out of this woman.

After a while she reaches back and grips my hip, squeezing tight.

I slow, but don't stop, relaxing into a lazy slide in and out, relishing each drag of my cock inside her soaked cunt. "Had enough?" I whisper in her ear.

I take my hand away and Brigid sucks in a breath. "You haven't come yet."

"You need to make yourself come one more time before I let go. You know why?"

She shakes her head.

"Because you get three orgasms for every one of mine. Because I am a motherfucking feminist."

A laugh bursts out from her lips, and she peeks back over her shoulder. "Well, Mr. Feminist, unfortunately for you even when I have a toy and am by myself the most I ever get is two, so I think you are going to have to settle for that."

I smack her ass again and her laugh turns from mirth to a moan. "That's for doubting me." Another on the other side. "That's because I know you love it. Now, you owe me a third."

"Holy shit, I think you might actually be able to do it." She meets my next thrust with a backward one of her own. "Only one way to find out."

"This time I want to watch your face as you come on my dick." I pull out, spinning her around once again and lifting her onto the counter.

"You know, I've been wondering how you managed to get me in from the car that day you picked us from the side of the road. I'm not exactly little. But seeing how you are tossing me around right now makes me kind of sad I missed being carried by you."

"Well, we can't have you sad when there is a third orgasm waiting to be had." I push my way inside her once again, Brigid gasping as I fill her probably very sensitive pussy. Once I'm seated to the hilt, I wrap her legs around my waist, then her arms around my neck, and lift her from the island.

Every push up, squat, curl, bench press and the dozens of other exercises I've tortured myself with over the years are all suddenly worth it. Because the truth is, Brigid is not a small girl. It's part of what I love about her. All those soft curves drive me fucking crazy. I may not have known it at the time, but I've built my body specifically so that I can throw this woman around however she pleases.

No, she's not a small woman, but bouncing her on my cock is no hardship. It's a fucking honor.

Within seconds, Brigid is right there on the edge again, and frankly, so am I. We're both getting loud, and I don't have a hand free to quiet us.

"Fuck, there is no way we're making it through this quietly." With Brigid still clinging to me and undulating on my dick, I turn and head toward the door.

"Holy shit, what are you doing?"

"Getting us someplace where we won't wake up the house." Brigid slips slightly when I have to release one hand to open the front door of the cabin, but in less than a second I am supporting her once again and stomping out to the middle of the clearing. "Scream all you want now, Sunshine. Let go."

Standing under the night sky, the grass under my feet, and Brigid wrapped around my body, is heady fucking stuff. I can feel the pressure building in my balls; the point of no return is closer than I want it. I need to follow through on my promise of three orgasms, and for that I need my hands.

Carefully, I lower myself to one knee, then the other, rearranging us until I am lying flat on my back in the grass and Brigid straddles me. "Ride me Brigid, ride my dick until you come."

No further encouragement is needed. She rolls her hips, grinding her clit against me then bouncing up and down on my dick several times, before grinding back down. No longer needing to worry about waking up Mica, her screams and moans fill the night air.

With my hands no longer occupied, I am free to caress her everywhere. Her hips, legs, stomach and chest are all fair game. I'm holding on by a thread with her body on display, her tits undulating with each thrust. I need that orgasm from her.

Reaching between us, I press my thumb to her clit, rubbing it in firm but gentle circles. Within seconds, she's detonating around me, her body collapsing onto my chest while I continue to massage her clit with my hand caught between us. I plant my feet and drive up into her, my own roars of pleasure mixing with hers as I let go and fill the condom.

We're a mess of limbs and sweat still writhing against each other, drawing out our mutual orgasms as long as possible.

Finally depleted, we gasp for air, pressed together, my arms wrapped tight around her back, her hands smoothing over my arms and shoulders.

As I stare up at the inky black sky dotted with stars, I realize there is no going back. I've fallen completely and totally in love with my neighbor.

* * *

"I'm serious, I'm making an entire furniture set for you. This is insane."

Brigid giggles in my arms, a sound I get the feeling she is not used to making. "I don't know, I kinda like that Mica has almost the entire cabin as his play area."

"I'm all for giving the kid space to roam, but you have nowhere to sit and relax. Two chairs that look like they might dissolve into sawdust and a rocking chair are not adequate cuddle options." With my feet planted on the floor I send us on a gentle sway in the rocking chair I gave Brigid after she moved in. After I saw her across the pond in that creaky old piece of shit, I knew I couldn't have her ass seated on anything but the best.

"But the rocking chair is working pretty well for me right now," she responds. Her head rests against my shoulder, one of the many quilts I've seen hanging around the cabin draped around the both of us. "Who knew you would be such a snuggler?"

I let a rumble of a chuckle be my answer. The truth is, I never used to want to cuddle with women before this. Sure, I gave the obligatory cool down and aftercare, never disrespected the women that I slept with, but cuddling was never a part of that.

After we caught our breath out in the yard, I carried Brigid back into the house and straight to this chair, only stopping to grab the quilt. Should I have deposited her back in bed to get some sleep and made my way to my own home? Yeah, probably. But the thought of leaving her made my stomach twist and turn sour.

"Besides, I'm not sure how much longer we'll be living up here."

I swear, my heart stops beating and the breath freezes in my lungs.

"Hopefully my application gets approved, and I'll need to be closer to town to start setting up the shop. I'd like to be open by Thanksgiving so I can cash in on the greatest capitalist holiday in the world, Black Friday."

"Yeah, that makes sense." Try as I might to keep my tone neutral, I know my displeasure at no longer having Brigid and Mica on the mountain with me comes through loud and clear.

"That's why as much as I appreciate you fixing the roof, and doing all the other little things around here I know you've fixed and haven't told me about but I have definitely noticed, you should probably stop. You're just improving the place for your stupid mayor. He'll probably turn around and rent this place out for twice the price now that it is actually half-livable." If I'm not mistaken, I get the sense Brigid doesn't love the thought of someone else living in the cabin either. Or maybe it is wishful thinking on my part. I know she said she was mine, no caution tape, but were those just words in the heat of the moment?

The words form on my tongue. I need to tell her that I'm about to buy the cabin and acre of land around it back from Burt. Lawyers are drafting the documents. Any day now I'll go down to Town Hall, hand over a huge chunk of my life savings, and this place will finally once again belong to my family as it was always intended. I should tell her, but I don't. Fear keeps me silent. Both of her reaction and that Burt will pull some of his antics and none of this will actually happen.

Brigid takes my silence as something other than the war of to tell or not to tell going on inside my head and tilts her face up to look at me. Her beauty nearly knocks me the fuck over. Nothing but the moonlight streaming in through the window illuminating her flawless, creamy skin. The nose ring in her septum, the piercings along her ear. I even spot a tiny little scar on her eyebrow where there must have been another piercing at one point.

"Just because Mica and I are going to move down to town doesn't mean this has to stop." She rubs her hand across my chest, it's a comforting gesture, but my dick takes it as something else altogether. We both ignore his valiant efforts to come back to life. "You hang out in town a lot. Now you'll just have

another reason. Besides, I'm pretty sure I'm going to need furniture for the store and whatever place we land."

She's right, of course she is. But why does this place without
her feel less like my home?

Chapter 30

Brigid

"Oh, this is getting crazy." The man that went from my annoying neighbor, to not so annoying neighbor, to whatever it is he is now. And he is at it once again.

Fixing shit.

It's like he can't help himself. No matter how many times I tell him it's not worth it, that I'll be moving out as soon as I find something suitable in town, he continues to make improvements.

Finding a new place is turning out to be harder than I thought. In a town this small there aren't a ton of opportunities for rentals. The house Roxy had called to tell me about was already snatched up by the time I got around to calling the owner.

A little part of my heart recognizes I might have dragged my feet a little bit on calling about the place. This little shit hole of a cabin has grown on me. So have the fringe benefits of a hot as hell neighbor whose favorite hobby appears to be giving me orgasms. And home improvements on a home that isn't even his.

Not to mention the way he always takes Mica into account. Whether it is cooking a meal or asking us to go on a walk, Orion always makes it clear Mica is not just a part of my life he has to deal with, but a part he welcomes and wants to incorporate into his life as well. Considering Mica's own father had no desire to meet him, Orion's efforts have me falling far faster than I am ready for.

"Listen, I can't stand the thought of you and Mica living here with a literal hole to the ground in one of the rooms. And since you refuse to move over to my cabin—" he looks at me with those puppy dog eyes that make me go a little mushy in my stomach and I shoot my most stern look back at him "—then the only other option is for me to fix it."

He first floated the idea of us moving over to his property two days after the incredible kitchen-slash-yard sexcapades. I turned him down before he could get the words fully out of his mouth. I don't care if he does spend most of his time here. Moving in together after knowing a man for a couple weeks is insane. I should know, I followed a man across the country after dating him for a few months.

True, I've been avoiding reading my own tarot cards for fear that they are going to show me what that little part of my heart keeps telling me. That Orion is different from any man I've ever known.

It's been a week since he first asked and he's dropped hints around the topic every single day. Not pressuring me necessarily, just little asides like mentioning the tub in his cabin has jets. Or that he could make an office for me in the workshop. That if we slept in the same bed I could wake up to orgasms, too. Yeah, that one was tempting.

"Okay, close your eyes." Orion stands with one hand on the handle of the bedroom door I haven't opened since the day we moved in. A sweet mixture of excitement and anxiety shows clear as day in his eyes. I love how his emotions are right there on the surface for the world to see. He doesn't shove them down and hide them like most men I know.

"Orion, you just patched the hole in the floor, I don't need a whole reveal." Mica and I spent yesterday in town looking at a couple of the open storefronts in the town square that have stood empty for years. My license application hasn't been approved yet, but I want to be ready when it is. And I think I found the perfect little place. It's right on the corner of the main road into the square, only two blocks away from the cafe. There is even a daycare center two blocks away where I could enroll Mica. He's almost a year and his first experience with other kids were with Paula and Sam's kids.

Apparently while we were gone exploring the town, Orion was here, hard at work fixing a house we may not be occupying for much longer.

"I might have done a little more than just the floor." While a slight blush creeps up his cheeks, Orion pushes the door open to reveal a completely different room than had been there the day before. Yes, the floor is patched. In fact, I wouldn't be able to tell you where the hole had been at this point. But besides that, the place has been totally scrubbed, blackout curtains hung in the window, complete with a tie back so that the sun can stream in when Mica isn't napping.

There is no mistaking this room is meant to be a nursery because sitting in the corner is a crib so gorgeous I actually gasp. The sides of it are a beautiful medium brown tone with spindles spaced far enough apart for Mica to be able to see through but not get stuck. The head and foot of the crib are solid pieces with decorative trim laid in gradually decreasing squares and painted black. There is even a mattress ready to go with a sheet in a dark green.

Above the crib are wooden letters spelling out Mica's name and they perfectly match the tones in the furniture. On the rest of the walls are black-and-white photos of trees and forest creatures that I have a sneaking suspicion were taken in this very forest. My favorite is one of Spruce sitting regally on the end of the dock looking into the distance. Each is placed in a beautiful gold frame that look similar to the ones on the mantel.

"Orion, this is incredible."

I turn to see the biggest smile stretching across his beautiful face. "I'm glad you like it. I designed the crib so we can convert it into a twin bed when the time comes for him to level up. Or we can just take one side off as a transition."

We.

Why does that one small word, just two letters, stir up so many emotions?

Excitement, because having someone give a gift as thoughtful as this is amazing and not something I'm used to from anyone outside my immediate family.

Hope, that maybe this thing with Orion isn't just a fleeting arrangement born from proximity and convenience.

Fear, because after everything William put me through, opening myself back up to entwining my life with another man could result in even more heartache. But also, because I'm a Single Mom. That title is something I take pride in. I don't need a man or partner to help me. Mica and I are our own little unit, and allowing Orion into that is scary as fuck.

"You just did this so you can fuck me in my bed finally," I tease, trying to diffuse some of the enormity this gesture holds.

It is the wrong thing to say, because despite no longer facing Orion, I can feel the shift in the air. That subtle static of hurt that fills the room.

"No. I did it because for now at least, you guys shouldn't live in a place open to the elements. And because the Pack 'n Play isn't meant to be a full-time sleep solution. But also, because it made me feel good to do it." He doesn't hide the pain my words caused, because that isn't who he is.

Orion doesn't hide things, he puts it all out there on the table for anyone to inspect and dissect.

"I'm sorry." I turn to him, trying to let my sincerity shine through as much as his hurt just did. "I'm not used to this." I wave to the room but also at him. "Accepting help and grand gestures isn't something I have a lot of experience in. It's hard to know how to react."

Over the last couple days, I've opened up to Orion more about Mica's father. It has become our routine to cuddle on the rocking chair together, me draped across his lap, and talk until both our eyes are drooping. It's made for some rough mornings, but we've gotten to know each other so fast thanks to those conversations. I told him about the cheating, the on again off again nature of our relationship, the manipulating. The way I dropped everything and gave up my future to support his dreams. My determination to not repeat the same mistakes.

"Plus, even though this place is where we live now, that is temporary. I get the feeling that you think if you can make this place livable, we'll stay up here permanently. I need you to know that isn't part of my plan, and I am sticking to my plan."

Understanding settles on his face. "I know that as soon as a place is open in town, you'll move out. But everything here is movable." He crosses the few feet separating us, cups my face in his huge hands. "Lucky for you, I know how to take the crib apart and put it back together. I just wanted you to know that I want this—" he leans his forehead down onto mine, hunching to bridge the gap in our heights "—isn't temporary for me. I know that you and Mica are a package deal and I want to take his needs into account as much as I take yours."

Tears burn behind my eyes. I'm not a crier. I'm a deal with shit and keep hustling person. Tears don't solve anything, they only blur your vision, making it harder to see the way forward. But these tears don't feel like something blocking my vision, they feel like a cleansing away of the grime years of pain have built to obscured how I see things.

So, I let them cascade down my cheeks as Orion silently wipes them away.

"Thank you," I sniff. "This room is amazing. The crib is incredible. You are pretty great, too." Gently, I tilt my head back and kiss Orion's lips. Unlike most of our other kisses, this isn't a kiss to ignite something. It's one that locks something into place. Maybe our hearts, as terrifying as that is.

"Let's see what the little man thinks." Orion kisses my forehead and then turns back to the tiny living room where Mica's play area still overwhelms the space.

I talked Orion out of building us a couch because it would have meant the area where Mica could play would have to shrink. I also like our cuddle session in the rocking chair. But in exchange, he made me promise as soon as I found a place in town, I would let him design something for my new space.

The man quickly stealing my heart returns a moment later with Mica perched on one of his muscled forearms, with the other arm banded around his tummy, keeping him secure against Orion's chest. Mica's eyes take in the room, but let's be real, he's nine months old so he could give two shits about what he sees.

Still, Orion walks him around to each of the pictures and tells him about them. They get to the photo of Spruce and Mica starts happily kicking his legs and babbling *pup pup pup.*

After they've toured the whole room, Orion puts Mica down in the crib, sitting him in the middle of the mattress. At first Mica appears totally affronted, as if he would say *how dare you put me down* if he had the words. But then he pulls himself to standing using the side of the crib and starts bouncing up and down, giggling at the funny face Orion makes through the bars.

I'm about to join them by the crib when my ringtone echoes in from where my phone sits charging on the kitchen counter. "I'll be right back, that's probably the warehouse manager. They were having some inventory issues."

Orion throws me a thumbs-up from over his shoulder and goes back to charming my baby.

But when I pick the phone up from the counter, the caller ID says "Town Hall" instead of "A&D Distribution". "Hello?"

"Is this Brigid Wolke?" I recognize the high-pitched, nasal voice instantly as the mayor's secretary. She spent nearly twenty minutes acting as a go-between for the mysterious Burt and I the day I got the business license application.

"Yes, it is." A sudden avalanche of nerves falls over me. Is this the call telling me my application has been rejected and we moved all this way for nothing? I turn to look through the new nursery door and recognize it wasn't totally for nothing.

"Mayor Lickinbill is happy to let you know that your application has been approved. We need you to come down to the office to sign your acceptance." She says the words totally flat, as if this isn't something worth celebrating.

"Oh my gosh, that is amazing!" I can't help but jump up and down a few times before getting a hold of myself. "What time does your office close? I can be there in like forty minutes."

"Take your time, I'm here until five."

I glance at the clock and see it is barely even lunch time. I don't that care this will be the second time I make the trek into town in as many days. I want the business license finalized as soon as humanly possible, before the mayor can reconsider, which I have heard happened in the past. "Great, I'll be there soon."

Orion is right there when I disconnect the call, looking at me with curiosity on his face and Mica in his arms. "What's going on?"

"My application was approved!" I circle my arms around Orion and Mica, gathering them into a giant hug.

"Holy shit, Brigid, that's amazing. Burt finally did something right for once."

"I need to head down there to pick up the official license before he can realize he just approved a shop that sells witchy paraphernalia."

All at once Orion goes still under my touch. "You're going down there now?"

"Absolutely, I might not have met my slum lord yet, but from everything I've heard I need to make this thing legally binding ASAP." I rush into my bedroom, pulling open the dresser to retrieve a plain long sleeve black t-shirt to cover all my tattoos. Should I take out the nose ring just in case? Deciding it can't hurt, I remove the small silver hoop and leave it on top of the dresser.

Orion stands in the doorway, Spruce at his feet and Mica in his arms. "Listen, there is something I should tell you before you head down there."

"Can it wait until I get back? I'll bring something from Dolly's and make you dinner to celebrate. I don't want to give him any more time to think than he's already had and it's such a long drive to town." I finish changing and slip on a simple pair of black flats that sit under my bed. "Do you mind watching Mica? I highly doubt he'll find signing paperwork entertaining, and it is getting close to nap time."

"Yeah, of course. But really, we need to talk."

"We will as soon as I get back." I plant my hands on his shoulders and press up onto my tip toes to give both my men pecks on the cheek. "I swear I won't be long."

Before he can get another word out, I'm rushing through the cabin, grabbing my keys from the hook by the door.

"Wish me luck!"

Chapter 31

Orion

Brigid left over two hours ago.

It takes half an hour to get to Town Hall. Probably an hour stuck there jumping through whatever bullshit hoops Burt is going to throw at her. Then a half hour back here. She should be back soon.

I should have told her.

There had been so many opportunities over the last week. Every time she said I was doing too much to improve someone I hate's property.

The countless times we laid together on the floor, the grass, in the rocking chair, basking in the post orgasm haze talking about our hopes and dreams. I could have told her then about one of my dreams coming true. Because, yes, I agreed to pay the high price for Burt's cabin because of Brigid. But the more I have to deal with Burt and his trying to weasel more out of me as we get closer to closing, the more I realize I want this for my family, too.

But I chickened out every time. I didn't want her to think I was trying to manipulate her into staying. After all the things her ex has done to tear her down, to destroy the trust in her own judgment, literally buying a cabin for her seemed like a pretty obvious way to manipulate her into staying. But now the lie of omission seems worse.

"Mica, let me give you a little advice." The little guy is sitting in a makeshift playpen I threw together made of couch cushions and boxes I had laying around the workshop. Spruce sits at his side taking his self-appointed role as baby bodyguard very seriously. I'm editing a video of me splitting wood from a few weeks ago that I've been procrastinating on. Another thing I've been keeping from the woman I love, like a fucking idiot.

The three of us have had a full day together. So far, we've crawled around in a pile of leaves, Mica giggling like crazy as I tossed handfuls into the air and Spruce tried to catch the leaves midair. Then we took a walk around the pond, had a snack, and made our way up to my office in the loft of the cabin so I could get some work done. Mica is starting to look sleepy, so I'm hoping he'll take a nap soon so his mom and I can talk when she gets back. "Don't start keeping secrets. Because once you start, it is really *really* hard to stop."

He gapes at me like he knows exactly what I'm talking about, so I keep going. Turns out the easiest person in the world to talk to is one that doesn't know what you're saying.

"Take for instance, my family." I turn back to the computer, continuing to shave down a clip where I'm splitting logs, making sure my face stays hidden either behind my hair or my arms as I swing. "I've been lying to them for years about the whole social media influencer thing. At first, I was embarrassed. I thought making videos online was something for teenagers and didn't want to get the inevitable ribbing from my siblings.

"But then everything kept getting bigger and bigger. Lying has become like a full-time job now. So not telling them about the cabin has become more normal to me than telling them. Keeping everything to myself is second nature. If I had just been honest in the beginning, I wouldn't have this constant debate of when and what to be honest about."

I turn to gauge Mica's reaction to my sage advice, but the guy is out like a light, breathing softly with one hand clutching Spruce's ear who sits protectively next to him. "Glad we had this talk, Buddy."

I turn back to the computer, whittling away at the video until it hits that sweet spot of being over a minute so it will be able to earn money, but keeping it short enough that people won't get bored and scroll away too soon. The whole shirtless thing tends to keep people tuned in, too.

The whole time my thoughts are consumed with how the meeting with Burt is going. Will he bring up selling the cabin to me? Will she be pissed?

Sure, at first I bought the cabin hoping I could improve it enough that she would stay longer, if not forever. But if the past few days have proved anything, it's that a longer commute will not make a difference in what we are. There may not be a label attached to it yet, but I know what it is for me. Everything.

We've spent nearly every day together. The four us, because yes, Spruce absolutely counts. We've gone on hikes, sat around the fire pit, caught lightning bugs, sat in my cabin and read. And yeah, we've had a shit ton of sex, just about everywhere except a bed. For some reason she's avoided coming to mine, and obviously hers won't work since Mica has been sharing a room with her.

So walls, floors, counters, tables, the dock, everywhere you can think of has become another surface to have my fill of Brigid. But we have yet to be in a bed. The closest we came was my couch while Mica slept in the stroller in my room.

Did I make the nursery in her cabin so we could finally make our way to a bed? No, all the reasons I gave her were the truth. But I would be lying if I said I wasn't hoping to be invited into her bedroom at some point.

Downstairs, the unmistakable squeak of my door opening then closing again echoes up to where I'm sitting in the loft. I'm on my feet and heading down the stairs before Brigid can so much as take two steps into the cabin.

"Hey, how'd it go?" I search her face for any hint of what could have happened with Burt. "Did you finally get to meet our infamous mayor?"

Her eyes shift from the papers in her hand up to mine. She knows. I can see it there behind her beautiful brown irises. Burt told her. Words are lost to me. Stuck in my throat are a million excuses and explanations. But not a single one can fight its way out.

"Yeah, it went fine. I got the license." She holds up the papers. "Even signed the lease for the storefront I liked in the town square."

I nod. Waiting for the other shoe to drop. It hangs there in the air between us, like a bubble floating around waiting for something to pop it.

"That's great, when do you get to start setting up?"

Brigid surveys the cabin, maybe looking for Mica, but I can't tell. "I already got the key to the shop from the landlord. Rose is her name, she said she'd been trying to rent it out for years."

"Yeah, she owns the B&B in town. I didn't realize she owned any other property in town though." This is the weirdest conversation ever. I keep wanting to look over my shoulder, expecting to see an actual huge elephant in the room waiting to be acknowledged. Both our words are stilted, dancing around the thing taking up all the oxygen in the room. "Maybe I can go down with you tomorrow and get some measurements, see if there are some shelving units in the workshop that might fit. Or I could make something custom."

She nods absently, her eyes totally unfocused. In an instant her gaze snaps up to mine. "Where's Mica?"

"Upstairs, sleeping in my office."

Without another word she's passing me by, heading up the stairs. "I should get him and head back. Thanks again for watching him."

"Yeah, I mean he's a great kid. Spruce did most of the heavy lifting keeping him entertained." I make it up to the loft just a few steps after Brigid, who is frozen in place by my computer. My computer that I never closed down and has my editing software open with a paused shot of me, shirtless, swinging an ax over my head. You may not be able to see my face, but only an idiot would fail to connect the dots. And Brigid is no idiot. "I can explain."

"You know, there was always a little part of me that wondered why you seemed so familiar." She huffs out one of those laughs that you know have no actual humor behind them and shakes her head. "I thought maybe we knew each other in a past life. That it was my soul recognizing yours. But this was just *another* secret you kept. I don't know how I didn't see it before. A friend of mine sent me an article once trying to figure out who you were."

Her words are defeated, not heated or angry. I hate it. I want her to be pissed, I could work with pissed. Diffusing tense situations is something I can handle. But what do I do with disappointed acceptance? Like she was expecting this.

"Brigid, I wasn't trying to hide it from you, at least not to, I don't know, trick you or something." I just want her to turn around, to look at me standing right here with her, not the man on the screen that has little to nothing to do with who I actually am.

"I'm not mad at you."

"It kinda seems like you might be."

"Seriously, I'm not. Keeping this secret." Brigid nods at the computer screen, sighs and finally turns to face me. "Keeping your plans for the cabin secret, it all makes sense. I get it. I'm mad at myself, not you."

"Why would you be mad at yourself?"

She looks down at Mica, who is still sleeping soundly, no clue the turmoil that's going on around him. "Today was the first time I left Mica alone with someone that wasn't one of my parents. I didn't even think about it. I went rushing out, *knowing* you would take care of him. There wasn't a *single* hesitation."

I want to treasure those words. Make them physical and tuck them into my pocket to keep with me always. But she says them like she's absolutely devastated by the words. "That's a good thing. You can trust me with him. Look, he's good. We had lunch, we played, had a very one-sided chat. Why would you be mad at yourself for leaving your son with someone who cares about him?"

"Because I swore to myself that I would never again put my trust somewhere other than myself. I let William lie to me over and over again. I ignored my intuition and the incredibly obvious signs he didn't care enough to cover. I believed, truly believed him every time he told me he would change, would stop sleeping with his students, would help me get back into art school, that he loved me, and would do anything to get me back." She shakes her head and bends to pick up Mica.

His eyes flutter open for a moment, just long enough to see it's his mother. Then they close again, a tiny smile on his face as he nestles in against her chest. Brigid lays her cheek on top of his head and closes her eyes.

"When Mica was born, I promised him that it was just the two of us for life. Hearing William say he didn't want Mica, wanted me to get rid of him in whatever way I preferred, it broke me from the spell that man had me under. I finally saw him for what he was; a man that was one way on the surface but something completely different deep down inside. No more second and third chances. First chances were off the table, too. If the man who helped create him couldn't find it in himself to love Mica as much as I do, what chance would a stranger have?"

"I'm not a stranger."

Brigid finally opens her eyes and looks at me with pity. "You might as well be." The disappointment in that one sentence is like a punch to the gut. "Yes, I understand keeping your internet fame and buying the cabin a secret. But it proves what I should have already known, I can't trust what I see on the surface. That is where I should have kept things, on the surface. We were neighbors with benefits, it shouldn't have gone any deeper than that. I promise, I won't tell anyone your secrets."

As I search for a response, a way to combat the parallels she has drawn between myself and her shithead ex, Brigid makes her way down the stairs. Spruce follows her down, but I'm frozen in my spot. Weighed down by the literal nausea rumbling in my stomach at the thought that I could be anything like the man that turned his back on this amazing woman and his son.

Brigid's shitty old Honda rumbling to life and Spruce's whining bark finally snap me out of the war happening in my body.

Then I'm moving faster than I have ever before.

Chapter 32

Brigid

If there is one thing I'm sure of, it is that Orion will come after me. Not in a creepy stalker way, but in a caring, make sure I'm okay way.

Turning down the main street, I head toward the town square. The trees in the little park that is the center of town are well on their way to displaying their full fall brilliance.

On the left, I pass the store. My store. Right now, it is an empty shell, but I *will* turn it into something special. Nothing will sidetrack me from achieving that dream.

It isn't my destination now, though.

There is one place I know for sure Orion won't come looking for me. One place I know for a fact his entire family avoids. The library where Wesley works.

Pulling into the little parking lot, I go to pull the stroller from the trunk and remember I left it on Orion's front porch so they could take a walk while I was in town earlier. Orion can't figure out the baby wrap, no matter how many times I've shown him.

When I open the backseat door, Mica blinks his sleepy eyes open, holding out his arms for me as I unbuckle him from the car seat. I didn't bring anything with me. No diaper bag, no bottles, no snacks. Mica is fine now, but he'll be hungry soon. He'll need to be changed. Shame washes over me. Not only did I trust my son with a near stranger, but now I'm letting my relationship with that stranger affect Mica. This is why I swore it would just be the two of us, forever. I can't trust my judgment with men.

We push through the doors of the library and are instantly greeted with the soft reassurance libraries always inspire. Inside the doors is a long, waist-height counter covered in marble. Behind the desk are rows of towering wooden bookshelves filling the main room. Each shelf is stuffed to the brim with books of all shapes and colors, each with the telltale label on the spine. The building is obviously as old as the town itself, but it has been maintained beautifully with the unique touches of the original structure melded perfectly with modern updates to make it usable.

"Hey there, coming to get your official Amoresville Library card?" Wesley stands from a chair behind the desk. He pushes up his glasses with one finger and gives me a warm, welcoming smile.

"Sure, we'll take one."

There must be something in my voice, because Wesley tilts his head and squints his brown eyes at me.

"Why are you really here?"

"Hiding from anyone with the last name of Halsted," I mumble, a little embarrassed that I've come to the library with ulterior motives.

Wesley nods in understanding and chuckles a little. "Well, you came to the right place. I can't remember the last time a Halsted walked through those doors." He glances up at the analog clock above the desk. "Lucky for you I have about forty-five minutes before Minecraft club descends on us. Want the tour?"

I nod, not sure what else to say.

Together, we walk around the main floor, Wesley pointing out the different sections. "Newspapers and periodicals are in the corner, though we don't get a ton of takers for those anymore. Non-fiction is here including the sciences, politics, and history." He indicates a large section dominating the back half of the library. There are tables grouped together with partitions for people to use for studying or working. "Here is the computer lab. In a rural area like this we get lots of school kids that don't have access to reliable internet, so this room tends to be pretty busy." There are at least five computers currently in use out of the dozen spread throughout the room. "We also have a program to help teach our older citizens how to use them to apply for things like Medicare and Social Security."

"Wow, I didn't think a small-town library would be so tech-y."

"Trust me, it wasn't like this before I got the Director position three years ago." We keep walking down the main aisle, with Wesley pointing out all the different sections of the fiction area. "For romance you'll need to head down the street to the cafe. I've been able to change a lot of things around here, but the mayor and city council won't budge on the decency laws."

"I can't believe you aren't allowed to have any romance novels. What about clean romances? Or thrillers with sex? Or women's fiction that aren't actually romance? Or classics? Or heck, the Bible has tons of sex."

Wesley raises both hands and turns around to walk backward in front of me. "Trust me, preaching to the choir, Brigid. I've been singing the same song to the town leadership for years. I've been able to do some *creative* shelving in some cases. But for books that I can't slip by the stodgy folks in town, well I hand them off to Roxy for the cafe."

"You supply her with all those books?" She had hundreds of books in her cafe, I assumed she stocked them all herself. "Does your uncle know?"

He shrugs and turns back around, climbing a wide staircase at the back of the building. "Roxy and I are extremely good at keeping secrets. I hope you are as well."

I just smile slightly and nod. This town trades in secrets. It's not my place to reveal Wesley's private dealings any more than Orion's. But I hate that I have been put in a place to lie not only to Roxy about Orion's career and the cabin, but now the whole town, including Orion, about Wesley and Roxy's romance library annex.

Mica pipes up with his usual babbles from where he's propped on my hip. "I promise he doesn't have the vocabulary to give you away either."

"Well, if he hangs out here, we will change that."

At the top of the stairs it's like we've walked into a new world. Unlike the sedate beige pallet of the first floor, the second floor is an explosion of color. Each wall is painted in a different bright primary color. There are fake clouds hanging from the ceiling along with paper airplanes hanging by fishing wire. The bookcases here are much lower, easier for little hands to reach and adults to see over. There are rugs placed sporadically around with enormous bean bag chairs and cushions for sitting and reading. Against one wall there are short tables and chairs set up for puzzles and arts and crafts.

Themed displays are set up at the end of each row of bookcases. *Raptors vs. Raptors*—a whole section comparing the raptor class of birds to the dinosaurs. *Squirrel Month* with informative and fiction books about the furry little creatures. And an *ADD Awareness Month* display featuring books for both kids and parents.

"This is incredible." Mica appears to agree as he practically tries to dive out of my arms to get to a bin of toys sitting on a low table.

"Thanks. When I first got hired after college I was the children's librarian. This was my magnum opus."

"Seriously, this would put the children's library in Pittsburgh to shame."

Wesley tucks his chin down to his chest, hiding a smile that I don't miss. "Let the man loose." He nods to Mica still fighting my hold on him. "There's a reason we have the blocks and toys on the lowest shelves."

I put Mica down on the floor and he immediately crawls over to the bins and starts grabbing at the blocks and tossing them toward Wesley and I. Together we catch each one and begin stacking them, settling in cross-legged on the floor.

"So, you wanna talk about why you're hiding from every Halsted in town?" He keeps his eyes on the task of growing his tower, not looking at me directly, which puts me at ease for some reason.

Honestly, I'm not sure how much I want to go into this with Wesley. Coming here seemed like a good idea at the time, but now I can see how it would hurt Orion, which isn't my intent. "I needed some distance from Orion."

The tower Wesley had been working on tumbles over and he makes a big fake surprised face, sending Mica into a fit of laughter as he crawls over to inspect the damage. "The Halsteds are like royalty in this town. If you plan on staying, it's going to be hard avoiding them."

I sigh, knowing he is right.

"But the Halsteds are also people of their word. If you tell Orion you don't want to be around him anymore, he'll respect that. So will his family." Wesley slowly puts one block on top of the other, letting Mica see how he positions it.

"You know, you talk about them in a much more positive light than they do about your family."

Wesley lets out a chuckle. "That is a complicated story going back far longer than anyone currently alive. But in this generation, they have reason to dislike my family. To dislike me."

"Roxy seems to like you just fine."

"True. We made peace with each other years ago, but I insisted we keep it a secret from the rest of the town. Mostly from my uncle. But that story is not entirely mine to tell."

"This must be a very complicated story because Orion said the same thing when I asked him why he hated you so much."

"Did he tell you any of it?"

"Just that the two of you got in a fight at school, he punched you, and because of that on his record he lost his football scholarship and went into the Marines instead."

Wesley nods sadly. "I tried like hell to make sure he didn't get punished for that punch. I deserved it and more. But when your uncle, the mayor of the town, is best friends with the school district superintendent, well let's just say they didn't care what I had to say about it."

"I doubt you deserved getting punched."

"You would be wrong. When I came here as a teenager, I was messed up. Both my parents had just died and I was shipped off to live with the uncle my mother almost never talked about in the town she had nothing but bad things to say about. I felt like an outsider. Burt didn't know the first thing about raising a teenager. But everyone here was so damn nice, and I hated them for being so different from the picture my mother had painted. I wanted to hate it here as much as she did. Thought it would honor her memory. But I didn't. I loved it here. Loved the people." Wesley stares at the blocks in front of him as if he's not actually seeing them. "I did things I'm not proud of. I promise you, I deserved a much more severe beating than what I got from Orion. He's a loyal guy, and he was doing what he thought was right."

"He's buying your uncle's cabin. The one I've been staying in." The words fall from my mouth before I can stop them. But I won't give away his other secret. That one has nothing to do with me. "He didn't tell me. I found out when I went to finish the business license paperwork. I tried to talk to Burt about fixing some things around the cabin and he told me to take it up with the new owner, my neighbor."

Wesley shakes his head in disappointment.

"Then your uncle seemed to realize I didn't know and dug in, talking about how Orion was paying way too much for the place and he couldn't figure out why." He knew why. It was obvious to us both.

"I'm sorry about my uncle. I wish I could do more to make him even a little bit human." Wesley turns to face me. "So, you're mad at Orion for buying the cabin you're living in?" He says the words neutrally, but I can tell he doesn't understand why the whole thing bothers me so much.

"No, I'm not mad at him. I'm mad at me."

This seems to confuse him even more. Join the club, buddy.

"Believe it or not, I understand why Orion bought the cabin. Or at least part of it. He saw a way he could help, a way he could make a difference for someone he has feelings for and he took it." I smile as Mica knocks over the tower of blocks in front of me and gives me a gummy grin. "When your uncle let the whole cabin secret slip, it broke loose a dam that was holding back a host of things I've been in denial over."

Mica picks up some of the blocks and begins trying to stack them, but not quite managing it.

"I should be nothing but excited right now, my dreams are coming true. I'm opening my shop. Planting roots in a place that I truly believe is where Mica and I belong." Those damn tears that make me feel too human prickle behind my eyes once again. "But suddenly my dreams have morphed, stretched to make room for a tall, overly helpful lumberjack. That scares the shit out of me."

Wesley silently builds a tower with me, letting the sudden onslaught of over-information pour from me without judgment.

"The last man I thought I loved, Mica's biological father, devastated me when he wanted nothing to do with us. It's a long story, but I swore that I would never let a man have that power over me again, not when I have Mica to protect. And here I am, trusting a man I shouldn't all over again." A single tear rolls down my cheek. I tilt my head back to the puffy cotton clouds and paper airplanes above us, willing the tears to disappear. "A man that it turns out keeps secrets a little too well. A man that effortlessly cares for me and my son. I fell so easily I didn't even notice it happening. I didn't move here looking for a romance. The opposite actually. It's supposed to be Mica and me forever. But the first man that showed interest in this town and I quite literally jumped him."

Wesley clears his throat in a nervous little chuckle. "Well, this is a town founded on love. I'm not entirely surprised that's what you found here."

"No, it isn't love." The words feel hollow, false as soon as I say them. "It can't be."

"I didn't clock you as someone who lies to themself." He says it with no judgment, but the slightest edge of something like pity. "Trust me, I know something about being in love when you don't want to be. You can fight it all you want, but it never really goes away. Love finds a way to grow even when you don't want it to."

Am I in love with Orion? I close my eyes and picture his face. Tap into the way I felt being in his arms. It isn't the heady rush of excitement that burns so bright you can't see past it and then gets snuffed out just as fast. It's a warm glow, consistent and steady. A fueling fire that sustains and protects. It lights the way instead of obscuring your path.

"Shit."

"Yeah." Mica pushes over Wesley's tower again, and keeps pushing it over when he tries to build it again, verging on tantrum territory.

"He's probably hungry." I gather Mica in my arms, immediately clocking the squishy diaper as I do. "And obviously needs a diaper change."

Wesley returns the blocks to the bin and places them back in their place on the shelf. "Yeah, you probably want to get out of here before a dozen pre-teens needing their Minecraft fix descend on this place, too."

Together we make our way back downstairs. At the front desk Wesley pauses, pushing his glasses back up his nose once again. "Listen, I'm not trying to convince you to do anything you don't want to, but maybe give Orion the benefit of the doubt. Like all of us, he has his baggage that he's carrying. You just need to decide if you're willing to share the burden of what he's carrying. And if you are willing to let him share in yours."

"Who knew small town librarians were so wise?"

He chuckles, nervously pushing at the bridge of his glasses even though they are still firmly in place. "Well, we do have lots of time to read."

Chapter 33

Orion

Brigid wasn't at the cafe. Mom was incredibly confused when I walked in, looked around the whole place, even the kitchen, then walked back out without saying a word.

The only other place I can think she would go is her shop, but there isn't a single light on and most of the windows are covered with brown paper. I check the perimeter of the building, hoping to find another way in.

Back in the day, when I was in high school, I'm pretty sure this was a barber shop, but Mom always cut our hair, so I don't think I've ever actually been in the space.

Where else would she go?

"Orion?" My brother's voice calls to me from the park across the street. "Dude, what are you doing?"

The last thing I want is to get slowed down by my brother, but behind him I see June, Delia, and Paula. They've been friendly with Brigid ever since the day we spent fixing up the cabin, could she have talked to one of them?

The thought spurs me on, jogging across the street, totally ignoring the insane stoplight and crosswalk Burt insisted on installing years ago and every single town resident has ignored since.

"Hey, June, have you seen Brigid?"

My future sister-in-law shakes her head, giving me a curious look. "No, we've been out here doing some wedding planning all day."

"Shit."

"What did you do?" my sister pipes up with her usual unhelpful two cents.

"None of your business." I don't want to get into this with them.

"Why are you carrying a purse?" Knox flicks the diaper bag I grabbed before leaving the cabin and now have slung over my shoulder.

"Also, none of your business."

Delia points a finger behind me. "Isn't that her coming out of the library?" Her voice turns icy. "With Wesley smiling at her from the front doors?"

My whole body whips around so fast I'm a little worried I tweaked something. Sure enough, the woman I've been frantically searching for the last forty-five minutes is waving over her shoulder to Wesley with Mica propped on her hip.

I don't think, just move. Because there is so much I need to explain to her. So much we need to clear up. By the time I make it the block to the small parking lot behind the library, she's popped the trunk on her shitty little car and is digging around in the mound of boxes searching for something. Mica fusses, teetering on the edge of a full meltdown.

"Brigid." I try to say it softly, not wanting to startle her; even still, she jumps at my voice. "Listen, we need to talk. I have a lot I need to explain."

She doesn't turn to face me, just keeps her body halfway in the truck shifting stuff around. Was following her down here the wrong move? I'm no expert at women or relationships, is this bordering on creepy stalker behavior?

Well, too late now. In for a penny, in for a pound.

"I know we need to talk, but Mica needs a bottle and a diaper change and I forgot the diaper bag at the cabin. There has to be a spare diaper in here somewhere. I need to clean this thing out." She says the last bit mostly to herself, but I make a note to myself to organize everything in there for her tonight while she sleeps.

Shit, this is creepy stalker stuff, isn't it?

I take the diaper bag from my shoulder. "Here, I realized I still had it when you left."

Finally, she stands from the trunk and turns to face me, immediately deflating when she sees me holding the bag of supplies out to her. "Thank you."

Instead of handing the bag to her, I walk to her side and close the trunk, then spread the blankie that is always stashed in the bag out on the car. Brigid lays Mica down on the blanket.

"Listen, I know I've kept some things to myself that I should have been upfront with you about, but it was never malicious. I wasn't hiding these things because I was trying to trick you."

Brigid keeps her focus entirely on Mica as I talk, okay maybe plead, with her. But I have to believe that she is hearing me. I hand her the wipes when she has the dirty diaper off and rolled up.

Hesitantly, she takes them from me, with a look on her face that I can't interpret. But I don't think the groveling that I'm in the middle of is doing the trick.

She puts the old diaper to the side and I grab it, depositing it in one of the plastic bags she keeps in the side pocket I've come to think of as the poop pocket. For some reason Brigid pauses cleaning up Mica and watches as I stow the diaper away.

"I know you said you didn't want to give men second chances, or even first, but I swear, if you make an exception for me, I will never keep something from you again."

I grab a clean diaper, open it, and hand it to her as soon as she's got Mica cleaned up, putting the wipes away in the diaper bag. The used wipes go in the plastic bag with the soiled diaper before I tie the whole thing closed and shove it into the poop pocket to dispose of later.

"I'll lay everything out on the table. Yes, at first I bought the cabin in part because I wanted to be able to make real changes to it so it would be safer for you and Mica. And yeah maybe I was hoping those changes would make you want to stay on the mountain a little longer. But I also bought the cabin because it *should* belong to someone in my family. That whole piece of land has been a part of my father's family for generations and being the one to put it back together felt like I was doing something to make up for the fact that I wasn't here while Dad was sick. That I only made it back when he was so close to death he barely knew who I was."

Now that the words have started I can't seem to stop them. My hands itch to do something, so I pull an empty bottle from the main compartment of the bag along with the tub of formula and the canister of water I refilled before leaving. She stands silently, watching me scoop the correct amount of formula into the bottle.

"The whole internet influencer thing, honestly, I've kept it a secret for so long because I was embarrassed. I went from having a full ride to college, to losing it because I was an idiot, to joining the Marines because I didn't see any other options, to failing my family by not being able to help in one of the worst times of our lives, to stumbling into a weird career where I chop up wood shirtless on the internet. It felt like one more way to embarrass my family. So, I kept it secret from them and the whole town. It never occurred to me I could choose to *not* keep it a secret from you. And when it did occur to me, I thought it was too late and you would think I was hiding things from you on purpose." I put the cap on the bottle and start shaking it vigorously to mix the contents. "The secret has become just as much part of the job as actually filming the videos themselves."

With the bottle all mixed up, and probably shaken vigorously enough it could have turned into butter, I hand it to Brigid. Slowly she takes the bottle from my hand and stares at it, an expression I've never seen before on her face.

"As long as I'm laying everything on the table, the day we met I made a plan to win you over. It started off as a way to convince you I wasn't a total asshole after that disaster of an introduction. But after a couple days it turned into a plan to make you love me. We're talking multiple phases, flow charts, progress reports. It might be a little crazy, but I'm so fucking crazy about you."

As quickly as they started, the words stop. It dawns on me that dumping all of this on her at once might be the wrong tactic. Too late now. There is one more thing I need to lay out there.

Gathering more courage than I needed in all my time deployed overseas or as I sat next to my father as he died, I look up at Brigid. She's staring at me like I have two heads. That tracks. She's still holding the bottle in one hand, and Mica is reaching for it from her other hip. "The truth is, I'm in love with you. I know that isn't part of your plan and that I'm probably digging myself more in a hole here. But I need you to know that every secret is out now. There is nothing else I'm hiding from you. There might be things you don't know about me yet, but that is simply because it takes a lifetime to learn every corner of someone's heart. I just hope you want to know more. I hope you'll let me in enough that I can learn everything about you, too."

A line of moisture glitters on the edge of Brigid's lower lid before falling down over her round cheeks. Fuck, I made her cry.

"I'm sor—"

"Stop." Brigid sucks in a breath, tears trailing down her face in rivulets now. Mica has managed to get the bottle into his mouth, Brigid half holding it while he does the rest, his gaze swings back and forth between us. I hope he grows up to be better about this stuff than I am. "You just made Mica a bottle. And you know where everything is in the diaper bag. Hell, you *brought* the diaper bag."

"Is that bad?" How did I fuck this up? I glance at the diaper bag still sitting on the trunk and back at her. "Shit, is this over-stepping?"

Brigid opens her mouth to respond but I surge on.

"Like the roof and the hole in the floor and the other stuff I keep doing without your permission. I'm sorry, I've just watched how you do these things and took note. And I knew you would need the diaper bag and since it was my fault you left it, I just figured—"

"I love you, too," she has to practically yell the words over my word vomit. They do the job. I shut up immediately. "I have a great father and I don't think he knew how to make a bottle after living with me for weeks after Mica was born."

"It took Sam months to figure out how to open a diaper without ripping off the little tabs on the side," Paula pipes up from behind us. Which is when I turn to see not only my entire family, but yeah, a good bit of the town all standing there.

Delia waves at me, and I see that she too is crying. "Our dad could never remember where all our school stuff was, let alone remember to grab it when he drove us instead of Mom."

"You did all that for Mica like it was second nature. Didn't even think about it. It might—" Brigid peers up at the sky and blows out a shaky breath before returning her eyes to me. "—It could be possible that I might have been wrong. Maybe you are different under the surface. Maybe you are better than I could ever imagine. Maybe I am just really scared." Her voice hitches as fat tears continue to cover her face.

I can't be not touching her any longer. I step forward and cup her face in my hands. "I promise, I am not going to hurt you. Or Mica."

She nods and sniffles. "There is a lot more to say," Brigid continues. "But maybe we save the rest of it for when half the town isn't here to witness it." Her gaze shifts from me to our audience over my shoulder.

Mom is standing next to Knox, whose arm is around her shoulder as she too cries. "We need to talk about some of that absolute bullshit you said about letting your family down, too."

"Also, everyone knows about your TikTok account," Paula pipes up. "Did you actually think none of your millions of followers were locals?"

"Excuse me, I didn't know my brother was taking his shirt off on the internet for money." Knox is trying his best not to laugh his ass off.

"I tried to tell you when I first met your family, but you said I was crazy." June pokes Knox.

"Well, who would want to watch someone chop wood shirtless, it's weird." Knox barely dodges Mom's attempt to smack him upside the head.

She walks to my side, kissing me on the cheek, then hugs Brigid. "Give me this baby and kiss my son, honey."

The second Mica is passed off to my mom, Brigid leaps into my arms, our lips meeting in a kiss not at all appropriate given we have an audience.

Judging by the absolute roar of applause and wolf whistles, they don't seem to mind.

Chapter 34

Brigid

We leave Orion's truck parked behind the cafe and drive back to the cabin together. The whole drive back, he has one hand gripping my thigh, high enough to send very dirty thoughts pouring through my mind, but not high enough to quench the thirst quickly enveloping me.

Considering a little while ago we were both agreeing that there was more to talk about, the interior of the car is awfully quiet, except for Mica in the backseat with Spruce babbling to the dog as if they've been separated for weeks instead of a couple hours.

Roxy offered to keep Mica overnight so we could have some alone time, but I'm not ready for that, yet. Thankfully, she wasn't insulted.

"Have you really never had someone besides your parents watch Mica?" It's the first question he's asked since leaving the square that was quickly passing the story of our little public display of insanity through town.

"Yeah, even then Mom had to force me to take naps or leave the apartment without him. She was the one that made my tattoo appointment the day before they left. Otherwise, I never would have gone. It was my decision to be a single mom, I didn't want to take the easy way out by hoisting him off on other people." I glance in the rearview mirror, smiling as his hand pats at the dog's head in his lap. "And honestly it wasn't a hardship. Motherhood was always something I knew I wanted, I just didn't expect it to happen quite like this."

"You know taking time to yourself isn't half-assing motherhood, right?"

I don't respond, because despite being told the same thing from my family, and friends, it is still hard for me to accept.

"Listen, I'm not saying you leave him home alone while you go have a spa day, but when was the last time you got the chance to only think about what you need?"

"Before moving here? Never. Since moving into that shitty little cabin? Quite a bit actually. Every time your hands were on me. Right up until my little meltdown, I had no doubt Mica was in good hands and wasn't worried one bit about how he was doing."

Orion squeezes my thigh.

"I'm sorry that is how you found out I was keeping secrets. I'd been telling myself for days that I needed to come clean before the papers were officially signed."

"I appreciate the apology. I'm afraid you have some choppy waters to work your way through thanks to the man who came before you."

"Well, good thing I'm a strong swimmer." He moves his hand a little bit higher, and I'm suddenly highly regretting my decision to wear jeans today. "As you probably remember."

The gas pedal inches closer to the floor of my car seemingly all by itself. *Calm down.* It's not like we can go at it the minute we step in the door anyway. Mica still needs dinner, a bath, and put to bed. I'm sure Orion has things he needs to do, too.

Suddenly, the "Lumberjack Song" from Monty Python fills the car. "What the hell is that?"

Orion laughs as he pulls his phone from his pocket. "My ring town, Delia thought it was hilarious to steal my phone and change it last time we had family dinner, and well, it grew on me." He glances at the screen as he silences the music. "Hello?"

The conversation doesn't last long, but I try my best to not eavesdrop. Hard to do in my tiny little Civic. After a few *yeahs* and one *thank you,* Orion ends the call and starts scrolling around on his phone.

Curiosity gets the better of me. "What was that all about?"

"Well, after you left, I called Burt to give him a piece of my mind while I drove to town. Told him he either had to stop dicking around and finalize the sale or I would take my offer back and send him the bill for everything I'd already done around the cabin." He continues tapping away at his phone, not looking up from the screen. "Magically, that was his lawyer letting me know all the contracts were emailed over by e-doc. So right now I am buying the cabin."

"What? Now? On the phone?"

He nods, a wry little smile on his face. "Yup, amazing what you can do when you're paying cash."

Um excuse me? Cash? "Are you some billionaire recluse lumberjack like in the books your mom has at the cafe? Is this the next deep dark secret you need to tell me?"

Orion's laugh fills the car, making my stomach do a little swoop. "Hardly, but my apparently not-so-secret side hustle has been very good to me. Considering my living expenses are next to nothing, and the only things I spend money on are tools and books, *and* I got a really good investment guy, I do pretty well." He does two final taps on the phone screen. "There. That cabin is mine."

"Holy shit." I can't believe he just bought a fucking cabin.

"Yeah." Something in that one word makes all my senses prick to attention.

"You okay?" Now I reach over to grab his thigh.

"Yeah. I'm weirdly emotional about finally putting my family's land back as it should be."

"I didn't know him, but I'm sure your dad would be proud of you."

Orion turns to face the window, but his hand covers mine on his leg and he entwines our fingers. "Thanks." In the window's reflection I see tears track down his face.

The rest of the ride goes by in an easy silence. The closer to the cabin we get, the more my stomach starts doing somersaults. We said some big things back at the library. Declaring my love for an internet famous lumberjack in front of half the town wasn't on my bingo card when I moved to Amoresville, but here we are.

Now the question is, where do we go from here?

I pull the car up beside the cabin just as the sky is turning the pinks and purples of twilight despite it only being seven. I love the shorter days of fall. We sit in silence for a moment, both gazing out at the beautiful pond and trees.

After a minute Orion turns to face me, resting his temple against the headrest. "I have a couple steaks and some asparagus from Knox's farm back at my cabin. Can I bring it over and make you dinner?"

I turn to match his position, taking in his beautiful face. The somersaults in my stomach turn to an effervescence, like someone popped a bottle of champagne inside me and it is sending fizzy bubbles through my veins. "I'd like that."

Within twenty minutes, Orion is hard at work searing the steaks in a cast iron skillet in my tiny kitchen. I have Mica in the highchair Orion made and am serving up his much simpler dinner when a thought occurs to me. "This highchair matches the crib almost perfectly. Was it really a left-over piece?"

Orion's cheeks turn a bright red, and I don't think it's from the heat radiating from the stove. "No. I made it with him in mind. Full disclosure, I'm also working on a king bedframe for you, dining table, and I've got ideas for bookshelves in your store. I have a whole notebook of designs inspired by the witch next door."

Something about being his inspiration makes me strangely proud. Mica settled in with his dinner, I walk up behind Orion and lay my cheek against his flannel-clad back, hooking my thumbs into the belt loops of his jeans. "I'd love to see your sketches."

With one hand, he reaches back and grips my hip. "I'll bring them over later. But, Sunshine, if you keep touching me, more meat than just these steaks is gonna get cooked."

The rest of the evening unfolds comfortably. I'm doing my best to let myself get used to it. I only resist a little when Orion says he'll clean up after dinner while I get Mica ready for bed. Don't resist at all when he wants me to show him how to use the baby wrap again and he wears Mica for a walk around the pond to wind down after playing with Spruce.

I love having him in my space.

As I sit, rocking Mica in his new nursery, Orion settles on the floor, his back propped against the wall next to us as we take turns reading books out loud, Spruce curled next to his side. The excitement of the day means Mica falls asleep faster than normal, and he barely stirs as I transfer him into the new crib.

Quietly, we back out of the room, Spruce curling up directly in front of the crib like a sentry.

With Mica down for the night, it's like the atmosphere in the cabin shifts in an instant. The cozy warmth of the domesticated night turns hot with the snick of the door latch sliding into place behind me.

I turn, knowing Orion will be there, and my arms reach up to wrap around his neck. His lips find mine with ease, as if they've known the way for a lifetime instead of only a few weeks.

"Fuck, Brigid, I've been thinking about getting my hands on you all fucking afternoon." His hands grip my ass, pulling me up so my legs can wrap around his waist. With a single spin, he has me pressed up against the wall, freeing his hands to wander across my body in greedy sweeps. "I can't get enough of you. Want to touch you all the time," he says between kisses to my neck and shoulders.

Everything inside me tightens, squeezes in need. "Yes. I need your hands on me. Please."

I push his flannel shirt down off his shoulders as he pulls my shirt up. He has to put me down to make the sudden mutual need to rid ourselves of our clothes work. After a little fumbling and breathy laughs, we finally manage to get down to nothing but my bra and panties and his boxer briefs.

"Goddamn, woman." He holds both my hands and rocks back a little on his feet, eyes tracking up and down my body. "I should be embarrassed by how many times a day I get rock hard remembering this exact sight. But I'm really not."

How does he manage to make me want to laugh and moan at the same time?

I close the small gap between our bodies, pressing my-self against him and moving our entwined hands behind his back. "You know, there's something I've been wanting to do with you."

Orion has a good foot on me in height, and enough muscle that the idea of me being able to push him around is laughable. Yet when I begin walking forward, he doesn't hesitate but matches me step for step backward until he is pressed against my bedroom door.

I swear his breathing picks up pace, and we're so tightly pressed together I can feel his heart pounding beneath his muscled chest.

"I'll do anything you want." He stoops down, taking my mouth in a filthy kiss, his hands held tightly in my grip. It would take next to nothing for him to free himself, but he doesn't so much as strain, perfectly content to have me direct things.

"Good, then I want you to fuck me in my bed until I scream." I kiss a line up along his neck, sucking on a spot that makes his dick twitch against me. "Then I want you to fall asleep next to me all night."

His green eyes peer down at me, a small, hesitant smile curling the corners of his mouth. "You sure?"

"Absolutely."

Chapter 35

Orion

I have had Brigid on nearly every flat—and not so flat—surface in both her cabin and mine. Each and every time has been damn near transcending. The kind of sex that makes me want to start journaling so I can document every detail to preserve in time for future generations to find and blush over.

But the prospect of finally getting to make love with Brigid in a bed is fucking with my head. I'm so Goddamn nervous. Gone is the smooth, dirty talking man that she's enjoyed the past few weeks. Instead she gets a bumbling idiot that very well might blow his load way too early.

Her hand tracks down my naked body, gripping my painfully hard cock through the cotton of my boxer briefs. And she fuck-ing *squeezes*.

"Fuck, Sunshine, you keep that up and this is going to be over way faster than either of us wants."

She does it again, stroking and squeezing me from root to tip. My knees go weak and I collapse back against the frankly criminally hard mattress of her bed. I'm replacing that thing tomorrow.

As Brigid pulls my underwear down over my hips, I add more items to the to-do list for getting the cabin worthy of Brigid living here.

New electrical.

She kisses a line up the underside of my shaft.

Upgrade the heating.

The wet heat of her mouth closes over my swollen head.

Replace the windows.

One hand grips my balls, fingers working figure eights around and between them.

Buy a fucking couch.

"Watch me, Orion. You know I love it when you watch."

I'm not going to last, but I'm also not going to deny her. Never. Propping myself up on my elbows, our gazes connect over the plains of my chest and stomach. Brigid on her knees, her mouth stuffed full of my cock, is one of the three best things I have ever seen. The other two are her too. As soon as I give her what she wants, she takes me even further back into her mouth, until I'm pressing against the entrance to her throat.

Her only goal must be to kill me because with a fucking wink, she fucking swallows. "Holy shit, you suck my cock so good I might lose my mind."

Slowly, she draws back, swirling her tongue around each inch of my length as she goes. "Good." She dives back down, bobbing up and down on my cock like she can't get enough.

I know the feeling.

For a few more minutes, I let her have her way with my cock, all the while holding on by the slimmest of threads. But the very second I feel the tingling at the base of my spine that lets me know the point of no return isn't far off, I grip the black strands of her hair in my fist and lift her from my cock. I swear, if the appendage between my legs could talk, he'd be cussing me out right now for stopping a blowjob for the record books.

"Your turn, Sunshine." I let go of her hair, pulling her up from the as I stand as well, pressing our bodies together, covering her neck and shoulder in kisses.

"But I was having fun," an uncharacteristic whine fills her voice.

"Too much. I wasn't going to last, and I'll be damned if we finally make it to a bed and I don't last for more than a minute." She's so damn short, I have to nearly bend in half to make my way down to her chest, still criminally covered in a utilitarian black cotton bra. "You are wearing far too many clothes still." I unclasp the bra and let it fall to the floor, then sit on the edge of the bed, pulling her to stand between my legs. Her tits are finally at mouth level, and I take my time tasting every inch of the beauties.

"Oh...holy...Orion." Brigid grips the back of my head as I suck on one nipple. Sliding my hands down her sides to hook my thumbs into the waistband of her panties, I push them down to pool around her ankles.

In one motion, I scoop her up into my arms and turn to toss her on the bed. She giggles, her limbs and hair landing in disarray around her. "I love that you're strong enough to toss me around."

Maybe all this time I've been working out twice a day it wasn't out of boredom, but in preparation to treat this woman the way she deserves. To be able to carry her when she falls asleep in the car and throw her in the bed when I can't wait to get inside her.

"Spread your legs, Sunshine. I'm hungry."

A sinful expression takes over the amusement from just a moment ago and she presses her legs together, knees bent, giving me absolutely zero access. "Make. Me."

My cock bounces between us, and her eyes slide there, one eyebrow arching in interest.

"You're asking for trouble, Brigid."

She nods slowly. "Yup." She enunciates the *P* with a loud pop.

With a growl, I dive across the mattress. But I don't pry her legs apart with brute force like I think she's expecting me to. Instead, I hook both of her calves over one shoulder and press my whole body forward, folding in her in half until her knees are almost parallel with her ear. My bare cock rubs her pussy, exposed by the position.

"Motherfucker." She gasps, her breaths coming out harshly.

"Yeah, there's more than one way to get to your pussy and believe me when I say I have imagined every single one." Leaning back a little, so she's not quite so compressed beneath me, I rub one hand down her side until it cups around her generous ass. Then I pull back, slapping that ass just enough to make it sting. "I'll find a way to this pussy no matter what obstacle you throw in front of me."

I start shallow thrusts, sliding my cock between her folds, but not entering her yet. Which is when I remember my fucking pants are out in the living room. And in those pants are the condoms I have optimistically started carrying in my wallet in case the opportunity to fuck Brigid presents itself.

"Fuck, sweetheart, I need to go grab a condom from my pants." I start to pull away, already planning to break land speed records to get there and back as fast as possible.

"No." Her hand grips my forearm, preventing me from leaving. "We don't need one. I have an IUD, and I was tested when I was pregnant. Are you clean?"

Fuck yes. I was bare inside Brigid once, the time we played our dangerous game of just the tip. The thought of being inside her completely and bare has me suddenly scared I might blow on the spot. "I'm clean. Got tested the last time I was at the VA for a checkup and haven't been with anyone since." And that was a fucking long time ago.

In a move that will play on repeat every day until I day, Brigid lifts one leg from my shoulder and swings it around until planting it on the bed beside me, leaving the other leg still on my shoulder, but her pussy totally open.

"Then what are you waiting for?"

God damn. Not one to make a lady wait, I reach down to grip my cock and line it up with Brigid's entrance. I manage to control myself while I slide inch by inch into her tight, warm, wet pussy, all the way until I fill her completely. The sensation of being bare inside her, nothing between us, nearly takes my breath away.

Brigid moans and pulses her hips, trying to get more friction. "Fuck me, Orion, pleeease."

Is there anything more intoxicating than my woman begging me to fuck her brains out?

Her words are the equivalent of throwing gasoline on a fire. I grip the leg still on my shoulder, pull out slowly until my cock nearly falls from the warmth of her, then slam home. Then again.

Brigid's mouth falls open, her back arching. "Yeeessss."

I wish I could say my mind is only on her pleasure. That my goal is nothing but getting her off. But that would be the biggest lie of my fucking life. I'm lost to the orgasm barreling down on me. Fighting off for one more minute so I can be inside her that much longer.

"Fucking incredible, Bridge. I can't get enough." I drop her leg to the side so she's spread wide open for me. Dropping down, I press my chest down onto her, taking her mouth in a kiss to muffle her moans rapidly increasing in volume, but also because I just need to be closer to her.

When the pleasure gets so great that I can't keep up with kissing, I nuzzle my face into her neck, pumping my hips, grinding against her clit each time I bottom out inside her. Her arms and legs come up to wrap around me, holding me to her in a tight grip.

"Oh god, Orion, I'm going to come, don't stop."

I don't change a thing. Just keep pounding away at her as her pussy flutters and closes around my bare cock. A sharp sting barely breaks through the absolute euphoria of fucking my woman as she digs her nails into my back.

In a rush, she holds me just that much tighter, nearly convulsing on the orgasm crashing over her. She screams once before biting down on my shoulder to hide her cries of bliss. That edge of pain mixed with pleasure takes me to the point of no return, and my own orgasm takes over.

All control is lost. I slam into her, emptying myself into her beautiful fucking pussy. My hands are in her hair, then on her hips, touching each place I can reach, searching for a point to anchor me to the earth as the rest of me cartwheels into the atmosphere. Her hands find mine, and our fingers entwine, pressing into the pillows next her head.

It could be seconds, minutes, or hours later, I'm not sure, when I finally return to myself. I'm lying boneless on her, the realization that I must be crushing her beneath my bulk slowly seeping in around that part of logic that still exists in my brain. But when I go to move off her, she wraps her legs around my waist, hooking her ankles together so I can't move.

"Don't move, stay here, inside me, on top of me. Maybe forever, but let's start with a few more minutes."

We're both sweaty, sticky, and panting, a complete mess. But our mess, so it doesn't seem weird.

"I'll stay as long as you let me," I whisper into her ear.

"Forever, then," she breathes into mine.

Hard to believe just a month ago, I didn't believe in magic. Now proof of it is lying beneath me in the shape of the woman I love.

Epilogue

Brigid

Six Months Later

Pride swells almost painfully in my chest. The front windows of my store reflect the pristine, cloudless morning sky of late April in Amoresville. Perfect for a grand opening.

The comically huge pair of scissors are heavy in my hand, a physical presence of the weight of this moment.

It took far longer to open the store than I wanted. Once Burt figured out that I wasn't in fact opening a high-end gem and mineral shop but a metaphysical store catering to the magically inclined, he tried to throw up roadblocks at every turn.

There was the time he tried to fine me for not getting a building permit for painting the interior of the store.

The approval process for my sign took weeks longer than it should have.

He even tried to revoke the business license by uncovering a literally ancient law still on the books in Pennsylvania that said it is illegal to charge money for fortune telling. There were lawyers, and a lot of truly awful words thrown around by Orion and the mayor, but in the end, he relented when the fight started to garner the interest of the county newspaper.

But six months later, the day has finally come to open the store. Our grand opening ceremony is in no way official or town sponsored, not a surprise given my history with the government in this town. But June, Roxy, and Delia insisted that I should be given the same pomp and circumstance that any other newly opened business was, so they organized this whole thing.

"Okay everyone, gather around." Orion stands beside me, a rapidly growing Mica perched on his hip, Spruce sitting politely at his feet. "It's time to open the store."

Beside him are my parents and sister, all in from Arizona for the occasion. They are staying in the now completely renovated cabin Mica and I had lived in for the first three months after our move.

That was when Orion asked us to move in with him again, but not at his cabin. Instead, we bought a cute, but rundown, house on the edge of town. Just close enough to downtown that I could walk to the store when the weather was nice enough, but also not too far from the mountain top where we fell in love so Orion could go up to work on his projects.

It is perfect.

Just like this day.

I think half the town has come out for the ribbon cutting. Many of the faces in the crowd I could now count as true friends. Even Harley has graced us with her presence before noon, but we had to ply her with Roxy's strongest drink—the Instalove, coffee mixed with espresso.

Murphy even drove up from Maryland for the weekend. He sneaks glances across the crowd at Harley, and I swear I can almost see the invisible thread that connects the two most shut-down people I've ever met.

Even Wesley has come out from the library to stand at the edges of the fray. I count him among my friends in town, much to Orion and his siblings' chagrin.

"Thank you for coming to the opening of the Tiger's Eye Boutique." I start in on the short remarks I agonized over since the girls started organizing this thing. "Six months ago, I packed everything important to me into my trunk and turned my car north. I'm someone that believes in the pull of something invisible that connects us all. Since the day I learned about this town, I felt that pull drawing me here. Every day since has proven to me that following my gut is always the right move. This store is the culmination of every dream I have had for myself. I hope it will become a safe place for all of you, and any visitors to town, to gather, learn, and grow. Whether you believe in the mystical or not, everyone is welcome in the Tiger's Eye."

Right on cue, Roxy and Delia appear with a huge red ribbon, stretching it out in front of me. With a little bit of effort, I place the open scissors around the ribbon, ready to snip it in half.

"So, by the power vested in me by all the goddesses, I pronounce the Tiger's Eye open for business!" With one strong tug, I close the scissors, and the ribbon falls away.

All around me people are clapping and hooting. Slowly as the claps die down, Burt emerges through the crowd. Roxy started a countdown to his last day in office in the coffee shop. Only two hundred and fifty-five days to go.

"Congratulations, Brigid." He says it like the words leave a bad taste in his mouth.

"Thank you, Burt, that is big of you." Honestly, I have no idea why he decided to make an appearance. His antics have not been popular on the local rumor circuit, with most people taking my side. "Why don't you come in, and I will give you a tour."

He sneers in the general direction of the store. "Some other time." Yeah, probably not. "I wanted to swing by because I thought this little...event...would be the perfect opportunity to make an exciting announcement."

Movement from the corner of the crowd pulls my attention. Wesley is pushing his way through the throng of people, who seem to have gathered a little closer now that something dramatic is going down.

"Burt, now is not the time." Wesley's face has gone nearly paper white, his eyes wide with unmistakable fear.

"Nonsense, this is the perfect time considering what an advocate you were for this unusual store." He gives his nephew a pointed look. I knew Wesley had spoken to his uncle in my defense but apparently wasn't aware of the obvious tension that had caused between the two. "What better time to announce that the proud Lickinbill line of mayors will continue with you, my boy."

Wesley's head falls, his chin tucking in tight against his chest, his jaw popping as he grinds his teeth together.

Around us people begin murmuring. I glance at all the Halsteds, gauging their reactions. Roxy is looking at her secret friend with pity. Knox looks annoyed. Orion appears surprisingly sympathetic to the man that he has slowly been letting go of his anger toward.

Delia, however, is another story. Her pale, freckled face is positively crimson, both hands clenched in fists by her side, the ribbon crinkled among her fingers. "This is bullshit," she seethes. With that, she turns, stomping up the street, probably to the cafe.

Truthfully, I think Wesley would make a great mayor. "Well, congratulations, Wes." I close the few feet between us and give him a loose, awkward hug. "Why don't we all head inside. There are refreshments and everyone gets ten percent off for opening day."

A few hours later, I'm showing Mrs. Winchester the fertility idols in one corner of the store when a strong pair of arms wrap around my waist from behind. I'm not sure exactly what Mrs. Winchester's interest in the idols is considering she has to be well on her way to eighty, so I'm happy for the distraction Orion offers.

"Sorry, Mrs. Winchester, could you spare my partner for a moment?" I'll never get tired of him calling me that, his partner. For life. We've talked about getting married eventually, but neither of us feels the need to rush. Especially after seeing the stress of wedding planning June and Knox had gone through last November. "I have a surprise for her outside."

"Go ahead, Orion. You two are so cute." She pats his forearm, giving it a little squeeze that is slightly on the groping side, and turns back to the shelves of statues.

After Orion's not so secret, secret identity was revealed last year, he stopped trying to hide his face in his videos. The first video that he appeared in with no obstacle went mega-viral, getting three million views in one day. These days his videos focus more on the renovations to our house, though his workouts and Spruce are still the favorites among his fans. They've even welcomed my presence, something I was nervous about the first time I appeared in a video.

"A surprise? How on earth have you been able to keep a surprise secret from me?" He is the literal worst at withholding any information from me now. Our Christmas-Yule-Solstice mash up holiday celebration had been a real struggle for him to keep any of my gifts under wraps.

"Hey, I am a steel trap. Nothing escapes." We both chuckle, and he takes my hand, leading me out onto the sidewalk. But we don't stop there. Instead, he steers us toward the park, jogging through the intersection even though the light is red. There are no cars on the street, everyone is at the store most likely.

"What are you doing?" I can't help but giggle at his excitement. He tries to slow his steps for my much shorter legs but keeps accidentally speeding up in his excitement.

"Something I've been thinking about since the day we met." Finally, we pull to a stop beside the fountain. The one with a statue of his ancestors, the settlers of this town. The one built on the very spot where they first made love. I've heard the story a couple times since moving here. First from Roxy at family dinner night, then again when June read an excerpt from her book about the town that was released on Valentine's Day.

Orion pushes one hand into his pocket, pulling out two-quarters.

"But it's still turned off for the season." I knew he wanted to complete the ritual with me as soon as it got turned back on, and since I love a good ritual, I am all for it. But Burt hasn't announced when that would be yet.

With a slight nod indicating something over my shoulder, I turn to see Wesley standing by, looking a little shy.

"Hit it."

Wesley nods and ducks down to fiddle with something set back into the wall of the fountain before standing and walking away quietly. All of a sudden, water starts pouring out from the spouts at the base of the fountain.

"Brigid, you are the love of my life. Will you seal our love by contributing to Amoresville's pothole fund?"

"Of course," I say with a laugh and a very enthusiastic nod.

In unison, we both kiss the coins and flick them into the quickly filling fountain. Orion gathers me in his arms, pressing his lips against mine. The kiss starts out innocent but quickly turns heated.

"I've also arranged for Mica and Spruce to spend the night with their grandparents up at the cabin." He kisses down my neck, pulling me flush against him.

"Great idea, we can get that wallpapering done in the dining room."

A sharp sting spreads over my ass cheek as he lands a slap right on target.

"Sure, if you would rather wallpaper than scream down the walls with never-ending orgasms. No worries about waking up the little freeloaders down the hall."

An errant moan slips through my lips. "On second thought, I like your plan better."

"That's what I thought." He takes my hands and slowly, we walk back to the store.

I look back over my shoulder at the fountain once more, sending a silent thank you to those two figures who fucked in a field and decided to stay. If it weren't for them, I might never have found the love of my life.

It might not have been part of my plan, but I wouldn't change a thing.

About the author

Brandy Ayers has been inventing stories in one form or another since childhood. Whether telling soap-opera-level-dramatic lies to her new neighbors at the tender age of six or daydreaming about how she would definitely run into and marry Keanu Reeves (her very age-appropriate crush in eighth grade), there was always something brewing in that weird little brain. After becoming a mother, Brandy decided she needed to do something other than care for her baby and go to work. Something for herself. That something ended up being writing down her crazy stories. More than ten years and fifteen books later, she's still at it.

When Brandy isn't writing, you can find her drinking way too much coffee, making jokes that produce groans and eye rolls from her kids, and growing her hodge-podge crew of pets. Lucky enough to have found two great loves in her life, Brandy lives with her second husband and fellow author James W. Farley in southern Pennsylvania.

https://www.brandyayersauthor.com/
Facebook: https://www.facebook.com/BrandyAyersAuthor
TikTok: @BrandyAyersAuthor

Instagram: @BrandyAyersWrites
Newsletter

Also by

Stand Alone Books:
Piece by Piece: A Modern Retelling of Jack and the Beanstalk
Wanted: No Strings
Unwrapping Her
The O Doctor
Taking Over

Blue Line Series:
Reckless Conduct
Possession
Intoxication
Disturbing the Peace